PRAISE FOR SC

In true Zoe Blake style, she's pulled off another perfectly written masterpiece, which was so hard to put down!

- Lyndsey W.

Wrench my heart out.... another masterpiece. I could taste the wine & smell the warmth of Italy on a breeze. But WOW the combustible heat between Baron & Amara .... explosive.

- Panda G.

Zoe Blake gives us another rich character drama with all the spice. Her detailed descriptions of the village, the language, the wine, and the food have me craving a trip to Italy.

- Jen D.

Zoe Blake has such a distinct voice that brings anything that comes out of her pen to life. I wanted to be in Italy. I wanted to taste the wine. I wanted to tend to the orchard. And I wanted to feel the possessive gaze of Barone Cavalieri trained solely on me.

- Morgan

SCANDALS OF THE FATHER

A DARK ENEMIES TO LOVERS ROMANCE

CAVALIERI BILLIONAIRE LEGACY
BOOK ONE

ZOE BLAKE

Poison Ink Publications

Blake, Zoe
Poison Ink Publications
Scandals of the Father
Cover Design by Dark City Designs
Model Wander Aguiar
Photographer Juliana Andrade

CONTENTS

CHAPTER 1

AMARA

No good came from attracting the attention of a man like Barone Cavalieri.

The prosecco flutes on my tray rattled as I caught sight of his glare.

The Barone Cavalieri, powerful patriarch of the Cavalieri family, was staring at me. No, not staring, glaring.

Shifting my gaze away, I tried to swallow past the dry fear which had turned my throat to dust. The flutes clattered again. I pressed my hand over their tops, stilling them. I inhaled a shaky breath and held it, trying to calm my racing heart. A piece of hair escaped my loose bun and tickled the side of my neck. I desperately wanted to flick it aside but was afraid to release my grip on my passing tray.

Despite it being late autumn, the sultry Italian sun would not release its hot grip on our little mountain valley in Abruzzo. A bead of sweat trickled between my shoulder blades. I shrugged one shoulder, trying to relieve the icky, itching sensation on my skin. Then froze. Had my motion drawn more of his unwanted attention? I was afraid to look.

What had I done wrong to warrant his glare?

Internally, I rolled my eyes.

Dammit, why had I agreed to work this awful wedding?

Everyone in the village knew it was doomed from the start.

The answer was simple.

Money, of course.

Stupid, completely-necessary-for-survival money.

I dared a glance out of the corner of my eye. Barone had turned away, his attention drawn by a handful of disreputable looking guests.

I let out the breath I was holding.

Maybe it had all been in my imagination?

After all, why on earth would Barone Cavalieri be glaring at me, one of the village catering servants, at his eldest son's wedding? I mean sure, I had been friends with his youngest son at school, but that was years ago. It wasn't like our families hung out in the same circles.

There were the rich as hell Cavalieris.

There was everyone else below them.

And at the very top was Barone Cavalieri.

The man was practically a legend in his own time.

Known as much for his kindness as his temper, he watched over our village like a feudal lord, harkening back to the power of his ancestors. I guessed it made sense, they even named our village after his family, who owned literally millions of acres of land across Italy and countless businesses, besides the ancestral winery that was the Cavalieri legacy.

It didn't hurt that the man was also tall, imposing, and handsome as sin.

Still, with that kind of power and wealth, there was always an undercurrent of treachery and fear.

It was this that had me shivering in the afternoon sun.

I headed inside to get more prosecco.

Later, I would be expected to pass glasses of the famous, and insanely expensive, *Vino Nobile di Montepulciano d'Abruzzo dei Cavalieri* made from old vines dating back to the thirteenth century, but for now the guests were supposed to be drinking prosecco to celebrate the happy couple.

Except nobody wanted any.

Irritated, I pulled out the band holding my hair back, relieved when the tight tension eased.

My best friend approached, carrying a full tray of uneaten appetizers. She lifted one poached pear half filled with creamy ricotta and drizzled with local sideritis honey and took a bite. "These are really quite tasty. A total waste on that boring crowd out there," she said after swallowing and licking her lips. "Have you ever seen a more somber and tense wedding? You'd think it was a funeral. Although it serves Enzo right for marrying such a bitc—"

I gestured with my head toward Signora Rossi, our supervisor who was standing nearby, as I whispered harshly through tightly closed teeth, "Milana!"

Milana's eyes widened. She tossed her tray aside so haphazardly, the contents slid over the tray lip and toppled onto the Carrara marble table surface. She swallowed a laugh. "Oops."

Milana used the flat of her hand to sweep the pear halves back onto the silver passing tray. The once elegant display was now a jumbled mess of overturned pears and smeared ricotta. She turned to face me, leaning her hip against the table. She licked a drop of honey off the tip of her finger as she raised one elegantly arched eyebrow. "You think the rumors are true?"

I finished wiping my tray and reached for several clean glasses. Distracted, I asked, "What rumors?" as I arranged the flutes on the tray.

"You know the rumors!" She leaned in close and in a hushed, conspiratorial tone whispered, "About the father and the scandal."

I lifted the green glass bottle of prosecco and carefully poured one hundred and eighty milliliters in the first flute.

Oh God.

Those rumors.

Warmth crept up my cheeks.

Barone Cavalieri's late wife, the mother of his sons Enzo and Cesare, died under mysterious circumstances over fifteen years ago. It caused a huge scandal. The topic tore the *I pettegolezzi del villaggio* in different directions. Some said she killed herself because she was a religious woman and could no longer bear to satisfy her husband's ungodly tastes in the bedroom. Others said he accidentally killed her in the middle of some rather vigorous, to put it mildly, lovemaking. Still others said he straight up murdered her.

The image of Barone's tall, powerful body looming over me as his dark, piercing glare held me in thrall clashed with all the salacious stories I had heard about his sexual kinks and appetites over the years.

The flute I had been filling bubbled over with crisp, white foam as I overfilled the glass, toppling it. I stepped out of the way as fizzing prosecco covered the white marble tabletop and dripped onto the floor. "*Che due palle!*"

Milana helped me lift the flutes off the tray. "I, for one, don't think he's a murderer. I'm sure it was just rumors started by a bunch of jealous bitches who were angry, because they couldn't tempt Barone and his legendary coc—"

"Milana!" I hissed again, furiously turning my head to make sure we weren't being overheard. I swept the spilled prosecco into the nearby porcelain sink with a towel.

"—to their beds," she finished in a rush before stuffing another pear in her mouth to stop herself from saying anything more.

I used the towel to cover my mouth as I laughed. "You're a terrible influence."

She laughed as she unabashedly talked around the appetizer in her mouth. "The worst."

The sound of voices coming closer echoed down the carved stone corridor to our left.

Milana scurried to finish righting as many of the pear halves as she could. "We better hurry or Signora Rossi will have our heads for not doing our jobs."

I splashed the bare minimum amount of prosecco in the flutes and lifted the tray. It wasn't like it mattered, no one was interested in drinking it anyway.

I headed toward the stone corridor to the right, away from the incoming voices. The lower level of the villa was a labyrinth of narrow corridors and small, cave-like rooms radiating from the center of the vast catering kitchen reserved for special events, like spokes on a wheel.

As I neared an intersecting corridor, voices raised in anger reached me.

"I will not stand for it, Renata!"

I started. It was Enzo Cavalieri, the groom, yelling at his bride. Hissing air through my teeth, I covered my mouth and looked around, hoping they had not heard me.

Renata cackled in return. "There's nothing you can do about it now, *husband.*"

I peeked around the corner and watched as Enzo snatched her around the upper arm and dragged her into one of the cave rooms. Its heavy oak door, hung with ancient wrought iron hinges, slammed shut behind them.

I tightened my grip on the tray as I was forced to walk past the door to get back outside, where I was supposed to be passing out drinks.

Even though I knew I shouldn't... I couldn't resist pausing just outside the door to see if I could hear anything more.

The thickness of the door muffled much of what they were saying, or technically, shouting.

"Stuck with—"

"Baby."

"—if it's even mine."

"—ruin my name—"

"*Vaffanculo!*"

I was so caught up in the drama, I didn't hear the heavy footsteps behind me until it was too late.

CHAPTER 2

AMARA

"*W*hat do you think you're doing?"
At the sound of Barone Cavalieri's commanding voice, I screamed and dropped my tray of glasses. *"Madonna santa!"* I exclaimed as I bent to retrieve the broken pieces.

"Leave it. I'll find a servant," he ordered.

Surveying the scattered pieces of broken glass, my cheeks burned as I responded quietly, "I *am* the servant, Don Cavalieri."

I glanced up at him through my eyelashes. He lowered his brow in a deep scowl. No doubt angry at me for eavesdropping and breaking all these expensive crystal flutes. Despite being in his mid-forties he looked like he could easily best any man half his age. An entire life spent working the vines, side by side with his men, had tanned his skin and honed his muscles. Normally, tall men were lean and almost wiry, but not Barone Cavalieri. His height only made his obvious strength that much more imposing. Going prematurely gray did not diminish his handsome features; in fact, it made him all that much more god-like. When I was a child, I'd often pictured Don Cavalieri as the embodiment of Jupiter, with his Roman nose and sharp, angular features, looking as if he was always scowling.

Kind of like he was doing now.

Determined to remove the mess as quickly as possible and then dig a deep hole in the earth, crawl in, and die, I said, "I'm sorry, sir. I'll clean it up right away."

In my haste, I lowered my knee onto a sharp piece of glass. The jagged edge tore through my silk stocking and stabbed deep into my skin. Startled by the pain, I rocked backward, unbalanced.

He moved so fast it was just a blur of color.

Don Cavalieri's large hand cradled my skull, stopping my momentum before my head could connect with the stone wall. I blinked several times in shock as I realized he had crouched down to save me from further injury, wedging my body between his open knees. My hand gripped the hard muscle of his thigh. My shoulder was against his... *dio santo!*

I struggled to rise. "I'm fine! I'm fine. Really, I'm fine!"

Don Cavalieri tightened his grip. "Stop fighting me."

I stilled instantly. My rapid heartbeat made it hard to breathe. I closed my eyes and sent a prayer up to the Madonna. *Please don't let me pass out.* I would never survive the embarrassment.

Placing one arm around my back and the other under my knees, he lifted me with ease. I tilted my head back at the same moment he looked down. Our lips were so close we were breathing the same air.

For one crazy moment, I thought he was going to kiss me.

It was pure insanity, of course.

Don Cavalieri hadn't known I existed before now. Not really. That moment earlier was probably nothing. More than likely he'd been staring at one of the guests, or annoyed that I had passed a guest and not offered them a glass, or something like that.

Powerful men like him didn't notice little mice like me.

The moment was broken when the oak door behind us swung open.

Before Enzo could say anything, Renata scrambled past him and down the corridor. He looked between me and his father. *"Che cavolo è successo?"*

Don Cavalieri's words rumbled through his chest and against my side as he spoke. " *Nulla. Me ne occupo io. Stai trascurando i tuoi ospiti."*

Enzo ran a hand through his hair. His knuckles were scraped and torn. My eyes widened. He looked like he had punched a wall. After hesitating, he nodded. *"Sì, Papà."*

He stormed down the corridor.

Leaving me alone with his imposing father.

I stared straight ahead, worried I would say something stupid if I looked into his dark eyes. "You can put me down, sir. I'm sure I can walk."

His only response was to stride down the corridor in the opposite direction of Enzo. He carried me for several minutes, taking a dizzying array of left and right turns into ever-darkening corridors which seemed to take us deeper and deeper inside the mountain.

Finally, we came to an ancient stone archway that was clearly Roman. The open archway had been closed off, probably in the fifteenth century, with a pair of massive oak doors which looked like someone had fashioned them from old wine barrels.

Don Cavalieri kicked the doors open. He strode into the room and placed me on the edge of a large executive desk the size of a bed before ordering, "Stay there," over his shoulder as he turned toward a cabinet with a painted scenic panel depicting the Abruzzo countryside, surrounded by gold-leaf scrollwork on its front.

I glanced down to where my palm touched the cool, polished surface of the desk. It was a beautiful walnut, intricately carved into an elaborate Gothic pattern of scrolls and fauna. The inlaid surface was in the *pieta dura* fashion with agate, marble, and lapis lazuli depicting a grape and vine motif. This desk probably cost more than all my ancestors had ever made in their combined lifetimes.

While it may be the twenty-first century around the rest of the world, in our village, tucked into a fertile valley at the foot of the Apennine mountains, it might as well still be the fifteenth century. The Cavalieri family had ruled over this valley since there were kings and princes on Italian soil.

The Cavalieri legacy was the legacy of wine making in Italy.

And Don Barone Cavalieri was the master of it all.

He and his two sons, Lorenzo and Cesare, were revered in my village. Their winery was the primary source of employment and wealth for the villagers. If you didn't work the vines, then you probably worked in one of their other innumerable businesses or fed off the scraps of their luxury lifestyle.

Like me.

I immediately tried to leap off the desk.

Don Cavalieri was there in an instant, clasping the tops of my thighs to hold me in place.

The breath left my body.

He then leaned down to my ear and gently scolded me. "I am tiring of you disobeying me, *dolcezza*. If you were not injured, I'd take you over my knee like an errant child."

My cheeks flamed as I lowered my head, hiding my embarrassment behind my hair. "Sorry, Don Cavalieri."

He turned back to the cabinet. The warmth from his hands lingered on my thighs. As he rummaged through the first aid contents, I glanced around the room.

It was a blending of sumptuous luxury and raw nature, not unlike the Cavalieri men.

The walls were sandstone, no doubt carved out by hand hundreds of years ago. They reached high above us, where they ended in an arched cathedral ceiling, a brass and crystal chandelier dangling from a heavy gilt chain in the center. A fresco of the sky at dawn was painted on the ceiling, as if to bring sunshine into the darkness. There were even a few chubby cherubs peeking out from behind the clouds. Behind the desk stood an elaborate bookcase with a large space in the center to accommodate a gilt-framed still-life painting of a vibrant arrangement of flowers with a realistic-looking glass of wine and a silver platter with a crust of bread near it.

The office was large enough to accommodate the massive desk and several oxblood leather sofas and chairs set before a vast stone fireplace. A black marble-inlaid vitrine with gold scrollwork was situated nearby, displaying bottles of Cavalieri wine from various vintages probably dating back centuries by the look of the dripping red wax-topped, slightly dusty bottles.

Everywhere I looked, it screamed old money.

The room was filled with impossibly expensive antique furniture, bronze statues on black marble pedestals, and priceless paintings depicting old agrarian scenes of laborers hunched over baskets laden with bunches of grapes and of donkey carts pulling barrels of wine down lonely, crushed-stone paths.

That was where I belonged.

As one of the faceless workers lost to time, whose labor made all this luxury possible.

Not here, sitting on his desk, bleeding on a carpet that was probably woven by actual Persians.

He turned back to me holding a roll of gauze, a bandage, and a small brown glass jar. Placing them to the side on the desk, he ran the tips of his fingers over my injured knee until he was almost touching the piece of glass which still protruded from my skin. With his free hand, he curved his finger under my chin, lifting my gaze. "I want you to look at me."

His dark eyes were too intense, too piercing, too all-knowing.

It was like staring straight into the dark side of the sun.

I lowered my gaze.

"Tsk. Tsk. Tsk. I said eyes on me, *dolcezza*."

Dolcezza.

Sweetness.

The word rolled off his tongue like warm honey.

One eyebrow arched. "Don't make me tell you again."

I licked my lips, then swallowed nervously.

His gaze briefly went to my mouth, then returned to my eyes. His eyes seemed even darker than before if that was even possible.

He stroked the edge of my jaw with his thumb. "I want you to take a deep breath. Then I'm going to count to three."

Instead of drawing air in, my lungs froze.

His lips quirked up on one side as he shifted his thumb to lightly stroke my lower lip. "Open your mouth and breathe, *piccola*."

Piccola. He spoke to me as if I were a child, and not a woman of twenty-four.

I opened my lips and, without thought, pressed just the barest tip of my tongue against his thumb, tasting the salt of his skin. My eyes widened. I couldn't believe I had just done that. I tried to snap my lips shut, but he pushed his thumb deeper into my mouth. His skin tasted slightly minty from the sage and provolone appetizers we were serving to the guests.

I was so mortified and distracted, I didn't even notice him pulling out the piece of glass until it was too late.

I cried out at the sharp sting of pain.

He shifted his hand to cradle my face. "It is almost over."

I shook my head.

No, it needed to be over now.

I couldn't take much more of his nearness, of the intimacy of it. "I need to get back to work. Signora Rossi will be angry as it is when she learns I broke the glasses. Thank you for taking the shard out. I can manage from here."

"What is my name?" he asked abruptly.

My brow furrowed. As if everyone in Italy didn't know who he was. "Don Cavalieri."

He nodded. "*Sì, the boss.* And who owns this villa?"

I bit my lip. "You do."

"And who owns the village and all the surrounding fields as far as the eye can see?"

"You do," I whispered.

"And who is paying your wage for this event?"

"You are."

"So, you understand then? I am the master of everything... *and everyone...* in my domain. It would be foolish to defy me."

My body trembled slightly. "Sì, Don Cavalieri."

"Brava ragazza."

Good girl.

His hands reached for my black skirt. He shifted the hem above my knee by several inches. When he went to shift it higher, I flattened my palms on my thighs. "What are you doing?"

"I need to remove your stocking to cleanse the wound."

Uncaring if I had any further objections, he shifted the skirt until the fabric bunched at the tops of my thighs, exposing the edge of my black silk stockings and my black with pink ribbon garter belt. Everyone knew that no matter how poor an Italian woman may be, she still spent money on quality fashion, and that included lingerie.

The tips of his fingers brushed my exposed skin as he reached under the garter strap and unlatched it. I clenched my stomach to stop the butterflies which were forming inside of me at his touch.

He lifted my leg and ran his hand along the underside of my calf before pulling off my high heel. He then gently rolled the nylons down over my toes. His warm hand lingered on the sensitive spot behind my knee. "It looks as though I owe you a new pair of stockings."

I blinked. "No. No. This was all my fault. I shouldn't have been... lingering... in the hallway like that."

Again, his eyebrow arched. "You mean eavesdropping."

I opened my mouth to deny it, but then thought better of it. There would be no point; not only did he catch me at it, but I also had a feeling he'd know I was lying.

"You should be very careful, *dolcezza*. An ancient villa like this has many secrets. Dangerous ones. I would hate to see you get hurt."

Is he threatening me?

Dio santo!

This is bad. Really bad.

The scandal over his wife's death raced across my brain.

I needed to get as far away from Don Cavalieri as possible.

He leaned in close and reached past me. A slight gasp of fear escaped my lips at the sudden movement.

He held up a cobalt blue glass pitcher. After pouring some water on a bunched-up piece of gauze, he cleaned the wound. He then opened the brown glass jar. "Yarrow, basil, and olive oil. We've used it as a salve for cuts for generations."

I nodded stiffly.

The warmth of his fingers melted the salve until it glistened on my skin, immersing us in a sweet, earthy scent. I hardly felt any twinge of pain as he gently bandaged the wound.

The moment he was done, I blurted out, "Can I leave now?"

"No."

"No?"

"No."

His hand brushed my bare thigh.

Out of panic, I snapped my knees closed, wincing at the

sharp stab of pain it caused. Before I could push my skirt back down into place, he put both hands on my thighs just above my knees and forced my legs open again.

Primal fear and awareness coursed up my spine.

His thumbs caressed my inner thighs. "What is your name?"

"Why do you need to know?"

"Because I want to know—and I always get what I want."

Seeing no option around it, my lips barely moved. "Amara Beneventi."

"Amara." He rolled my name around in his mouth, as if he were tasting it. "What does it mean?"

My lips thinned. "Bitter."

His gaze moved to my mouth.

I instinctively licked my lips.

"I cannot agree. I think you would taste sweet, with just a hint of tart, like a grape warmed in the sun. Its juice bursting onto your tongue the moment you pierce its soft skin."

His fingers tightened on my thighs.

The breath left my lungs on a sigh as I leaned forward, my eyelids lowering. I was entranced.

"*Dolcezza.*"

"Barone."

"*Papà!*"

I blinked as cold reality crashed over us like an icy wall of water.

"*Papà*, are you in there?"

It was Cesare, his son and my former schoolmate.

I barely had time to push my skirt back into place before he burst through the office doors.

CHAPTER 3

BARONE

The moment the office doors flew open, I shifted my stance so my body was blocking Amara from view. I didn't want anyone to catch even a glimpse of her open thighs.

I had captured a vulnerable little bird with a broken wing, and I had no intention of sharing my new pet.

She was entrancing. Her thick black hair fell in waves halfway down her back. A very unfashionable length for women today, which only added to her almost otherworldly appeal. But it wasn't her full pink lips or her soft features which most intrigued me.

It was her beautiful dark eyes.

There was a somber light emanating from them which I found captivating. It was the look of someone who had experienced enormous sadness but remained astonishingly hopeful. I had seen the look before, but never in one so young.

Had we not been interrupted, I would have given in to

temptation and kissed her deeply, if only from curiosity. To see if I could chase away the sadness and replace it with desire.

Cesare flopped down into one of the soft leather chairs near the stone fireplace. He threw his head back with laughter. "If Renata continues flirting with the tradesmen, we are going to need to find a new label maker and machinist, because Enzo is going to kill them both."

I closed my eyes for a moment and prayed for patience. I had fiercely argued with Lorenzo, until the very moment they needed him at the altar, against this wedding. I rubbed my jaw where it was still a little sore from the fistfight that resulted from our last *conversation*.

The Cavalieri legacy was important, but not more important than my son's happiness. She was not the right woman for him. We all knew it. She would never make him happy. I knew she would tarnish the Cavalieri name far more than a baby born out of wedlock ever could. And it's not as if we would not accept the child. But while my son may have inherited my late wife's eyes, he also inherited my stubbornness. There was no deterring him.

"Go out there and keep the peace. And for fuck's sake, keep Renata away from other men, at least until the wedding feast is over. We have business associates here. We don't need more scandal."

Cesare shook his head as he waved his hand in the air. "Keeping that woman away from men would be like throwing a fish into the woods. Speaking of business, Sebastian Diamanti just arrived. He's looking for you."

I nodded. "Go into the private cellar and grab a bottle of the

2005 and give it to Antonella to decant. I'll meet Sebastian on the terrace soon."

Cesare rose and buttoned his beige linen blazer. "I'll also have the men prepare a case of the 2011, since that is the closest vintage ready to drink and—hold on, is that Amara hiding behind you?"

Cesare looked around my shoulder. "It is you! Amara Beneventi... looking as beautiful as ever."

He went to step around me, but I shifted to block him.

Cesare's brow creased.

"Hello, Cesare," said Amara softly from over my shoulder as she tried to slide off the desk.

I reached back and placed a proprietary hand on her thigh.

Squeezing my fingers gently as a warning. She stilled.

Cesare's gaze shifted from my eyes to just over my shoulder, then back again.

I narrowed my gaze on my son, daring him to test my authority. "Amara had a small accident. I'm attending to her injury."

Amara shifted again. "I'm fine, really. I should get back to work."

I kept my eyes locked on Cesare's. "Stay right where you are. *Cesare was leaving to do as I asked*, and I still haven't finished with your bandage."

There was a long, awkward silence.

Cesare's jaw clicked from side to side, as if he were chewing over my words. His eyes narrowed as he cocked his head, assessing me. "Of course, but first, *I would like to say hello to Amara*."

Insisting he leave without talking to my captured little bird would only raise questions I had no intention of answering. I crossed my arms over my chest and stepped slightly to one side, allowing Cesare to see Amara, who was still sitting demurely on the edge of my desk.

He grabbed both of her hands and greeted her warmly, giving her a kiss on each cheek. He whispered something in her ear, which I couldn't hear. I held my breath, waiting for her response. After a moment's hesitation, she shook her head no.

I released the tension I was holding in my shoulders.

It was clear they were old friends. So, it would make sense for him to greet her affectionately if he hadn't seen her in a while. At least that was what I told myself to tamp down the completely irrational jealousy which was clawing inside my chest.

Cesare straightened and cast a sidelong glance at me. "Amara and I have known one another for years." He turned back to Amara. "It broke my heart when you chose *Liceo classico* over *Istituto commerciale*. It took me months to find another pretty girl who was willing to share her notes. You had such a keen business mind. Far better than mine. Why didn't you take the commerce track?"

"I wanted to, but my stepfather wouldn't allow it. He said no one would want to marry an ugly girl who keeps her nose in a ledger." Amara's eyes widened. She then lowered her head, letting her silky raven's-wing hair partially hide her features, as if her own bold honesty startled her.

I caught a glimpse of her eyes before she dipped her head. There it was again, that sweet sadness.

Cesare placed a hand over his heart. "I was very sorry to

hear about your mother's passing. I wanted to pay my respects, but work—"

Amara cut him off by placing a hand on his forearm. "It's fine. It was years ago. I'm fine."

I wrapped my hand around her wrist and pulled it off Cesare. "I need to finish with her bandage, and you need to see to that bottle of wine I requested for Sebastian."

Cesare smiled. "Yes, of course." He gave Amara a quick bow. "I will seek you out later so we can catch up. Dare I hope Milana is also here at the villa?"

A tentative, shy smile tugged at her closed lips. It was a thing of sweet beauty to see, and it angered me that Cesare caused it.

"She is."

"Does she still hate me?"

Amara nodded. "Probably."

Cesare once more placed his hand over his heart, but this time it was as if he were wounded. He then gave Amara a wink. "Maybe I will risk saying hello, anyway."

Amara pressed her hands to her cheeks as she shook her head. "Bring a weapon if you do."

Cesare winked and left, leaving the doors open behind him.

I followed him to the threshold, slammed the doors shut, and slid the ancient wrought iron bolt closed as well. When I turned back, Amara was on her feet, holding the torn remnants of her stocking while she put her shoe back on.

I scowled. "Who told you to get off that desk?"

She fidgeted with the stocking as she shifted her hips to keep her weight off her injured knee. "I need to go. Signora Rossi will be looking for me."

"I don't give a damn about Signora Rossi. Get your ass back up on that desk."

As I walked toward her, she scurried around the desk, standing behind my high-backed leather executive chair as if it would shield her from me... and my intentions.

"It's nice that you don't care about Signora Rossi, but I do. She's probably not going to pay me for this shift as it is because of the broken glasses, but I can't afford to be cut from her roster. The tourist season is almost over. I'll need the work."

I reached into my inside blazer pocket and pulled out my billfold. "Don't worry about the damn glasses. You're not going back to work. Not injured like that." I pulled out two one-hundred-euro bills and tossed them onto the desk. "There. I've paid you."

Her eyes widened as all the color drained from her pretty cheeks. Her body stiffened as she stared at the folded bills.

Fuck.

"Amara, I—"

Before I could apologize for the unintended insult, she bolted past me for the doors.

I couldn't let her leave. Not yet. Not with her thinking I believed she was no better than a whore to be bought with a few hundred euros.

I snatched her by the upper arm and spun her around until her back was against the door. I placed my hand on the curve of her waist and leaned in. "We're not finished."

"Don Cavalieri—"

"Barone."

"What?"

"You called me Barone a moment ago."

"I'm sorry."

"Stop apologizing."

"Don Cavalieri—"

"Barone."

She sighed in frustration.

I tucked an errant curl behind her ear before stroking the edge of her cheekbone with the backs of my knuckles. "I can do this all day."

"You have guests waiting."

"Let them wait."

Another frustrated sigh. She really was adorable when she was angry.

"I have to get back to work."

My brow furrowed. Regardless of how she interpreted my trying to give her money, I couldn't allow her to return to work. It wasn't her knee, that was just a bad scratch. It was the idea of her out there serving my guests. Serving the men I had invited to celebrate my son's wedding. Serving men getting drunk on my wine. Possibly putting herself in harm's way from their advances and grasping hands. The idea didn't sit right with me.

"No."

"No?"

"No."

"You can't say no."

"I think we've already established that in this villa and in fact for the entire village, my word is law. I'm the master here and I say no."

She crossed her arms over her chest. "Well... well, I say yes."

I ran my hand down the ugly black tie she wore as part of her catering uniform before tugging on the end. A woman this beautiful and intriguing should be draped in Gucci, Versace, and Armani, not boring white cotton blouses and serviceable black skirts. "Keep being impertinent and I will find another use for this tie."

The color came back to her cheeks.

"Please, Don... Barone... I must go."

I looked down at her. She was so tiny; the top of her head barely reached my chin. She was right. I had neglected my guests for far too long. The problem was, I didn't seem to care. I hadn't been this captivated by a woman in years.

"Say it again."

"I must go."

"No. My name. I want to hear it again."

I traced her bottom lip with my fingertip, wanting to feel the word as she said it.

After a moment's hesitation, she breathed, "Barone."

I leaned my hips in, pinning her to one of the doors, careful of her injured knee. "Again."

I watched her gaze as it lowered to my mouth. My cock lengthened.

"Barone."

I rested my forearm over her head against the door. "Again."

"Please...."

I leaned down and inhaled the light lemon verbena scent of her glossy hair as I gently but firmly applied pressure with my fingers against her waist. "Again, Amara."

"Barone."

I kissed her forehead.

"Barone."

I traced my lips to the side of her cheek.

"Barone."

I kissed the corner of her mouth before tracing the tip of my tongue along the seam. "Open your mouth for me, *dolcezza*."

I inhaled her sigh before tasting her lips.

And it was all I was going to allow myself.

A taste.

She was too young, too innocent, too naïve for a man like me.

Too sweet.

My tongue slipped inside her mouth, and I couldn't suppress a groan as I pressed my body forward, needing to feel her soft body against my own.

The moment her tongue hesitantly twirled around mine, I was lost.

I moved my hand to grasp her jaw as I deepened the kiss, driving my free hand into her hair and tilting her head back as I pulled her away from the door. I walked her backward to the sofa. Our bodies fell together, my arm cushioning her. I kissed down her neck as I yanked her skirt up to her waist. Shifting my hips, I skimmed my hand over her body to reach between her thighs. The wet silk of her panties nearly drove me mad.

I placed an open-mouthed kiss along her jaw, resisting the urge to sink my teeth into her soft, scented flesh. "Mother of God, you taste as sweet as you look, *dolcezza*. I could eat you in one bite."

Her small hands gripped my shoulders. "I'm not sure... I...."

I claimed her mouth again as I rubbed the hard ridge of my cock against her hip, needing to ease the tension. Running my hand over her flat belly, I untucked her white blouse and then reached for her uniform tie.

I pulled on the loose knot as I growled, "I'm going to take you to my bed, tie you up by your wrists, and fuck you until your bones melt."

Amara stilled.

I closed my eyes.

Fuck.

She pushed against my chest. "Get off me."

I tried to secure her wrists without hurting her. "Amara—"

"No! Let me go!" she screamed as she bucked and kicked beneath me.

Not wanting her knee to bleed again with her struggles, I stood and offered her my hand.

Her breathing was heavy as she pushed her skirt back down into place before rising, but only after giving my outstretched hand a scathing look. She took a wobbly step and stumbled over the edge of the carpet. I gripped her upper arm to steady her but released it when she directed a furious look at me.

She marched to the doors. Her shoulders sagged when she quickly realized she could not pull back the heavy wrought iron bolt.

I watched her from behind as she straightened her shoulders and tilted her chin up. She took a deep breath, then requested in slow, even tones, "Please open the doors, *Don Cavalieri.*"

I stepped closer and leaned my shoulder against the door on the left. I studied her profile. She had the cutest little stubborn chin. It had the tiniest little cleft in it. I wanted to lick it.

Dammit, what the fuck was wrong with me?

I had practically called a woman young enough to be my daughter a whore... twice.

Yet, I still didn't want her to leave, not like this.

26

"Amara, look at me."

She tilted her head slightly in my direction, sending me a glare that was icy enough to freeze lava. "If you are *finished* with me, sir, I'd like to get back to my *real* duties."

I pulled on the iron bolt, unlocking the double doors. As she reached for the handle, I pressed an open palm to the door, keeping it closed. "This changes nothing. You are not to return to serving my guests. I want you to go to the stables behind the villa and ask for Alfonso. Tell him I said to drive you home."

She kept her gaze straight ahead.

After a moment of tense silence, I removed my hand and stood back.

She flung the doors open. As she crossed the threshold, I tossed out one final warning. "Don't disobey me, Amara, or there will be consequences."

She tossed one last look at me over her shoulder before disappearing into the dark corridor.

CHAPTER 4

AMARA

I smoothed my hair and took a deep breath before rounding the corner into the catering kitchen. It had taken me close to twenty minutes to navigate through the labyrinth of corridors back to civilization. Especially since I had to stop and remove my other stocking and garter belt.

Milana raced up to me. "Where have you been? Signora Rossi is having kittens over your disappearance."

Before I could respond, Signora Rossi approached me. "Silly, stupid girl. I do not pay you to lurk in dark corners and not work."

I tightened the knot on my black uniform tie. "I'm so sorry, Signora. I dropped some glasses and then cut myself trying to clean them up."

She waved her hand in the air. "Never mind the glasses. I'll send someone to clean up your mess. I need you to help with the platters. The Diamantis have arrived. We cannot have them thinking we are no better than a heathen backwater to Rome."

I glanced over my shoulder in case Barone had followed me. He hadn't. Still. His final warning echoed in my head. If I didn't return to work, I risked Signora Rossi's wrath. If I did, I risked Barone's, which would be significantly worse. Still... I needed the work. It wasn't like he'd even notice. I was one of over fifty staff assisting with the wedding feast.

I was probably nothing more than a pretty face to him.

Worse, he thought I was a slut who'd just fall into bed with him.

I gritted my teeth. No! It was even worse than that. He thought he could fuck me on an office sofa! A lowly peasant like me didn't even deserve his exalted bed. The humiliation stung. I couldn't believe I had allowed myself to become entranced by him. If he hadn't shocked me with his startling intentions about tying me up, I might very well have opened my legs for him. What a disgrace that would have been. My poor mother would have rolled in her grave if her daughter had done such a shameful thing.

Signora Rossi cut into my thoughts. "Stupid girl. Stop standing there with your mouth open catching flies! *Vai! Vai! Vai!*"

I bowed my head and grabbed a platter of roasted beets, burrata, and black walnuts and scurried through the door out into the waning sunlight.

The Cavalieri villa clung to the mountainside as if its warm, bread-colored walls, forest-green shutters, and iron balconies had sprung up from the earth with the rock itself. Like the Cavalieris. Their legacy stretched back further than anyone's memories. They were probably the ones to plant the first grape vine. The first to press an olive. The first to lift their faces to the warm Abruzzo sun and claim all within view as their own.

Stretched out onto the terraced lawns, tucked between the beech, pine, and oak trees, were long, sun-bleached wooden tables topped with elegant cream lace. Hand-carved wooden bowls spilled over with lavender, dahlia, gardenia, and honeysuckle flowers found within the fields. Heaping platters of *fusilli pinolati, tagliatelle con aragosta e zucchini, antipasto di rollatine di salame e carciofi and spiedini* were interspersed between the crystal flutes, sterling silver flatware, and bone china with the Cavalieri crest of a rearing horse emblazoned on their smooth ivory surfaces in gold and cobalt blue. And this was just the first course.

As I found a place next to some steamed artichokes with grilled lemon for the platter I was holding, a small army of staff brought in bottle after bottle of the Cavalieri Winery's finest vintage. Nothing but the best for the eldest son.

Before I could return for another platter, Cesare stopped me.

"Amara, a moment, please."

Glancing over his shoulder at a frowning Signora Rossi, I shook my head. "I really can't right now, Cesare."

He followed my glance. With only a look from him, Signora Rossi slunk away. He turned back to me, a charming smile on his face. "It seems you can."

I pulled at the collar of my blouse as I gave him barely a nod. It seemed all Cavalieri men were the same—charming and easygoing until they were told no. Then the fangs came out. That wasn't the alarming part. The alarming part was how easily they slipped back behind their civilized façade afterward, as if nothing had happened. It was like seeing a bolt of lightning in the middle of a summer day. A flash of power and strength that you were only half-certain even occurred.

He gestured for us to walk deeper into the trees, away from the guests. I glanced anxiously about, hoping his father was nowhere nearby.

Cesare lit a hand-rolled cigarette. "What was all that about earlier?"

"Nothing. A misunderstanding."

He studied me carefully. Keeping his eyes on me, he brought his cigarette to his lips and inhaled before blowing out a swirling cloud of blue smoke. "My father doesn't have *misunderstandings*."

"I don't know what to tell you, Cesare."

"How about the truth? Amara, we are friends."

I backed away a few steps. "No, Cesare. We were friends. We are no longer friends. We are not the same people we once were, back in school. You live high on a mountain in a world of privilege and luxury. And I am a servant and shopgirl."

He frowned. "Don't speak about yourself that way. You know I never treated—"

"I have to go."

He grabbed my upper arm as I tried to leave. "He is my father and I love and respect him, but if he hurt you somehow...."

"It's not like that. He—"

"What do you think you're doing?"

We both turned to see Milana approach. She pushed her hand down on Cesare's forearm, breaking his grasp. "Get away from her."

Cesare's entire demeanor tensed as he straightened his shoulders. "Milana."

Milana tugged on my wrist to pull me behind her. "You don't talk to me or my friend, Cesare. Do you understand me?"

His eyes narrowed. He wet his finger and thumb and crushed the hot ash at the tip of his cigarette. "One of these days, I will not find your anger so amusing."

Milana's fingers tightened around my wrist.

Wanting to protect my friend, I laid a comforting hand on her shoulder as I looked at Cesare. "You should go. We have work to do."

Keeping his gaze locked on Milana, he asked me, "Do you need me to speak to my father?"

My eyes widened. That was the last thing in the world I needed. "No. Really, Cesare. Thank you, but no. It really was just a silly thing not worth mentioning."

I held my breath and waited. His gaze shifted between the two of us. I knew he didn't believe me and sensed he wanted to say something more to Milana. Finally, he nodded and walked off.

We both let out a collective breath.

I leaned against the strong trunk of a nearby oak tree.

Navigating these Cavalieri men was exhausting.

I just wanted to go home, get a hot shower, climb into bed, and try not to repeatedly play over in my head what had happened in Barone's office.

Milana crossed her arms over her chest. "Why was he talking to you?"

Although she was my best friend, I wasn't quite ready to share with anyone what happened with Barone just yet, not until I'd had time to process it on my own. I shrugged. "We haven't really seen one another in years. He was saying he was sorry about Mama." It wasn't exactly a lie.

She glared over her shoulder at Cesare's retreating back.

As if feeling the heat of her gaze, he turned and gave her a mock salute, then turned back toward the guests.

I observed Milana's reaction. Her whole body stiffened in anger. "Are you ever going to tell me what he did to deserve your undying rage?"

The three of us were never close friends in school, but we were friends.

Until one day, everything changed.

Milana was different after that. She tried to hide it with wide smiles and loud laughs, but I could tell. Something hardened inside of her. Soon after, she stopped talking to many of our friends, but especially Cesare. She seemed to have a special hatred for him.

Milana headed back toward the villa as I followed closely behind. "He knows what he did," she whispered under her breath.

I left it at that, not wishing to fight.

Just then a chill ran down my spine, as if I were being watched.

I scanned the mingling guests but didn't catch the eye of anyone.

Most of the guests were clustering around the very glamorous Diamanti family, who had just arrived by helicopter. I'd heard the staff whispering earlier that the infamous Sebastian Diamanti and his brother Rafaello were certain to attend as their family was close with the Cavalieris.

The Diamantis controlled almost three quarters of the world's diamond trade. They had unfathomable amounts of money and influence... and if the rumors were true, were more dangerous than all the Italian mafia families combined.

Not wanting to get caught staring, I shifted my gaze to continue searching the crowd.

There was Renata still flirting with a group of men as Enzo seethed nearby, but no sign of Barone.

Shaking off the feeling, I went to get more food platters.

This really was the worst wedding ever.

CHAPTER 5

BARONE

I crossed the private terrace and clapped Sebastian on the upper arms. After giving him a kiss on each cheek, I cupped his jaw. "A face only the devil could love. Speaking of the devil, where is that reprobate father of yours?"

Sebastian shrugged out of his Armani blazer and placed it on the back of a nearby chair as I poured us both a glass from our 2005 vintage. "He sends his well wishes for the happy couple and his regrets."

I smirked as I handed Sebastian his glass. "Bullshit."

My old friend, Fabrizio Diamanti, had been nursing a grudge against me for years for not sanctioning a teenage marriage between my eldest son, Lorenzo, and his young daughter, Arabella. It would have been an epic union of two of Italy's most powerful families. Unfortunately for him, I was determined to let my children forge their own paths in life. I wanted them to have the choice I was never given. For Fabrizio, children were not family, they were pawns to be moved about a grand chessboard. Each move meant to garner him more wealth and influence for his Diamanti empire. Of course, one didn't secure the lion's share of the world's diamond trade by having morals or being timid.

We clinked glasses and sipped.

Sebastian smiled. "Excellent as always."

I nodded. "It was a good year for wine."

We both moved toward the wrought iron railing. My private terrace embodied the ancient story of Italy. On one side it was built into the mountain. On another was an Etruscan rock wall. On the final side was some of the finest wrought iron work in Italy. A masterpiece of scroll work which morphed into the Cavalieri family crest.

While ancient pines shaded the terrace, it overlooked the entire mountain valley, my own little piece of paradise. Below us, the wedding guests mingled among the food-laden tables as a quartet played Puccini's *La Boheme*, hardly fitting wedding music and yet somehow fitting for *this* wedding.

Sebastian gazed down at the guests. "My father prepared a file on Enzo's bride, Renata Moretti, and her father, Bruno. Apparently, he has some... unsavory business partners."

I stiffened. Sebastian was not much older than my own sons and, in many ways, I considered him like a son, but that wouldn't save him if he started trouble with my family. I swirled the wine in my glass, the ruby liquid picking up the faint, final rays of the sun and reflecting them back as glittering shimmers of light. "And?"

"And... I burned it. Your secrets are your own, my friend. My father's ways will not be mine. I took over the company a few months ago. Things are going to be different. That is, once I've finished cleaning up his messes," responded Sebastian secretively.

We both watched as Enzo approached his scandalous bride, my troublesome daughter-in-law.

Sebastian raised his chin and nodded in my son's direction. "Is he at least happy with his choice?"

I sipped my wine, savoring the wild plum and earthy character which was so emblematic of the Montepulciano grape grown in this region for centuries. Answering carefully, I stated, "I believe he is content to have done the honorable thing. Beyond that, I cannot say, other than this was entirely his choice, not mine."

Sebastian stared down into his glass. "Have you noticed how often the 'honorable thing' seems to bring happiness to one and misery to the other? As if honor needs a blood sacrifice to be honorable?"

I gave him a mirthless smile. "It is not honor which seeks the blood, but the wretched, entangled roots of our family trees which demand it. So, tell me, are you finally contemplating marriage?"

He set his glass aside and cupped one hand with the other. There was a distinctive crack of his knuckle. "Let's just say, I may have to make an *honorable* sacrifice soon."

I placed a hand on his shoulder. "Family is never easy. I too had to marry more out of obligation than choice. It was something I had hoped my sons would never have to face."

He gave me a sidelong glance. "Do you regret it?"

"I don't regret my sons." As I was saying this, I glimpsed Amara emerging from the trees with a heavy platter of food. Her legs were now bare, and she walked with only the slightest limp as she favored her cut knee. I ran the tip of my tongue over the inside of my bottom lip, tasting her with the wine.

Staring at the sway of Amara's hips as she weaved through the guests, heat pooled inside my chest. "I regret missing out on the true passions of life. I married per my father's wishes when I was impossibly young and was a dutiful husband until the day Angelina died. Then I was left with two young sons and a wine empire to run. There was no time for life... for love. It is not the big moments I regret, but the small ones. The soft feel of a woman's hand over my heart. The unguarded looks a woman truly in love gives that feed a man's soul. The peaceful security that comes from knowing you are loved by a good woman." I downed the rest of my wine in an inelegant gulp. Setting the glass aside, I buttoned my linen blazer and clapped Sebastian on the shoulder again. "Don't make my same mistake."

He finished his glass and set it aside. "I may not have a choice."

"Well, at least that is a decision for another day."

"True. Let's join the guests, I know Rafaello and Arabella are eager to say hello."

"In a moment. I have something I need to attend to first."

Some*one* would be closer to the truth.

After parting with Sebastian, I made my way deeper inside the cool interior of the villa. The waxed terracotta brick floors led the way through one open space to another until I reached the winding staircase that would take me down into the old wine cellar which I had converted into an event space.

The moment I appeared, a hush fell over the gathered staff.

An older woman pushed her way to the front. Her thin,

pinched lips barely moved as she asked, "Don Cavalieri, is there something I can assist you with?"

My eyes narrowed as I searched the faces of all the female staff. Each pretty in their own way, but none comparing with the subtle beauty of Amara's dark eyes. Finally, I spotted her. Her shoulders were hunched as she lowered her head and turned to sneak out of the room unseen.

Without looking at the older woman, I said, "No," as I made my way toward Amara, who had already crossed the threshold of the double glass doors to the outside and was hastily making her way across the lawn. She was carrying a large platter of confetti, the sugar-coated almonds painted gold and clustered to look like delicate flowers.

As she glanced over her shoulder and observed my pursuit, she quickened her pace.

I gritted my teeth, resisting the urge to shout her name, not wanting to draw the attention of my guests.

As I neared, her high heel caught in an uneven clump of grass. I reached out just as her ankle bent and her knee buckled. I quickly placed a flat hand under the tray, catching it before it spilled, as I steadied her with a grip on her upper arm.

I called over a passing servant. "Take this," I ordered as I shoved the platter into his empty hands.

I then turned my attention to Amara. I breathed in deeply through my clenched teeth as I tried to cool my anger. I had given her explicit instructions to leave and not to continue serving my guests. Instructions she disobeyed.

Her first instinct was to pull away from my grasp.

I pulled her close to my side and whispered harshly in her ear, "Don't you dare."

Only when she had stilled did I continue. "Can you walk, or did you hurt your ankle as well?"

She lowered her eyes. "I can walk."

I flexed my fingers before tightening my grip on her arm. "Good. Then walk."

I half dragged her across the lawn and around the villa to my stables.

"Where are you taking me?"

"You... don't get to talk."

"But...."

I glared down at her.

Her eyes widened as she closed her lips tightly.

The further we got away from the guests the more agitated she became.

"Don Cavalieri—"

"Barone."

"Fine, Barone. I need to return to the party. My friend will wonder—"

"You should have thought of that earlier. You had a chance to obey me your way. Now we are doing this my way."

She dug her heels in and pulled out of my grasp. She planted a hand on her hip. "You may own all this," she gestured wildly with her other arm, "but you don't own me. You don't get to tell me what to do! I don't care how rich and important you are!"

She was like an angry little sparrow hopping about with ruffled feathers.

I wrapped my arm around her waist and snatched her close, tilting her head back with my finger under her chin. "It's not that I am richer or more important, *dolcezza*. It's that *I'm bigger*."

I gave her a wink before notching my shoulder into her midsection and hoisting her high over my shoulder.

"Oh! You brute! You bully! Let me go!"

"No. You want to act like a petulant child, you will be treated like one."

She pounded on my back with her tiny fists. "I'll scream!"

"No, you won't."

She was far too concerned about what her employer, Signora Rossi, would say if she witnessed this scene because her scream drew attention to us.

As we crossed into the quiet interior of the stone-walled stables, I called out, "Alfonso!"

A tall man in overalls with a cap mostly shading his sun-weathered face appeared, wiping the grease off his hands with a rag. "Yes, Don Cavalieri?" He barely spared a glance at the squirming woman on my shoulder, as if this were an everyday occurrence. It was not. Still, nothing fazed the sixty-five-year-old who had been taking care of my family's automobiles and horses since he could barely walk.

"The keys."

Alfonso nodded. He leaned across the threshold of the room he had just exited and reached for something. The next second he was tossing me the keys to my Fiat 124 Spider Lusso.

"If anyone asks...."

Alfonso shrugged. "I know nothing. I saw nothing."

I smirked. "Good man."

The top was already down on the convertible, so I deposited Amara in the front passenger seat before crossing behind to the driver's side. The moment she touched the car door handle, I called out, "I wouldn't if I were you."

She glared at me over her shoulder before sitting back in the seat and crossing her arms over her chest.

I started the car and pulled out of the stable and onto the crushed white limestone drive, then down the winding road which led into the village.

"Where do you live?"

She tilted her chin high and remained silent.

"Tell me, *dolcezza*, or I will take you to one of my many private properties. Who knows when your friends will see you next?"

She gasped. "Fine. You take the road just past Santa Maria Church and follow it until you come to where the old mill used to be. You then turn at the Roman ruins. My house is the small terracotta one with green shutters set off to one side close to the dying olive tree."

I shifted gears and raced through the streets of Cavalieri. The village my ancestors founded centuries earlier had grown into a small mountainside town which flourished under our guardianship.

As we pulled away from the center of town, the houses grew much smaller and less well-kept. A stark reminder that not everyone flourished in Cavalieri. I turned at the ruins and pulled near to an old farmhouse. The terraced stone walls surrounding the property were falling down. There was an overgrown garden to the side, and shutters with faded, chipped green paint seemed to look on in mournful silence.

I made a mental note to have Signora Rossi quadruple whatever she was paying her staff for the wedding I was neglecting.

I slowed the car as we neared her home. I gripped the steering wheel, reminding myself that this was just that, *her home.* It may anger me to drop such a beautiful, vulnerable crea-ture off here, but that was no excuse to insult her pride.

The second the car stopped she once again turned and reached for the door handle.

I shook my head. "Stop." What kind of ignorant boys had this girl dated that she didn't know better than to not open her own car door?

I got out of the car and circled around. The moment I opened her door, she flew out, feathers ruffled. "There, you have driven me home. Thank you. I'll go now."

I wrapped my hand around her waist. Looking down at her small, angular nose and the little cleft in her chin, I commanded, "Invite me inside."

Her head turned sharply as she surveyed the home and grounds as if searching for something... or someone.

My fingers tightened around her waist. It had never occurred to me that someone had claimed my little sparrow. The thought was... unsettling. "Tell me now. Is there a man who watches over you?"

She bit her lip. I could tell she was preparing to lie to me.

"I want the truth, Amara."

"Shouldn't you be getting back to your son's wedding? They will be missing you soon."

"The wedding can wait." I placed a hand on her lower back and propelled her toward the dilapidated, double-door entrance.

"Wait. We can't!"

My hand curled into a fist. "Who is behind this door that you don't want me to know about?"

I had no right to be making such demands on her.

Still, that wasn't stopping me.

There was something about her. My little wounded bird, who continued to peck and fight at those trying to help her.

"Nothing. No one. It's not like that. It's just that my... my stepfather and stepbrother live here as well, and they can be... difficult... about guests."

It was not unusual in Italy for an unmarried woman in her twenties to still be living at home. Most children lived with their parents until they married. However, I didn't like the fact that she lived with two men who were not blood relatives. I would have to change that and very soon.

I pushed her along. "Well, then. Let's meet these *difficult* men in your life."

If her stepfather and stepbrother were at home and I sensed even the slightest thing wrong with either of them, I was yanking her out of here, kicking and screaming if necessary.

She pushed open the unlocked door and let out a sigh of relief when it was evident the home was deserted. The structure clearly dated back to just after the war. Despite its shabby appearance, it was obvious someone was trying to keep up appearances. There were carefully mended lace curtains on the windows and a slightly chipped porcelain vase with wildflowers on a sideboard.

She stepped forward and turned her rigid back on me. "Thank you for escorting me home. You can leave now."

"Turn around."

"Why?"

"Because I said so."

With a frustrated sigh, she turned around. Her lower lip thrust out in a pout.

"I want a kiss before I leave."

She blinked. "What?"

"You heard me."

"What if I say no?"

I stroked her lower lip with the pad of my thumb. "I'd take one anyway."

"Why are you doing this? Do you think I owe you some kind of payment for the broken glasses?"

She walked over to a kitchen cupboard and pulled down an earthenware jug with a metal lid. She threw off the lid and dumped the contents onto the table. There was a small stack of neatly folded euros and a handful of coins. She gestured to the pile with disgust. "Here! Here is your payment. Take it and leave."

In this exact moment, I couldn't decide if I deserved her anger or not.

But truthfully, I didn't give a damn.

It was time to teach my little bird a lesson.

I shrugged out of my blazer and tossed it aside. I then watched her as I slowly unbuttoned my cuffs and rolled up the linen sleeves of my shirt.

She backed away until her hip hit the white porcelain farmhouse sink. "What do you think you are doing?"

I snatched her around the waist and placed my hand over her mouth to muffle her scream. "Taking my payment."

CHAPTER 6

AMARA

I clawed at the hand covering my mouth as I kicked out. The moment his palm slipped I screamed, but it was cut short when he hauled me over his shoulder again. Not that it would matter. My neighbors were far too used to the sounds of screams and fights coming from this farmhouse to react. They were as afraid of my stepfather and stepbrother as my poor mother had been.

"Which way is your room?"

My only response was a grunt as I tried to lift my torso to get some leverage to kick him again. My high heels fell to the floor with my effort, making my kicks as ineffective as a feather flapping against a tree trunk.

He slapped my ass. "Which way, brat?"

"Ow!"

He slapped my ass again.

"Behind the kitchen," I hissed through clenched teeth as my

tender flesh burned more from humiliation than the actual spanks.

He crossed the smooth brick floor and was forced to bend his tall body practically in half, as he still held me firmly, just to enter my room. He lowered me to my feet and closed the door before standing in front of it, arms crossed over his chest. There was no point in trying to escape. He was blocking the only exit in the narrow, windowless space. My room was actually an old storage room, meant to keep root vegetables and hanging meat as evidenced by the exposed-wood ceiling beams with their simple iron hooks. I had managed to make it my own as best I could with a bright comforter covered in cheery yellow sunflowers, and cornflower blue paint on the crumbling plaster walls.

Barone looked down at my single bed with its simple wrought iron frame covered in faded white paint and frowned. "This cannot be where you sleep."

My back stiffened. "I'm so very sorry the accommodations are not up to your exalted standards, *your kingship*, but I didn't exactly invite you into my bedroom."

He leaned his shoulder against the door as he studied me. I held my breath as his gaze swept over me from the top of my head to the tips of my toes and back, lingering on my mouth. Under his heated scrutiny, my tongue instinctively flicked out to lick my upper lip. His eyes narrowed at the movement. My body trembled slightly from the effort to keep still. This must be what it felt like to be a mouse caught in a predator's trap.

When he finally spoke, I gave a small start at the deep, commanding tone of his voice, which seemed to echo around the small chamber.

"Tell me, *dolcezza*. How have I managed to offend you so deeply?" he asked, quirking one eyebrow up. He waved his right hand in front of him in a dismissive gesture. "I caught you spying on my son in a private moment. Instead of scolding you, as I should have, I bandaged your knee. I then graciously offered you enough money for you to feel at ease in taking the rest of the day off to nurse your sore limb. When you refused my offer, I neglected my guests and gave you a ride home, sparing you any further discomfort." He then gave a slight bow of the head. "I even escorted you safely into your home, as any gentlemen would be expected to do."

At first, I was too stunned to speak. I then turned in a circle, looking for something to throw at him. Unfortunately, I had precious few possessions and nothing that I wanted to lose breaking over his stubborn, arrogant skull. I set my hands on my hips and leaned forward. "Are you serious?"

When his only response was a smirk, I threw my hands up in disgust.

"Where do I begin?" I tapped the items off on my fingers. "You refused to let me just do my job and pick up the broken glass. You *kidnapped me* back to your *lair* where you held me prisoner. *You kissed me without asking permission.* You then *insulted me* by tossing money at me, basically calling me a whore, before trying to have sex with me on a sofa. Then you kidnapped me *again* and dragged me away from work *against my will,* only to then insult my home!"

I leaned a hip against the side of my bed as I tried to catch my breath from my rant. Before he could speak, I raised my finger and pointed at him. "Oh! Oh! And... and... *you spanked me!*"

51

He straightened.

I inched around the end of my bed, away from him. It was as if he had suddenly swallowed up all the air in the room. With his superior height, his head almost brushed the low ceiling. "Are you finished?"

Thinking to brazen it out, I tilted my chin up as I white-knuckled the footboard behind me. I inhaled deeply before saying slowly and evenly, with as much authority as I could muster given my quaking limbs, "Yes, I believe I am. You may go now."

Barone chuckled as he rubbed his jaw. He then reached down and turned the tarnished brass key to lock the door.

I bit my lower lip to stop it from trembling as I stared at him with wide eyes.

What did I just do?

What was I thinking, mouthing off to one of the most powerful men in Italy?

He could squash me and my meager existence like a bug without the slightest effort.

He stepped forward and I skittered around the bed away from him, but only trapped myself in a corner.

Barone flattened both palms against the painted plaster walls, caging me in.

He leaned down and gently kissed my forehead, then the corner of my eye.

I tightened my abdomen to quell the butterflies in my stomach as my fingernails dug bright red crescent marks into my palms.

The bristle of his beard brushed my cheek as he tilted his

head to whisper in my right ear, "Know this, my sweet little bird, I will never ask for permission before kissing you." He lowered his hand to wrap it around the left side of my neck. His fingers delved into my hair, twisting until my head fell back. As his head lowered, I tightened my lips and turned my face to the side as much as his grip would allow.

Barone chuckled. "Always the hard way with you, *piccola*."

He released his grip on my hair. For one fleeting moment, I thought he was going to depart.

I was wrong.

He wrenched at the tie around my throat, loosening it. He whipped it from my blouse collar and held the length between his two fists.

My eyes widened as realization dawned.

I lifted my hands and pounded against his chest, yelling nonsensical curses at him.

Unfortunately, I played right into his plan.

Before I could fight back, he easily secured my narrow wrists. He had my tie wrapped securely around them and stretched my arms so high over my head it forced me up onto my toes. He looped my tied wrists over one of the iron ceiling hooks meant for hanging meat.

He stepped back and observed my dangling form while he lowered his hands to his belt buckle.

I pulled on the tie around my wrists. "What are you doing?"

He unbuckled his belt and whipped it through his belt loops before tossing it aside on my tiny bed. He unbuttoned the first few buttons of his shirt, then untucked it and pulled it over his head. The movement drew my eyes to his waist... and lower.

The unmistakable press of his engorged cock was outlined against his thin, linen trousers.

Oh my God. His length stretched halfway down his thigh.

The fucking rumors were true.

I frantically pulled my wrists again.

He stepped forward. His warm, muscular chest pressed against mine as he ran his hands over my arms up to my wrists. "Stop fighting, *dolcezza*. You'll only hurt yourself."

Tears spilled down my cheeks. "Please. I'm sorry I talked back. I'm sorry I disobeyed you. Just let me go."

He lowered one hand to caress the skin of my neck where it touched the edge of my blouse collar. "Not until I have taken my *full* payment."

"I offered you all the money I have."

"I'm not interested in your money."

He tucked his fingers inside my collar and wrenched downward. The cheap buttons easily gave way, scattering across the brick floor the moment the thin threads securing them snapped. He then pulled my skirt down and over my ankles. It left me with nothing on but my mismatched white lace bra and pink silk panties. The torn blouse offered no protection; its remaining shreds dangled uselessly from my shoulders.

He cupped his hands under my knees and lowered his body until my thighs were straddling his shoulders. My sex pressed almost against his mouth. He straightened. The tight pressure on my wrists abated, but I still could not leverage them off the iron hook.

"Since you will not let me kiss your mouth, I'll have to kiss you in other ways."

His warm breath caressed my pussy through the silk of my panties.

Despite his rough handling, I was already wet. Almost against my will. I would be mortified if he learned of my arousal. I bucked my hips, trying to dislodge his grasp.

It was to no avail.

His large hands moved to cup my ass, pushing the juncture of my thighs even closer to his mouth. He inhaled deeply. "The sweet scent of your musk is like wine to me."

My cheeks burned with humiliation. I wasn't used to this kind of intense scrutiny from a man. I had had only one boyfriend, and the experience was not nearly as exciting as all those love scenes in the movies. It was awkward and... quick. And he certainly never kissed me *there*.

Barone pressed his lips against my panties and breathed out. His hot breath caressed my clit. A shiver ran up my spine as I clenched my thighs around his head.

Dio santo.

He opened his lips wider and pressed the tip of his tongue along my seam. Even with the barrier of my panties, I could feel the deliciously wicked pressure of his mouth. He moved his tongue faster and faster in a steadily growing rhythm. My hips bucked again, although this time I wasn't trying to get away.

I closed my eyes as my head fell back. My entire weight resting on his firm shoulders, I could no longer fight the warm arousal swirling low in my stomach and between my thighs. The orgasm that was building inside of me was so intense, I fought against its effect. "I can't... I don't... please...." I shook my head from side to side, trying to fight his power over me. Somehow, I knew if I gave in, I would be lost. He would forever own a piece of me. I couldn't let that happen.

Barone growled, "Still you fight me, *piccola.*"

"This is wrong," I whimpered.

Everything about this was wrong. He was a man used to taking what he wanted. I couldn't let him take me. I wasn't a possession to be claimed. I breathed heavily as I fought back against the rising wave of endorphins.

"Dammit, *dolcezza.* Don't you dare deny me this."

My eyes sprang open as I defiantly met his dark, angry gaze over my prone body.

His eyes narrowed. In one furious movement, he lifted me high, freeing my wrists from the iron hook. My limited freedom was short-lived. With my wrists still bound, he sat on my narrow bed and flipped me over his knees.

I tried to rise, but a strong hand at my lower back kept me in place.

"Since you won't accept the pleasure, you will endure the pain," he threatened.

I looked over my shoulder to watch in horror as he picked up his leather belt. "No! You can't!"

"Watch me."

He wrenched down my panties until they stretched between my upper thighs.

He raised his arm and brought his belt down across my exposed cheeks.

I cried out in alarm as I struggled to move off his lap.

The belt came down again and again. Each time, it struck my flesh with a loud *thwack*. My skin was on fire, sharp stings radiating up my thighs and over my punishment-warmed ass.

Even more humiliating than his spanking me with his belt like a misbehaving child were the vibrations it sent to my clit. With each strike, my pussy rubbed against the edge of his hard thigh. Every time I squirmed, my stomach pressed against the heavy length of his cock.

I raised my tied wrists to my cheeks to brush away tears as he relentlessly punished me.

After several more strikes of the belt, he finally tossed it aside. I was so relieved I sobbed.

My ass and upper thighs were swollen and hot from his punishment.

My skin was so sensitive, the caress of his hand as he pushed it between my thighs felt like the harsh bristles of a brush against my skin.

He slipped a fingertip between the wet seam of my pussy lips.

I gasped.

"Let's try this again. And if you try to deny me the beautiful sound of your release, I will pry your thighs open, tie your ankles to this bed, and whip your pussy until you scream for mercy."

A sob lodged in my throat. I was caught between heaven and hell, tormented by his threats and the sinful feel of his fingers.

The pad of his thumb teased my clit as he pushed one finger inside of me.

It had been so long. I bit my lower lip until I tasted blood, stifling a groan.

He slipped a second thick finger inside of me. "*Madonna santa*, you are so tight. I can barely get two fingers inside of you."

He twisted his wrist, shifting his fingers deep inside of me as his thumb continued to apply subtle pressure to my clit. His forearm brushed the now sensitive skin of my ass. The mixture of pleasure and pain almost sent me over the edge. I wouldn't be able to fight my orgasm this time. It was too demanding, too strong, too intense.

"Are you a virgin, Amara?"

I gritted my teeth, refusing to answer.

He circled my throat with his free hand and tilted my head back, forcing my torso up as he pushed his fingers in painfully deep. "Answer me."

"No."

"But you cannot be very experienced."

I refused to respond, although it was true. None of the eligible men my age had ever really piqued my interest enough to put myself through the clumsy and bumbling act of sex.

His fingers tightened around my throat.

"Why do you care?" I whispered past the pressure of his hand.

"If you don't understand yet, you soon will," he answered cryptically.

Keeping his hand on my throat, he increased the rhythm of his other hand, thrusting in deep and fast.

I did not stand a chance.

I cried out as my whole body was swallowed beneath the wave of my orgasm.

Barone flipped my body until he was cradling me on his lap. This time, when he lowered his mouth to claim mine, I didn't resist.

His tongue swept inside, tasting my cries. I was breathless when he finally relented.

Looking down at me, he warned, "Next time, do not deny me."

Next time?

He stood and turned, lowering my curled body onto the center of the bed. He flipped a corner of my sunflower blanket over my mostly naked form.

I watched him shrug into his shirt and put his belt back on as the wet tears cooled on my cheeks.

He went down on his haunches and finally untied my wrists. He kissed the slight red marks the cheap cotton tie had caused. "What is your mobile number?"

I blinked. "What? Why?"

He smiled. It was a charming smile meant to be given across a cafe table on a bright sunny day. A casual, carefree smile. As if we had just shared an espresso and pastry this past hour instead of a belt-spanking from him until he forced an orgasm from my resistant body. "Because I dislike being kept waiting. I will call before I come to get you tomorrow. For now, I must return to my son's wedding, otherwise I would not have untied you for the world until you had given me at least two more of those sweet releases of yours."

There isn't a chance in hell I am ever letting myself be alone in a room with this man ever again.

I shook my head as I pulled the blanket more firmly over my shoulders. "I don't have a mobile."

He frowned. "How can that be?"

"Not all of us have the money to spare, *Don Cavalieri*."

He rose. As he buttoned his cuffs, he said sternly, "I will have one delivered here later this evening with my number programmed in. I warn you, Amara. Do not fail to answer it when I call."

He then kissed me on the top of my head and left without another word.

CHAPTER 7

AMARA

*T*hree days. Seventy-two hours. Four thousand, three hundred twenty minutes.

That was how long I had been avoiding Barone... and I was exhausted from the effort.

First there was the mobile phone delivery later that evening.

The delivery man practically quaked in his boots when I refused to accept it. It was only by the grace of God that my stepfather, Rocco, and my stepbrother, Mario, had already left for work the next morning when Barone came storming back to the house. Pounding on the locked double doors, demanding entry.

I hid, out of sight, in my windowless bedroom until long after I heard his car skid away down our weed-laden drive.

Next came more gifts. Flowers I had a hard time explaining. Jewelry I was forced to mail back to his villa since I didn't dare answer the door for the delivery man, not even to refuse the package, lest Barone be close by.

Thankfully, after the first two days, the gifts stopped. Still, I remained vigilant. I knew a man like Barone was only interested in me because of the novelty. He probably wasn't used to a woman telling him no. Soon that novelty would wear off and he would focus his attention elsewhere. I tried not to think how that idea made my stomach clench.

I had confessed none of this to Milana yet. She'd think I was crazy. Barone Cavalieri was every girl's dream. A tall, rich, handsome older man. The perfect package... except for those strange rumors. And truly it wasn't the scandalous gossip that made me resist his efforts, although after the other night I was definitely closer to believing them than I ever had been. I mean, who knew that people actually did the stuff I read about in *Fifty Shades* in *real life*? Or that it would be so... stimulating. I never even thought it was possible to orgasm that hard or that completely, and the man didn't even take my damn panties off to do it.

A man like that was not for a woman like me. I was self-aware enough to know when I was out of my league. And it wasn't the money or the luxurious lifestyle. I may be from a small mountainside Italian village, but that didn't mean I wasn't educated or cultured. I knew which fork to use and the finer points of Shakespeare. I knew I'd be able to hold my own with his rich friends from Rome. Sort of. Well, maybe. Probably. I just didn't want to. I had only spent a few hours in the man's presence and already I was exhausted and overwhelmed by the intensity of it all.

A small, inner voice whispered *bullshit*.

That traitorous inner voice knew I found Barone Cavalieri fascinating. He was big and strong and intelligent and handsome. He was a man who knew how to go after what he wanted, and I'd have to be made of stone to not be flattered that, at least for a few hours a few days ago, I was what he wanted.

Me.

Little old nobody Amara Beneventi from the wrong side of town.

That same inner voice knew that unlike Barone, I was afraid to go after what I wanted. Why else would I still be living in my mother's old house with my terrible stepfather and stepbrother, still dreaming of a future but not doing anything about it? I kept using my lack of money as an excuse, but plenty of people with no money succeeded in life. I was smart. I had a great business mind. I was meant for better things than working as a shopgirl at a souvenir store.

And yet it was like my life was clouded in a cold fog. Still. Unmoving. Stagnant.

Barone had seared away that fog with the light of a thousand suns and instead of rejoicing in the warmth, I turned and ran deeper back into the clouds.

I just wasn't ready for the light yet... and I hated myself for that, but it was the truth. Especially not a light like Barone's, which was sure to burn me to cinders, leaving me as nothing but a pile of ashes when he was done with me. And eventually, he would be done with me.

Over the last few days, I had gone to work early and stayed late. Although I wasn't getting much done. Every time the bell over the door rang, I jumped out of my skin, thinking Barone had found out where I worked. My boss finally got so annoyed he banished me to the back room to do inventory. He was stocking up for the final tourist push. Soon the Cavalieri Winery would harvest this year's grapes, creating a festive atmosphere that always drew tourists to the area. After that, winter would set in, and I'd be let go for the season until spring.

It was already dark when I locked the back door of the souvenir shop and made my way home. It had become my habit to avoid the crowded piazza just in case, preferring to take the long way home that circled around the town square. Although I had heard through village gossip Barone had left on the train to Rome this morning on business, I still wasn't taking any chances.

Dim lights were visible through the closed shutters of my house. My shoulders sagged. I had hoped Rocco and Mario would be out drinking and playing *Scopa* as was their habit on Friday evenings. I was in no mood for the tense atmosphere their presence always caused.

There was no love lost between me and my stepfather and stepbrother. They had taken advantage of my mother from the moment they entered our lives. Promising safety and security, all they brought was violence and poverty. Technically, this wasn't even their house. It was mine, but they refused to leave after my mother's death, and I did not have the money to hire a lawyer to force them to go. It was the Italian way. Laws and regulations were only enforced for those who shouted the loudest or had the most money. The rest of us could just fuck off and continue on with our lives while complaining to anyone who would listen what saintly martyrs we were for being so wronged.

At first it was the usual misery. Dodging fists if the pasta was too cold or too hot. Covering my ears with a pillow at night to block out their drunken shouts. Staying away from the house as much as possible from dawn until dusk. But in the last few years, things had changed.

They had gotten more dangerous.

On more than one occasion, one or the other had blocked my path in the narrow hallway leading to the bathroom. Or had *accidentally* burst into my bedroom while I was changing. There were sly comments, wayward brushes, and sometimes even crude gestures.

I knew it was only a matter of time before one of them crossed the line, which was why I was saving every euro I made to be able to afford the cost of moving out. I hated leaving my inheritance behind, but I had long ago accepted it was the only way.

In the meantime, I purchased a padlock for the inside of my bedroom door.

I trudged up the worn path and listened at the double doors before carefully pushing one side open. The house seemed unusually quiet. Holding my breath, I tiptoed across the entryway toward the kitchen. Hopefully, I could grab some bread and cheese and lock myself in my room before they even knew I was home.

"Welcome home, *puttana*."

I turned with a gasp.

Rocco was leaning against the doorjamb. Mario lurked behind him.

"What did you call me?"

Had they learned about Barone and the shameful things we did?

Rocco tossed a ripped-open package onto the center of our kitchen table. An expensive pair of silk stockings fell out.

My eyes widened.

Rocco tore the lid off the box and crushed the silk lingerie inside in his fist. He crossed the room and held it under my nose. "A man only gives his whore such things."

I smacked his hand away from my face. "Get away from me. My private life is none of your business."

He sneered. "Always playing the ice queen. Acting like you are too good to sleep with my son, all the while you are spreading your legs for the men of the village."

Ew.

Bile rose in my throat at the thought of being with Mario.

"He's my brother!"

"In name, not blood."

Mario crept further into the room. They both were crowding me into a corner.

Rocco leered at me as his pudgy hands circled his fat belly. He licked his lips. "I think it's time you start paying your way in this house."

Anger got the best of me. "Paying my way? *This is my house!* My mother left it to me, not you. You are the lazy, cheap free-loaders who can't hold down a job. Not me. I'm the one who pays for the food on the table and the roof over our heads."

Rocco slapped me so hard across the face, my head slammed into the wall, making my ears ring.

He flipped me around and pushed my front against the wall as he twisted my arm behind my back. He pulled so hard, I was afraid he was going to break it. His breath reeked of stale tobacco as he spoke so harshly his spittle hit my cheek. "I'm going to teach you a lesson, *brutta puttana.*"

His calloused hand reached under the hem of my dress.

I screamed as I threw my head back as hard as I could. I could hear the sickening crack of bone as my skull connected with his nose. I spun around just in time to see blood gush from his broken nose. His hands flew to his face as he yelled out to Mario, "Get her!"

I circled the kitchen table with Mario in pursuit.

As I tried to sprint past him, he tripped me. I fell to the floor, knocking over a nearby table. Mario clawed at my dress as I tried to crawl away from him. He turned me onto my back and straddled my hips. He slapped me once. Then again. Tears blurred my vision.

He grabbed his cock through his jeans as he leered down at me. "I'm going to make you choke on my cock, *little sister.*"

As he fumbled with his zipper, I stretched out my arm, reaching for the Chianti bottle I used as a candleholder which had toppled off the overturned table. I wrapped my fingers around the neck and swung my arm as hard as I could, catching Mario on the side of his head.

Glass showered down over my torso as he fell forward on top of me.

Screaming, I pushed him off me and struggled to my feet. I picked up the broken bottle and held it before me like a weapon as Rocco stormed toward me like a bull. It stopped him in his tracks.

"Get back or I swear to God, I'll gut you like a fish."

I backed away toward the front door.

Blood oozed from his broken nose as he balked. "You better leave and if you ever come back, I'll kill you."

The moment the cool night air hit my back, I turned, dropped the bottle, and ran.

* * *

AFTER TAKING several narrow alleyways and hiding behind an ancient fountain of a Roman goddess holding a pouring pitcher of water, I finally made my way to Milana's apartment. She lived above the leather goods store where she worked, just off the piazza. Having no way to contact her, I picked up a handful of pebbles and lobbed them at her open shutters. The lights were on, but that didn't mean anything. I knew Milana slept with all the lights on, it was a strange quirk of hers. I turned my head from side to side, scanning the dark streets each time, looking for either the police or my stepfather and stepbrother. After several minutes, I gave up trying to wake her.

Having nowhere else to go, I made my way to the Cavalieri Porta Nuova train station, as I had done many times before when I felt unsafe at home. There was something welcoming about its highly polished gray marble floors with their mirror finish, and its faded maps of Italy showing the twisted routes of iron ways leading to Rome, Verona, Milan, and beyond. Sometimes, I liked to imagine getting on one of those trains and escaping.

The problem was, I loved everything about my little village, from the Renaissance architecture to the perpetual widows, dressed all in black, who sat in the piazza each day fanning themselves as they scowled at the tourists. It was home and always would be. One day, I would scrape together enough money to open a little bookshop or some other type of business. That was my dream. To own a little business I could be proud of, perhaps with a little apartment above it, where I would live in peace, away from—I gave myself a mental shake.

It served no purpose dwelling on the horror of what just happened.

I would get some sleep and figure out what to do next in the morning. Fortunately, the train station was mostly deserted for the night. Only the sleeping *capostazione*, the stationmaster, with his gold-lace-band cap pulled low over his eyes, remained to greet the final *Interregionale* train from Rome which wouldn't be arriving until midnight.

Pushing aside a discarded copy of *La Gazzetta dello Sport*, I sat down on one of the outside wooden benches that was tucked under the overhang on the platform and leaned my head against the stone wall of the station ticket window. I lifted my fingertips to gingerly touch my sore cheekbone. No doubt I'd have a black eye tomorrow. It wouldn't be the first time. As soon as it was light, I'd make my way back to Milana's. She'd lend me some of her makeup to cover it.

I closed my eyes. I refused to cry or feel sorry for myself.

Tomorrow I would sneak back into the house and gather my meager belongings and my money from its hiding place in the kitchen. I was sure Milana would let me stay at her apartment until I could figure something out.

Everything is going to be okay.

It has to be.

I have no other choice.

A tear slipped past my closed lids.

I wrapped my arms tighter around my middle as my stomach growled. I thought about the half-eaten *piadina* carefully wrapped up in my discarded bag at home with its wedge of *prosciutto crudo* and soft *Gregoriano* cheese which was to be my supper. Between the late hour and having no money, I would have to wait until morning to eat. My bruised and tired body slipped to the side as my head lowered to my chest. Worn out, I curled my legs up onto the bench and laid my head down on the rough wooden slats.

I had never felt more alone in my entire life.

Another tear slipped down my cheek.

Just before I fell into an exhausted sleep, my scattered mind latched onto one wayward thought.

Barone.

CHAPTER 8

BARONE

*A*lthough Sebastian had offered the use of his helicopter for my trip to Rome, I preferred the train. Like most Italians, I was more accustomed to the energy and chatter of the carriages than I was to a solitary automobile or helicopter ride over the fertile fields of home.

Sure, the regional trains meant for citizens were not as well maintained as the more touristy ones, and often smelled of an odd mixture of disinfectant, urine, and stale cigarette smoke. The latter despite smoking being banned for decades, which indicated the age of the carriage cars. But it was in the open carriages where you could mix with everyman and chat, or more accurately argue, about football, politics, the latest government scandal. It was where the true humanity of Italy could be met.

But not this late at night. This late, there was only the monotonous thump of metal wheels on an almost-two-hundred-year-old track and the gentle rhythmic sway of the carriage as I stared out at the red, beady eyes of the *lumini* flickering over the graves in the cemeteries that passed, like ghostly sentinels.

While usually preferring the animation of the open carriage cars, when on the late schedule, I chose one of the few remaining trains with private compartments. Pushing the antiquated varnished door with its thin pane of glass along its wobbly track, I stepped inside a narrow compartment furnished with two facing wooden benches and brushed nickel luggage racks. I tossed my black, wool overcoat and compact suitcase on the luggage rack above the seat and closed the door behind me. Hopefully, the closed door and mostly empty late-night train would discourage any passenger from trying to join me for some conversation. I was in no mood this evening.

I did occasionally choose the compartment trains for some solitary reading and had in fact brought the celebrated Ignazio Silone's *Bread and Wine* with me to read, but the book remained unopened next to me on the wooden bench.

My thoughts were occupied by a pair of beautifully sad, dark eyes.

Amara.

The woman had consumed my every moment this past week.

If my meetings in Rome hadn't been scheduled months ago, I would have cancelled them just to remain in Cavalieri to pursue her. In the few days I'd had after the wedding to be with her before I had to leave, she had thwarted me at every turn. Refusing the mobile phone I purchased to communicate with her. Returning the many gifts I sent.

Even literally hiding from me when I went in search of her.

I curled my right hand into a fist and cupped it with my left as I stared at my reflection in the dark window.

Her hiding from me ended tomorrow.

My business in Rome, which had kept me from her side, was concluded. The harvest, my busiest time of year, didn't start for several weeks yet, which meant I had plenty of time to focus all my attention on caging my little bird.

The memory of her taste had faded.

I opened my palm and rubbed the center.

I could no longer imagine the cool feel of her soft skin or hear her startled intake of breath at my touch.

I needed to see her.

To touch her.

To taste her.

To fuck her.

I had denied myself the pleasure of sinking my cock deep inside her tight, warm flesh and had regretted it ever since. It had become an obsession. At night I tossed in my bed, my cock hard and raging at just the thought of what it would feel like to have her tied up, lying prone and vulnerable beneath me. I would grip my cock and imagine it was her throat as I straddled her face and thrust. Night after night, I would wake up in a cold sweat after dreaming of the feel of her sleek thighs pressing against my jaw as my tongue licked and laved her pussy.

I shifted in my seat and adjusted my cock which had length-ened at just the thought of her and was now pressing against the tight confines of my bespoke Brioni suit.

There was just something about the woman.

Her sweet innocence mixed with a haunting sadness.

The way her intelligent eyes flashed with defiance.

The cute way she raised her chin with the tiny cleft in it when angry.

The tight feel of her pussy as it gripped my finger.

The siren's song of her orgasm the moment she finally let go.

The way her cheek fit in the palm of my hand as I spanked her pert ass for defying me.

I was obsessed with all of it.

She had become like a drug, and I needed another fix.

It would be all I could do not to tear the goddamn doors of her little shack off their hinges the moment I arrived back in the village, although it would be past midnight, just to get at her.

I was like a beast about to slip its leash.

I had only enough restraint left in me to wait until morning.

But then all bets were fucking off.

The very moment the sun rose, I was going to claim what was mine.

And she was mine.

Whether she knew it or not.

Whether she liked it or not.

Amara Beneventi was mine.

In all my life, despite having the pleasure that riches and good looks brought a man like me when it came to women, I had never met a woman who fascinated and engrossed me like Amara.

She was a unique and rare bird, one I planned to make my pet.

That she was fighting me at every turn only made me more determined to win.

I would tear the town apart until I found her and carried her to my bed.

I would chain her to it if necessary.

She'd be lucky if I gave her time to eat or sleep once I finally got to slip between those thighs.

I already had my staff preparing one of the cottages I owned on the edge of my winery for her. I'd prefer her at the villa where I'd have unfettered access to her charms at all times, but my former sister-in-law, Gabriella, was currently staying there, not to mention Cesare, who lived nearby in a one-story house attached to the main villa via a courtyard overlooking a heated grotto.

I had no intention of sharing even a glimpse of Amara with anyone.

I also couldn't risk anyone hearing her screams for help if I needed a few days to... persuade her... to my way of thinking.

She was intelligent and independent enough to fight me on my insisting that she no longer work and focus all her attention on me, but I was confident I would, in the end, convince her that I had her best interests in mind. Besides, I had every intention of spoiling the hell out of her. I'd start with the cottage and a new wardrobe from the best designers, and of course a new car and a hefty bank account with additional letters of credit she could draw upon at all the best stores in Rome and Milan.

And when we finally parted ways, I would see that she had plenty of financial security and perhaps a nice apartment in Rome. I had it all worked out.

The train started to slow its approach.

Out of habit, I looked at my watch, with its familiar black face, dial, and worn brown leather band, even though it didn't work. It was my great-grandfather's old Panerai Radiomir watch, which he received when he was in the Italian Royal Navy. I wore it for sentimental reasons, and because I hated the annoying computers we now called phones. It was a nice reminder of our family's legacy. It had worked until a year ago. Unfortunately, because of the toxic radium in the dial, I could not have it repaired.

Sighing, I took out the phone I was always reluctant to carry and checked the time.

It was almost midnight.

We were pulling into the Cavalieri Porta Nuova train station uncharacteristically on time.

In less than eight hours I would have Amara in my arms again... and perhaps over my knee.

I stood to stretch my legs, pulling on my black overcoat, more to cover the erection that had not abated than to ward off any chill in the air. I lowered the compartment window and stuck my head out to see if I could spot either my black Maserati Quattroporte or Alfonso, who was scheduled to pick me up.

As my eyes scanned the darkness beyond the faded flickering lamps of the train station, they stopped on a small, huddled mass on the bench nearby.

I immediately recognized the soft raven hair, the curve of her hip, the edge of her jaw.

My God, it was Amara.

Not giving a damn about my suitcase, I raced off the train, shoving the few passengers disembarking aside. I fell to my knees at her side. "Amara?"

When she didn't stir, cold, hard fear iced through my chest like a lance.

I pushed the hair partially obscuring her face aside... and that was when I saw it.

The bruise on her cheek.

Cold fear was immediately replaced with white hot, uncontrollable rage.

I cradled her face, grateful that while chilled, her skin had the warmth of life to it. "Amara, babygirl, wake up."

Her thick black eyelashes twitched as her eyelids fluttered.

I gently stroked her cheek, careful to avoid the dark bruise just beneath her eye.

Finally, she opened her eyes, but then quickly shut them with a whimper.

"Amara?"

"Please, it hurts," she moaned softly.

My gut twisted.

Before I could say anything the *capostazione* approached. "Hey, what are you doing to that girl?"

I stood and turned on him, fists drawn.

He raised both palms up. "I'm sorry, Don Cavalieri. I didn't see it was you."

I shrugged out of my overcoat. "How long has she been here?"

The *capostazione* scratched his head and shrugged. "I didn't see her come in, but it's not the first time. Please. She doesn't hurt or bother anyone. She just needs a place to stay till her father cools off."

"Stepfather," I growled as I wrapped my coat over her curled form before sweeping her into my arms.

Amara groaned and shifted, but then quieted.

I gestured with my head. "Find my driver."

The *capostazione* stood up at attention. "Yes, sir. Right away, sir."

My narrowed gaze sent the other curious passersby scrambling.

I leaned down and kissed the top of her head. "I'm so sorry, *dolcezza*. I should never have left you in that hovel. I'll never forgive myself for this."

I closed my eyes and sent a prayer up to God that they did not hurt her in other ways.

This was my fault.

She was my responsibility.

True, I had met her just a few days ago, but it had only taken one look into her upturned face and those unfathomable eyes to know I was going to make her mine. And from that moment on, she had also become mine to protect. And I had failed her. Against my better judgment, I allowed her to have her pride and to stay at that wretched farmhouse with those non-blood male relatives.

I hugged her tighter to my body.

They were going to pay for this.

The roar of a Maserati engine broke the evening silence. Alfonso broke through a dilapidated wooden fence, jumped a curb, and drove my car onto the cement train platform to a stop directly in front of me.

The *capostazione* knew better than to complain. He rushed forward to open the passenger door for me. I ducked low to slip inside, careful of Amara's head. "Go!" I ordered as I settled back into the warmed black leather seat with her in my arms.

Alfonso cast me a concerned look but didn't speak as he shifted the car into gear and raced off into the dark night, through the winding country lanes outside the village which led to the winery. Although the trip was less than fifteen minutes, it felt like an eternity. Amara didn't stir the entire time.

Alerted to the emergency by Alfonso, my staff were waiting at the villa entrance when the car pulled into the loose-stone drive. I barely waited for the car to come to a complete stop before I stepped out and raced inside. Heading across the Roman tile mosaic to the curved, wrought iron staircase, I took the stairs two at a time as I called over my shoulder, "Get Dr. Pontano here. Now."

Striding down the long hallway, I kicked open the double doors which led to the primary suite, my bedroom. Marching through the various antechambers, I carried Amara to my bed and placed her gently in the center.

I carefully removed my overcoat and her shoes, then started on the buttons down the front of her torn dress. I wanted her to be comfortable, plus I needed to check for further injuries.

Her eyes sprang open. They were unfocused and wild.

With a shriek, she jumped off the bed and flew backward until her back hit the far wall. Clutching her dress front, she stared at me with wide eyes. "What are you doing?"

"I'm here to help."

She shook her head. "I don't need your help." Her frenzied gaze settled on the doorway. Her only means of escape.

Before I could caution her against it, she bolted for the door.

I snatched her around the waist just as she reached the threshold. Ignoring her curses and cries, I hauled her back into the room. Shifting her squirming weight to one hip, I used my free arm to close and bolt the door. I then grasped her more firmly and brought her back to the bed.

Her struggle intensified.

We both fell onto the mattress.

I used my weight to pin her down. Careful to avoid truly hurting her, I stretched her arms over her head and secured her wrists in my hand as I used my legs to stop her kicking.

"Let me go!"

"No."

"Let me go!"

"No."

Already exhausted from her earlier ordeal, she only had the energy to struggle for a minute longer before she subsided. Her chest rose and fell as she sucked in large gulps of air.

My gaze searched her face. In the dim light on the train platform, I couldn't quite make out her injuries. In the brighter light of my bedroom, I could more clearly see the swollen bruise under her right eye and the cut on her left cheekbone. "Tell me."

Her gaze shifted to the left. "Tell you what?"

I tightened my grasp on her wrists. "Don't play games with me, Amara. Tell me who hurt you."

Her eyes shimmered with tears. She sniffed before whispering, "It's nothing. I'm fine. Really."

My stomach twisted so violently with disgust I thought I might vomit. "It's not fucking nothing. Someone laid hands on you, and they are going to pay for it."

"It's none of your concern."

"The hell it isn't," I snarled.

"You don't own me. I'm not your responsibility."

My jaw tightened. "Now that's where you're wrong."

She shook her head. "No. I'm not. I'm just some staff member you tried to seduce at a party. I'm nobody. Now, please just let me go."

"Not on your life. You want to do this the hard way, little bird? Fine."

Using my free hand, I tore at the buttons of her dress.

CHAPTER 9

AMARA

$\mathcal{M}$y cheeks flamed as I pulled on my wrists. I couldn't dislodge his grasp. "Stop. What are you doing?"

Barone's brow furrowed as he ignored my struggles and continued to tear at my simple cotton dress. It was cornflower blue with a row of pink pearl buttons down the front. Mario had torn one of the capped sleeves, leaving it hanging limply from my shoulder.

I twisted my torso and bucked my hips but could not dislodge him.

In no time, he had my dress open past the waist, exposing my pale pink lace bra and the white silk bow sewn to the top of my matching pink panties.

Barone shifted his weight off me.

I tried to take advantage of the moment and shot up, attempting to get off the bed. Turned out it was a trap. He used my movement to strip the dress off my shoulders. The thin cotton fabric easily tore and fell away.

He then used his forearm to pin me back to the bed by my waist. "Now, are you going to be a good girl and let me examine you for more injuries or are you going to force me to tie you up?"

My mouth dropped open. "You wouldn't dare."

"Try me."

I huffed as I crossed my arms over my chest and stared at the ceiling. "I'm not injured. Can't you take my word for it?"

"No."

I tightened my jaw. "Fine," I pushed out through clenched teeth.

Lying on his bed in only my panties and bra and the torn fragments of my dress, my whole body burned with humiliation. I prayed the earth would split open and swallow me whole. Of all the people in the world to stumble across me on that stupid train platform, why did it have to be Barone Cavalieri?

He ran his warm fingers up my right arm and across my collarbone, hesitating briefly over the rapid pulse in my throat before tracing the left collarbone and down my left arm. "Are you going to tell me what happened?"

I turned my head to the side. "You said I had to endure your examination, not your questions."

He may have found me at one of my lowest points, but I still had my pride.

His fingertips trailed down over my abdomen. I clenched my stomach muscles in response, trying to quell the fluttering his touch caused despite the strained circumstances.

He flicked one loop edge of the white bow on my panties.

I couldn't contain a shocked gasp.

My eyes flew to his.

His intense dark gaze stared down at me as his hand continued to move down over my thigh.

I held my breath.

After a moment, he broke his stare, to examine my legs for injuries.

Finding none, he delved his fingers into my hair, cupping the back of my skull. "Did you hit your head at all?"

Yes, when Rocco slammed it against the wall. "No."

His lips thinned.

Again, his eyes locked on mine.

I swallowed as I broke our gaze.

"Eyes on me," he commanded.

Like a forlorn puppy, I instantly obeyed.

He stroked my cheek, just below the bruise. "You should know better than to try lying to me, *piccola*."

The man truly had God-like omniscience.

"I'm not lying," I protested, even though I definitely was.

"We'll see what the doctor says when he arrives."

"Doctor? What the hell? I don't need a doctor, Barone. It's just a black eye. I'll recover."

Barone's eyes shifted as he inhaled slowly. I could feel the tight tension in his body.

After a few deep breaths, he looked down at me. He massaged my skull lightly as he spoke. "*Dolcezza*, I'm going to need you to listen to me very carefully. It is taking all the restraint I physically possess to stay here with you right now until the doctor arrives. The moment he does, I am going to that miserable shack you call a home and pulling your stepfather and stepbrother out of their beds by their shriveled balls. I'm then going to drag them to the center of the piazza where I will set them on fire and hope their screams of agony serve as a warning to every man throughout Italy and beyond to never again touch what is mine."

I blinked several times, stunned, not only by the brutality of his words, but the intensity with which he uttered them. When I could finally form words, they came out as a croaked whisper. "You can't do that, not over someone like me. You barely know me."

"I don't have to know you, to know that no woman should ever... *ever*... have to utter the reprehensible phrase *it's just a black eye*, but especially not a woman under my protection."

"I didn't say it was Rocco and Mario."

"You didn't have to."

It wasn't so much their blood on my hands as it was getting Barone in trouble with *la polizia* that I was worried about. If he went to prison, the winery would suffer and by extension the entire village, and then everyone would blame me. This was a nightmare. What a fucking mess! "Please, can't we just forget all about this? I appreciate your concern. Really, I do, but I'm fine. Thank you for offering to get a doctor, but I don't need one. If you could just give me a lift back into the village, I can stay with my friend Milana until this all blows over." I tried to shimmy off the side of the bed.

Barone placed a restraining hand on the curve of my waist and pulled me back to his side. "You're tired. You've had a long, trying evening so I'm going to explain this slowly, so you understand." He curved a finger under my chin and tilted my head back, so I was sure to meet his gaze. "You are *not* leaving this bed. You *will* see the doctor. Afterward, you *will* rest. You are *not* going anywhere. Do you understand me?"

"But—"

"This is not up for discussion. So help me God, Amara, you will not like the consequences if you try to disobey me in this."

Before I could argue further, there was a soft knock. A voice called through the door, "The doctor has arrived, Don Cavalieri."

Barone rose and cracked the door open slightly. I could hear him say, " *Un momento, dottore.*"

He returned to the bed and pulled the heavy down comforter out from under me and laid it over my half naked form, tucking it up under my chin. "Don't move."

He turned to walk back to the door. Without turning around, he tossed over his shoulder, "Don't test me on this, Amara."

He left the room.

For several minutes, I thought seriously about running, but it was the middle of the night, and he would probably catch me before I got off the villa grounds.

Barone returned with a woman who looked like Sophia Loren. She was probably in her late fifties and wore a crimson silk dressing gown with a matching turban. Despite the late hour, she was still in full makeup, and her large, gold hoop earrings matched her jangling wrist bangles. She was tightening her robe around her slim waist as she grumbled, "This better be good, Barone. Marco had finally found the right spot."

Barone gestured toward the bed where I was half hidden under the blankets. "Gabriella, this is Amara. Amara, this is my sister-in-law, Gabriella." He then turned toward Gabriella. "I need you to watch over her and keep her comfortable while the doctor examines her."

Gabriella brought her hands to her cheeks as she exclaimed, " *Oh, Madonna mia! Poverina. Ma che mostro ti ha fatto questo? Poverina. Certo, Barone. Certo.*"

She then rushed over to the bed. Sitting gingerly on the edge, she smoothed back my hair and clucked over me as she fussed with the edge of the blanket.

Over her shoulder, I watched Barone open the door wider and gesture for the doctor to enter. He then turned to leave. I rose on my elbows and called out, "Barone, where are you going?"

He looked at me with barely concealed rage. "Don't leave that bed, Amara."

With that final warning, he was gone.

CHAPTER 10

BARONE

*U*ncaring about the late hour, I barged into Cesare's house, making my way through the open floor plan to the back rooms. As I threw open the bedroom door, Cesare sprang up in bed.

"Call your brother and meet me at the stables."

Without saying a word, he jumped out of bed and reached for his jeans.

I stormed out and crossed the dark, terraced lawn to the back of the villa where we kept our vehicles and horses. I threw open the small cabinet near the doorway and grabbed both sets of keys for our Moto Guzzi V7 motorcycles. After I lost my wife, I worked for countless hours in the garage refurbishing one with my two young boys watching. Italian therapy. Later, when they were teenagers, I bought them each a Moto Guzzi that needed to be refurbished so we could continue working on them together. I straddled the bike and turned the key in the ignition. By then Cesare had joined me.

He started up his bike. "Enzo will join us as we cross into the piazza. Mind telling me what's going on?"

I threw back the kickstand. "We're going hunting."

The motorcycle jerked to life and I raced down the crushed-limestone path that led to the village, with Cesare close behind.

The village, with its mostly Medieval and Renaissance architecture, resembled a ghostly relic appearing out of the mists of time at this late hour. At two a.m., it was assured that even the bakers and farmers were still tucked in their beds. As we crossed into the piazza, Enzo fell in behind us on his own Moto Guzzi motorcycle.

Until his wedding, he had lived in the small farmer's cottage at the edge of our winery where I was planning for Amara to stay. The structure was over two hundred years old and had only five rooms including a kitchen and two bedrooms, as well as a beautiful, shaded veranda.

Enzo, who had always had an affinity for construction and architecture, painstakingly remodeled most of it by hand, using the traditional ways to honor the history of the property. The freshly plastered walls showed off vibrant frescoes reminiscent of Pompeii. Newly varnished ceiling beams in other rooms looked down on framed sixteenth century vistas of Abruzzo that somehow complimented odd market day finds like a set of cobalt blue swallow figurines or a seventies barrel chair in tarnished gold and emerald green fabric.

The place was a charming, eclectic work of art, a reflection of my son's unique talents... and his new bride hated every brick.

She had insisted he purchase a massive luxury seventeenth century building off the central piazza. Apparently, she required Murano chandeliers, marble fireplaces, and over sixty-five-hundred square meters of space with five floors of rooms to be truly happy.

As we turned onto the road just past Santa Maria Church, an automobile *della polizia* with its lights flashing blocked our path. Dressed in his rumpled uniform, his hat askew, Benito Ciccone leaned against the side of his car smoking a hand-rolled cigarette.

We slowed our motorcycles and cut the engines.

While Cesare and Enzo continued to straddle their bikes, I alighted and approached Benito.

He gave me a lazy smile as he blew smoke from his nostrils. "I cannot let you do this, Barone."

I crossed my arms over my chest as I looked down at him from my superior height. "And what is it I'm supposedly doing?"

"I heard what happened to the Beneventi girl."

Even in the middle of the night, gossip traveled fast in a mountain village.

He pulled off his hat and wiped his brow with the end of his sleeve before replacing it. "You must let me handle this."

I took a deep breath, attempting to calm my rage. "And tell me, old friend, how was it handled in the past? Were they thrown in jail for a few hours and told to behave before being unleashed on the village again?"

He shrugged. "Come on, Barone. You know how it is. Men will be men. You cannot lock up a man and his son for getting a little drunk and swinging their fists now and then. Even if I wanted to, they play cards with a judge. There is nothing I can do."

I nodded. "Well, you are right. There is nothing *you* can do." I raised an eyebrow as I stared down at him.

He shook his head mournfully as he crushed the cigarette beneath his boot while reaching for another. After carefully sprinkling the dried tobacco along the paper, he slowly rolled it before pinching the end between his lips. He pulled out a match and lit it. Taking a long drag, he tilted his head back and blew the smoke up at the full moon. He sighed. "You can't kill them. It would be a mess of paperwork and I'm in no mood to help you hide two bodies. Not to mention the harvest is coming up. The village needs you and your sons more."

I nodded. "Fine. Mark my words, they will glimpse hell's gate before the night is through... but they won't pass through."

Benito crushed his second cigarette beneath his boot and straightened as he righted his hat. Sparing a sly glance up at the darkened windows, knowing that their shuttered depths concealed eager, listening ears, he said loudly, "I hope you and your sons have a safe journey, Don Cavalieri. I am patrolling on the far side of the village before returning to my station for the night. Say hello to Gabriella for me."

I smirked as I shook his hand.

We watched him drive off before continuing up the road to Amara's home.

No, her former home.

I'd be damned if I would permit her ever to return to that wretched hovel.

The place looked deserted as we rode up, but a rusted, faded blue *Piaggio Ape* truck in the drive told me the bastards must be home.

We disembarked and approached the double-door entrance.

I tried a handle. The door swung open unimpeded. I supposed there was no reason to lock a door when you had nothing to steal.

We stood silently in the small parlor room, surveying the damage.

It was obvious a brutal fight had taken place. A table was overturned, and the shattered glass of a broken wine bottle littered the floor. Just beyond in the kitchen, I could see the package of lingerie I had sent earlier, torn up, its contents trampled on the floor.

For the second time that evening my stomach clenched so hard I thought I would wretch. It was impossible not to conclude that because of my gift, I had somehow played a part in this violent farce.

My hands curled into fists. "Find them."

Enzo and Cesare headed to the left, and I turned right. I kicked in the first door I encountered. Rocco was ignominiously passed out on top of what used to be a pile of clean, neatly folded laundry, probably done by Amara herself.

I kicked his partially unlaced boot. "Get up."

Rocco snorted as his bleary eyes blinked open.

I reached over and grabbed him by the front of his denim overalls and dragged him upright. "I said, get the fuck up." Pushing him forward, he slammed face-first into the wall near the door. I snatched him by the back and thrust him over the threshold, out into the parlor. Enzo and Cesare were already there with Amara's stepbrother, Mario, who was dressed in a dirty, white T-shirt and half-buttoned jeans.

Rocco snorted, then swallowed the phlegm before grousing, "Who the hell are you?"

Mario smirked as he lifted his T-shirt and rubbed his belly. "Don't you know, Father? We're in the presence of royalty. King Barone and the two princes."

Enzo shook his head in disgust. "*Che due coglioni*, Mario, how are you not dead yet?"

I gestured with my head. "You know this piece of garbage?"

Enzo laughed. "Only by reputation."

Cesare slapped Enzo on the shoulder. "Now I recognize him. *Cazzo*, Mario!"

Mario surged forward but tripped and fell to his knees when his unfastened jeans slipped down his thighs. "*Zitti, stronzi!*" he raged as his father helped him to his feet.

Enzo mockingly covered his eyes. "Please, Mario, we don't need to see your little dick again, we got an eyeful already."

Cesare laughed as he held up his hand and pinched his forefinger and thumb together. "Could you really call it an *eyeful*, though?"

I glanced at them, both eyebrows raised. Cesare gestured toward Mario and explained. "Mario here tried to force his pencil dick down Gina Falconi's throat during a football game back when we were in school. She didn't take too kindly to his amorous advances and taught him a lesson by tearing off his pants and chasing his half naked ass out onto the pitch in the middle of the game."

I did not find the story nearly as amusing as my sons. Cupping my right fist with my left, my voice was deceptively soft and low when I asked, "So is that what you tried to do to Amara tonight?"

Mario cupped his crotch. "Oh, my little sister was begging for it."

Rocco licked his lips. "She wanted us to take turns."

I lunged forward. "I'm going to rip both of your throats out."

Rocco and Mario skittered backward like cockroaches.

Enzo placed a restraining hand on my upper arm. "Now, *Papà*, let's be sensible here. It's hardly fair that you get to kill *both of them* yourself."

Cesare stepped forward. "I'll take Mario."

Mario sputtered as he raised his fists. "I'm going to—"

Enzo raised a hand, silencing him. He furrowed his brow as he turned to Cesare. "Why do you get Mario?"

I waved my hand in Rocco's direction. "Well, I'm clearly going to rip off Rocco's shriveled balls, shove them down his throat, and watch as he chokes on them. You two will have to decide who gets to do the same to his pitiful son."

Cesare laid a flat hand on his chest. "I haven't gotten into a decent fight in months. I need this, brother."

"You?" objected Enzo. "I was forced to watch my new wife flirt with half our workforce. And I wasn't allowed to kill any of them."

Cesare bowed his head slightly. "True. You win."

Rocco's beady little black eyes shifted between us. The precise moment it dawned on him that we seriously just might kill them both was obvious, and like any bully, he was a coward at heart.

He raised his palms up. "There is no need to fight. You don't need to worry about any argument from us over that stupid *puttana*. You can take her. Pass her around between the three of you for all I care."

Mario piped up helpfully, "She'd probably take all three of you on at once."

Rocco smiled and nodded like a buffoon. "Yes! Yes! Great idea. Use her with my blessing." He then tilted his head to the side as he raised his hand and pinched his fingers together. "And if perhaps you wanted to give me a small compensation for keeping quiet about the three of you fucking my stepdaughter, then I'm sure we can come to an arrangement."

I returned his smile as I stepped toward him. I placed my hand on his shoulder. "You have no idea how pleased I am you just said that."

CHAPTER 11

BARONE

I hissed through my teeth as the hot water hit my scraped knuckles. Turning the brushed gold shower nozzle to its hottest level, I leaned my palms against the cobalt blue tile and dipped my head low, letting the scalding water run over my head and down my back.

Pink liquid swirled over the white marble shower floor before rushing down the drain, washing away the dried blood from the various cuts I had sustained from beating Rocco to a pulp. We had deposited the crumpled, broken messes that were him and his son at the edge of town with instructions to never return or we'd put them both in the ground. Since my power and influence trumped their friendship with some low-level judge, I had no doubt they believed I would gladly murder them both and get away with it.

Because it was true.

It wasn't like I hadn't gotten away with murder before.

I still wasn't sure it was the correct decision to let them live, but I could easily hunt them down and rectify that another day.

For now, my primary concern had to be Amara.

Amara.

My poor little broken bird.

* * *

GABRIELLA WAS WATCHING over Amara's sleeping form when I returned. She placed her finger to her lips and motioned for me to follow her out to the terrace, which wrapped around the bedroom suite.

She clucked her tongue as she shook her head. "Such a stubborn girl." She then winked at me. "I like her."

She pulled a sterling silver cigarette case out of her dressing gown pocket and flicked it open, offering me one. I took it. Placing her own in a matching silver cigarette holder, she popped a slim lighter out from the side of the case.

I took the lighter from her and lit both of our cigarettes before returning it to her. I stared down at the red ash on the tip. "What did Dr. Pontano say?"

She tilted her head back and pursed her lips to blow a stream of blue smoke. "She is mostly fine. A bruised eye and a cut cheek. He thinks she may have a concussion, so he wants us to watch over her for the next few hours. Just in case."

"Did she tell him, or you, what happened?"

Gabriella bared her teeth as her upper lip curled. "Those pitiful excuses for men she lives with got angry. One slapped her, and she hit her head against the wall. I got the feeling there was more, but she wouldn't say beyond that."

My shoulders tensed. I inhaled a steadying breath before asking, "And was there any...."

She raised an eyebrow. "Interference?" she finished delicately.

I clenched my jaw and nodded.

"No." She raised her hands into the air. "Thank the Madonna, or I would have killed those two bastards myself. You did kill them, right?"

I let out the breath I had been holding. "Benito Ciccone caught wind of our plans. We thought it best to rough them up and chase them out of the village... for now."

She smiled wistfully. "Benito Ciccone. Great kisser, but terrible lover."

"He says hello. Should I be asking who the man is, who's currently sleeping under my roof?"

She took another drag on her cigarette. "Marco?"

I nodded.

"Oh, he's just some puppy who followed me home from the piazza today."

My sister-in-law was nothing like her much younger sister, my dead wife. Where Angelina had been shy, deeply religious, and reserved, Gabriella was vivacious and more than a little promiscuous. I had lost track of the number of lovers she'd had over the years. Still, she had been an adoring aunt to my sons and a great friend to me over the years, which was why I always made sure the staff kept a room ready for her use whenever she traveled in from Rome.

I raised an eyebrow. "A little young for you, don't you think?"

She smirked as she nodded in the direction of the open bedroom glass door. "I could say the same to you."

"It's not like that. She is... was... a foolish dalliance. I know better than to get involved with one so young and from the village."

"Well, I think it's about time you stopped messing with those casual flings in Rome and got serious for once."

"Says the woman who hasn't had a serious relationship her whole life."

She waved her hand in the air. "Posh, I'm different. I prefer to be alone and independent."

"I do as well."

"Liar." She leaned her hip against the railing. "Look, I loved my sister. And I know you at least cared for her, but let's be truthful with one another. She was boring. Sweet, and a good mother, but boring. If she hadn't—"

I gave Gabriella a hard look.

Over fifteen years later it was still something we did not talk about.

Had sworn never to discuss, in fact.

She cleared her throat. "If what happened hadn't happened, you would have eventually made each other miserable. It's been, what? Fifteen years? You must forgive yourself and allow yourself to live again. Angelina would have wanted you to. You know this is true. You deserve to love and to be loved or else what is life for?"

I took one final drag off my cigarette as I gazed into the dark bedroom. "It is not that easy."

Gabriella followed my gaze. "I think it may be easy with someone like her, no? She is feisty, that one. She has a fire in her belly. And she does not care one whit about all your wealth and power. You need someone like that in your life, Barone. You have been alone for far too long. I worry about you."

I cupped the back of Gabriella's neck and placed a chaste kiss on her forehead. "*Grazie per l'aiuto, sei un angelo.* Whatever would have been possible is no longer so. It's more complicated now. The whole village will be talking about tonight's events over their *caffè e pasticcini* tomorrow morning. I can't ruin her reputation like that. It would make it impossible for her to find a good young man to later marry and have babies with."

"You act like you are in your dotage. You are in your prime, Barone. You could still have another family."

"I am a grumpy old man who would always insist on getting his way. She needs a young man she can lead around by the nose. I know you women secretly like that."

It's what would be best for her.

At least I'm trying to convince myself of that.

She winked. "You are wrong. Take it from a woman who knows. Women like older, domineering men who take what they want, and don't let them get away with their nonsense. Not awkward young puppies who snivel at our feet and paw at us in the bedroom. Speaking of which, I need to get back to Marco." She gave me a kiss on the cheek. "*Buona notte*, Barone."

"*Buona notte*, Gabriella." I turned and made my way further down the terrace where there was another set of glass doors leading to the en suite bathroom.

* * *

101

I THOUGHT about Amara tucked safely in my bed as I reached for the bar of sandalwood soap. I rubbed it between my palms to generate a thick, rich lather. She was actually the first woman to sleep in that bed. When I was married, my wife chose to sleep in a separate bedroom rather than be subjected to *my needs* more than necessary. Afterward, I chose to only pursue casual engagements while I was in Rome, keeping my personal life away from my sons and village gossip.

It was odd how natural it felt to have Amara in my bed.

As if she belonged there.

In fact, the idea of moving her, even to the farmhouse cottage on my property as I originally planned, no longer appealed to me.

I ran my hand over my chest and abdomen.

Fuck.

No. I couldn't. It was unthinkable.

There was no way it was possible to keep her here beyond this evening. My ancestors founded this village. It bore my name. My winery was the primary employer and my other businesses made up the lion's share of the rest. I had a duty and responsibility to remain respectable and forthright. I couldn't be seen to be preying upon a young and vulnerable woman of the village, no matter how enticing and intriguing I found her. Not to mention what it would do to her reputation. Italy was still a very conservative country. She would probably be fired from her job, lose friends.

With my original plan, there might have been a chance to prevent that since I could have kept a short dalliance private.

Kept her secluded in the cottage.

My own little pet bird, waiting for me to come and play with her.

But not now.

By morning, the whole village would know the scandal of what happened here tonight.

I groaned, thinking of the wasted chance, of the moments I wouldn't have with her.

The things I would have done to that luscious, sweet body.

My hand dipped further to grab my already hard shaft. I fisted the length and squeezed.

Closing my eyes, I imagined Amara here in the shower with me. Her naked skin glistening with foamy soap. I would turn her to face the tiles and grip her breasts from behind, weighing them in my hands as I kissed her wet neck, relishing in how her long, damp curls tickled my chest.

I gripped my cock harder and shifted my hand up and down its length.

My right hand would wrap around her silky throat as my left roamed down her body, over her flat stomach to push between her thighs. My fingers would tease the seam of her tight pussy as I coaxed a moan from her lips.

I moved my hand over my cock harder as I threw my head back to let the hot water cascade over my chest.

Once I had coaxed at least two orgasms from her with my fingers, I would direct her to press her palms against the warm shower tiles as I pulled her hips toward me until she was bent almost in half. I would then drip rich, soapy lather down her back until it slipped over her hips and between her ass cheeks.

I let out a groan as I fisted my cock, squeezing the base

before torturing myself by slowly pulling my hand down to the head and back.

I would pry her cheeks open and tease her pert little asshole, opening it with my finger, but not too much. I'd want her to feel the pleasurable pain when I forced it open with my cock.

I'd grip my cock as I am now and lather it with silky suds before positioning myself behind her.

The second the head of my cock pressed against her forbidden hole, her head would turn as she looked over her shoulder. Her dark gaze would be filled with fear, desire, and trust. For I instinctively knew she would be a virgin back there. Good girls with tight pussies and barely any lovers didn't allow men to fuck them in the ass.

I would grip her wet hair at the base of her skull and push forward. Ignoring her cries, I would thrust hard and deep, claiming her as mine.

Just the thought of her virgin ass gripping my shaft had me furiously rubbing my cock. I rose on my toes as my balls tightened. The moment I imagined coming in her ass, I blew my seed over the blue shower tiles.

I rested my forehead against the tiles as I allowed my breathing to return to normal.

Christ, this woman was some of the best sex I'd ever had, and I hadn't even fucked her yet.

My cock was still semi-hard. The release wasn't enough. Somehow, I knew it would never be enough with Amara.

Turning off the shower, I dried off and wrapped a towel around my hips.

I stepped silently into the bedroom.

Amara was curled up on her side in the center of my bed.

I removed the towel and lifted the blankets to slip in behind her.

She was still wearing her bra and panties.

Careful not to wake her, I slipped my hand between our bodies and unclasped her bra. I pushed the strap over her free arm, letting the bra fall to the mattress, still wrapped around her other arm.

Nestling my body flush against hers, I wrapped my arm firmly around her middle and lifted my hand to cup the warm weight of her breast in my palm.

Amara sighed and wiggled her ass as she pressed herself more securely against me.

Deciding what to do with her was a problem for another day.

Tonight, I would hold her close and pray tomorrow never came.

CHAPTER 12

AMARA

*T*snuggled deeper into the warm softness. I could see the sunlight from behind my eyelids, but didn't want to open my eyes, because I knew once I did this dream would be over and the harsh reality of my life would crash down on me. It was an extremely odd sensation to have had both the best and worst night's sleep of my life on the same night.

Wait.

Why is that?

My eyes sprang open.

The haze of sleep gone in an instant.

There was no reason why I should feel warm and safe... was there?

Focus.

What the hell happened last night?

I tried to think but my head was pounding. I rubbed my eyes and looked around at my surroundings. On the bedside table there was a small crystal pitcher of water and two aspirin tablets. As I reached for them, the blanket fell away. The cool morning air hit my naked breasts.

What the hell?

I snatched the blanket up high, then pulled it away to look down at myself. My unhooked bra was wrapped around my left wrist. Thankfully, my panties were still on.

Seriously, what the hell happened last night?

I couldn't think past this pounding headache.

Again, I reached for the aspirin tablets and swallowed them with a gulp of water. Leaning back with my eyes closed, I inhaled deeply through my nose, waiting for the medicine to take effect.

And that was when I caught it.

The unmistakable masculine scent of sandalwood.

Barone's scent.

I opened my eyes and turned my head.

The pillow next to mine had the slightest indentation.

My hand flew to my mouth.

Dio Santo.

Dio Santo

DIO SANTO!

Barone had slept with me. I had slept with Barone. WE had slept together.

The reality I was trying so desperately to keep at bay crashed down on me like an icy waterfall.

My stepfather hitting me.

Mario's attempted assault.

My running to the train station.

Barone finding me.

The villa.

The doctor.

Barone leaving to confront my stepfather and stepbrother.

His sweet sister-in-law cooing over me and chastising the doctor for his cold hands and embarrassing questions.

All of it terrible, nasty, cold, painful, humiliating, confusing, and awful.

And then... warmth.

Security.

Safety.

Peaceful sleep.

Barone.

I remembered now.

I had fallen asleep and, in the night, Barone had crept into bed, pulled me close, and held me.

My brow furrowed. I really could not remember if he'd tried something or not. On the one hand, my bra was unhooked, but on the other, my panties were still on. I bit my lip. No. There was no way we'd had sex. I may not be the most experienced woman in the world, but I somehow knew that any woman who had sex with a man like Barone *remembered it...* no matter how hard she may have hit her head.

The small clock dial on the bedside table showed it was only seven a.m. I wasn't due at work until late in the afternoon. I wrapped the down comforter around my middle and scurried to the edge of the bed. Rising, I crept to the bathroom door and listened before entering. All was silent. I was fairly certain Barone would not be around.

Barone and his sons were notorious for being very hands-on owners. It was one reason why their laborers were so loyal and revered them. They usually could be found in the fields working side by side with them, so it stood to reason that Barone was an early riser.

And thank goodness for that. I absolutely did not want to face him. I knew eventually I'd have to face the embarrassing task of thanking him for helping me last night, but I was hoping I could put that off for as long as possible. Maybe I could get away with just sending him a nice card in the post?

Especially since I wanted to avoid any conversation about *us.*

I did not know if there was an *us.*

Or if he expected there would be an *us* after last night.

Or if I even wanted there to be an *us.*

It was all a bit too much for me to cope with along with this headache and having to deal with my stepfather and everything else. Those were all problems for tomorrow. Right now, I needed a shower and some food, in that order.

The bathroom was as gorgeous as the bedroom. All deep, dark blues and golds with white marble countertops and floors. I smiled when I saw the small pile of makeup products and lotions set out between the two sinks. There was a neatly folded note on top. As I picked it up, it smelled heavily of rose-scented perfume.

Amara,

Here are some essentials. I do not rise until at least noon.

We will have lunch before I leave for Roma.

- Gabriella

Gabriella was precisely the type of woman I aspired to be one day. She was sassy, opinionated, and elegant. It had been fascinating to watch her long, glossy red fingernails as she'd snapped her fingers ordering Dr. Pantona about as her gold bangles jangled and clanged. Afterward, sensing my anxiety over what was happening with Barone and my stepfather, she'd distracted me with stories of her life in Rome until my eyelids were too heavy to keep open.

Barone's shower was about half the size of my bedroom. It was strangely titillating to think of Barone standing within this same space... naked. He was just so ruggedly handsome and muscled and tanned and *big*. His white hair and closely trimmed beard and mustache gave him the perfect air of sophistication. I even liked the braided brown leather bracelets and the dark leather and silver watch he wore on his left wrist. I rolled my eyes. I sounded like a silly schoolgirl with a crush.

Not wanting to linger in the shower too long, I jumped out and wrapped one of his massive towels around me. I leaned over and wiped the steam off the mirror and groaned when I saw my reflection. Tilting my head to the right and left to catch my bruised eye at each angle. Well, it could definitely have been worse. Using the makeup Gabriella left me, I covered both it and the scratch up nicely with some powder foundation. Adding a bright, crimson lip and thick, black cat-eye eyeliner also pulled the focus away from my injuries to where they weren't really noticeable.

Returning to the bedroom, I realized with dismay that my torn dress was nowhere to be found. Crap. Gabriella hadn't left me any clothes. I walked over to the massive clothes cabinet which dominated the far wall and opened the door. After pushing his suits aside, I found Barone's work clothes. I selected a faded cotton denim shirt. It was butter soft from being worn and laundered so often. When I put it on, it reached almost to my knees. I then got one of his thick brown leather belts and wrapped it around my waist, tucking the excess into a loop and down. Cuffing the super-long sleeves, I left the first few buttons at the collar unbuttoned and pulled the collar up.

Checking my reflection in the mirror on the cabinet door, I fluffed my hair which was already drying in a riot of curls and waves. Not too bad. Never say an Italian woman couldn't make a fashionable outfit out of just about anything in a pinch. I found my light-brown suede flats near the bed and slipped them on before leaving the bedroom in search of food.

Now that I had showered and my headache had abated, I was starving, especially since I was denied my meager supper last night. I would eat first and then see about getting a ride back into the village.

I made my way down the elaborate, wrought iron spiral staircase and across the ancient Roman mosaic tile entrance to the back of the villa. The entire villa was an open floor plan to take advantage of the mountain breezes. It was filled with stunning artwork, frescoes, and sculptures. The best Italy offered, befitting a family that traced its roots back to when Italy was a kingdom. The kitchen was in the back. There was a small, scribbled note on the marble-topped island from the cook.

Gone to market. - Rosa

Like most Italian households, she probably only purchased enough food for a day or so, so that everything she cooked was as fresh as possible. I found the espresso maker and the milk and made myself a *caffè lungo*. Lifting a striped linen kitchen towel, I was delighted to see a platter of freshly baked *cornetti*. I slathered one with some plum jam and ate the buttery pastry with gusto.

I indulged in a second *caffè lungo* and went in search of someone who could give me a ride.

After peeking in several doorways, I entered a curious room.

Something just told me this was Barone's space.

I glanced nervously over my shoulder before venturing further inside.

It was obviously an old sunroom or greenhouse. The walls and ceiling were green glass with coppery green ironwork, bathing the entire room in warmth and sunlight. There were several pieces of mismatched furniture which looked as if they had seen years of loving use. In the center was a desk piled high with files and stacks of papers. I crossed to stand behind the desk.

The papers had no sense of order. There were invoices mixed with maintenance requests. Orders mixed with inventory sheets. The laptop was buried under a pile of what looked like staff files that were covered in a layer of dust. There was a mobile phone that looked like it was being used more as a paperweight than the essential tool most people found it to be. Out of curiosity I opened the deep desk drawers to either side of the leather executive chair. Both were filled with empty hanging folders, but no files.

I placed my cup on the leather desk blotter and sat in the chair. Sinking into the soft, cushioned seat, I stroked the armrests. This must be Barone's real office. The luxurious, cave-like one where he bandaged my knee the other day must be for show. To impress clients with the majesty and legacy of the Cavalieri name. This one was for the real work of running the winery. It was funny how both suited Barone's personality.

Knowing I had several hours before I needed to be at work and forgetting all about searching for someone to give me a lift, my natural driving need for organization and order sprang into action.

I grabbed a stack of files and sorted them into piles.

Two hours later, I had the entire office whipped into shape.

I had even updated his computer to the latest version of Microsoft. Shaking my head when I fired it up and his password was actually *password*. Really, I couldn't believe the Cavalieri name was a billion-euros industry. Although I knew most of the administrative matters for their multiple businesses took place in Rome. And it wasn't hard to make a fortune when you made one of the most recognized, expensive wines in the world. I guessed it was part of the charm for the business to be a little antiquated with paper invoices and such.

Still, my mind buzzed with all the ways I could help streamline his operation. I could automate his inventory. There was great scheduling and payroll software out there that would replace the Excel sheets he had printed out. And a quick check on Google showed that while *#Cavalieri* was pretty popular in wine circles, they had no social media accounts. How was that even possible?

I stretched my arms while flexing my fingers. I had a little more time before I had to leave, perhaps I would just set up a quick Instagram account and post a few of the pictures I found in a folder on his laptop. I really liked the one of Barone holding a glass of red wine up to the sunlight.

Yes, and then maybe I'd—

"What the hell are you doing in here?"

I looked up just in time to see Barone storming into the

room. He was dressed in a dusty pair of denim jeans, heavy work boots, and a white linen shirt, the cuffs rolled up to expose his strong forearms. He brought the scents of the earth, leather, and sunshine with him. My stomach did a flip-flop at the sight of him as my cheeks flamed.

I rose so quickly from the chair, it wheeled back and slammed against the glass wall. I grimaced, hoping it didn't crack the ancient glass.

Barone crossed to stand before me. "Answer me, Amara. What are you doing?"

I was angry at the tears that crept into my eyes. "I... well... I just thought I'd straighten things up a bit for you," I said, gesturing weakly at the now clean surface of his desk.

His gaze scanned the desk as his brow furrowed. He then turned his angry gaze on me. "First of all, you are supposed to be upstairs in my bed, resting. Second of all, no one asked you to mess with my things."

I planted my hands on my hips. "I wasn't *messing* with your things. I was *organizing* them."

"Well, no one asked you to *organize* them. Now get your ass back upstairs in bed." He stretched his arm out wide and pointed to the door.

"Stop speaking to me like I am a child. I'm not going back to bed. I feel fine. And someone needed to organize this place. It was a fucking mess."

"Watch your language," he growled before running a hand through his hair. "And everything was just as I liked it. I had a system. Now I won't be able to find anything. And you're not fine. You may have a concussion, so either march yourself back up to bed or I'll carry you up there myself."

"I—"

Barone stepped in close. Placing his hands on either side of my hips, caging me in against the edge of the desk. He leaned down low. He was so close I could smell the mint on his breath. "Go ahead, *dolcezza*. Talk back to me one more time, and I'll whip my belt off from around your waist and spank your ass so red you won't sit for a week."

I opened my mouth several times to fire back a retort, but all that came out was a tiny squeak.

He raised one eyebrow. "That's what I thought." He moved to the side and gestured with his arm again. "Now get your ass upstairs and the next time I come into this house you had better be in my bed, do you understand me?"

I jerked my head in a quick nod before squeezing past him. Without another word, I headed for the door.

Barone murmured a soft, "*Brava ragazza,*" as I left.

I briefly closed my eyes as a bolt of lightning shot straight between my legs. What was it about that simple phrase?

After crossing the threshold, I stood in the hallway for a few moments.

Away from his intense and judgmental gaze, I had a chance to think straight.

No.

I would not go back to bed like a good girl.

I was getting the hell out of here and away from Barone Cavalieri's confusing and overwhelming presence.

In a huff, I turned and stormed back into his office.

CHAPTER 13

BARONE

"*Y*ou know what? I don't care what you say. I'm not going upstairs. I'm not—"

I wrapped my hand around the back of her neck and snatched her to me. The moment her body slammed into mine, I claimed her mouth, silencing her protest. Placing my free hand on her jaw, I forced her mouth open and swept my tongue inside. Finally tasting what I had been craving since that first kiss.

It had been a shock to see her in my office, dressed in my shirt. With her tousled hair, red lips, and long, bare legs on display, it was all I could do not to bend her over my desk and fuck her raw. I felt like a complete asshole for thinking like that. She was a vulnerable young woman, injured and under my protection, and I was no better than a rutting beast with no morals.

In my defense, I had spent a brutal, sleepless night with a raging hard-on, unable to satisfy my lust. It had been a special torture holding her so close but only allowing myself the gentlest of touches. I should have just moved to one of the many spare bedrooms in the villa, but I couldn't bear the thought of not watching over her just in case she needed me. So, I'd stayed. Each sigh, each wiggle of her bottom, each rise of her chest pushing her breast into my palm its own punishment.

A twenty-minute cold shower this morning did nothing to ease my unsated desire for her. Yet, I was determined to leave her be until she had recovered, and until I could figure out what to do about her.

All morning long I wrestled with the decision.

Should I be the gentleman and let her go?

Or give in to my baser desires, take her to my bed, and to hell with the consequences?

I still hadn't decided what I was going to do when I walked in to see the object of my torment bathed in a halo of morning sunlight, with slightly damp hair that still smelled of rainwater and my soap, looking like an angel sent from heaven to condemn me for my unholy thoughts.

My only option was to pick a fight with her to get her out of my sight as quickly as possible.

And it had worked. But then she walked back in... and I was damned.

I was a man possessed.

Unleashed.

I couldn't get enough of her.

I wanted her air to be my air.

My lips pressed so hard against hers I tasted the coppery tang of blood, and it only spurred me to further heights of violent passion.

My arm encircled her waist as I pulled her petite frame off the floor. My fingers tore into her hair, allowing me to twist a fistful in my hand, wrenching her head back so I could claim her mouth even more deeply. I swung our bodies around, kicking the office door shut behind me and knocking over a chair as I carried her to my now empty desk.

I lifted her high and placed her on the smooth surface. Pushing her thighs open, I stepped in between them. Breaking the kiss only long enough to wrap both my hands around her neck just under her jaw, I tilted her head back so I could stare into her dark, volatile eyes. Breathing heavily, I panted, "You are driving me insane, *dolcezza*. All day. All night. All I can think about is kissing you. Holding you. Fucking you." I kissed the corner of her eye, her cheekbone, the tip of her nose, then claimed her mouth again.

Her small hands went to the buttons of my shirt.

It was all the encouragement I needed.

I stepped back, already missing her warmth, and wrenched the garment off. Uncaring as the buttons scattered across the marble tile floor. Tossing the shirt aside, I stepped back between her thighs. Centering my hand on her chest, I pushed her back until she was lying prone on my desk like a pagan offering on an altar.

I tore at the buttons shielding her flesh from my view. "Do you have any idea what it did to me, seeing you dressed in my shirt, knowing you had spent the night in my bed?"

I opened the shirt to her navel, right where my thick brown leather belt stopped me. Pushing her lace bra up, I exposed her beautiful breasts. Leaning over her gorgeous form, I sucked one perfect cherry nipple into my mouth, scraping the sensitive flesh gently with my teeth.

Amara let out a sweet groan as her legs rose to wrap around my hips.

I sucked harder as I palmed her other breast, pinching her nipple between my finger and thumb.

Her torso shot off the desk.

I forced her body back down as I swirled my tongue around her nipple and moved my hand to caress between her thighs.

Like a beast, I tore the delicate fabric of her panties off her body.

Kissing her breast, then her stomach, I then kneeled in front of the desk, in front of my pagan goddess. I ran my tongue along her inner thigh before inhaling the sweet musk of her pussy. I traced the seam with the tip of my tongue. She was already wet and ready for me.

"Wait," she breathed as she sat up on the desk.

I groaned as I rose to tower over her. I leaned in, my palms on either side of her hips as the tops of her thighs cradled my painfully hard cock. "Baby, I can't wait another minute. I need to taste you, to fuck you."

She slipped off the desk and kneeled before me. Her slim fingers went to the buckle of my belt. "You first."

The innocent sensuality of her offer rocked me to my core.

I watched in awe as she slipped my leather belt through the metal buckle and then slowly unzipped my jeans. She reached inside my pants and pulled my cock free. The turgid length looked even bigger in her small hand. I had a rush of male ego as her eyes widened at its length and girth.

She looked back up at me. In her eyes was a beguiling mixture of fear, desire... and uncertainty.

Again, I felt an arrogant rush of possession knowing she was mostly inexperienced in such things.

Stepping closer, until my booted feet straddled her kneeling form, I ran my thumb over her lower lip. "Open your mouth for daddy." Primal need made it a harsh, growling command.

With wide, doe-like eyes, she obeyed.

My body tensed as I fisted my shaft and directed the head to rest just inside her open lips. "Take a deep breath, baby."

I could feel her gentle breath sigh over my cock right before I pushed it deep inside her wet heat.

Instinctively, she yanked her head back.

I cupped the back of her head in my palm and held her in place as I pushed my hips forward.

Her tongue shifted under my cock as I thrust until the sensitive head felt the pressure of the back of her throat. Amara's shoulders jerked as she gagged. I pulled back slightly but pushed in again.

Her whimper sent a vibration up my shaft as I used my grip on her hair to force her head forward. I pushed in deeper. Her throat muscles tightened around the head of my cock. I clenched my jaw as sweat broke out on my brow over my effort to not violently thrust in straight to my balls.

Breathing heavily, I thrust slowly, opening her throat.

Her fingernails dug into my thighs. The tiny sparks of pain only added to my pleasure.

The edges of her teeth scraped along my shaft as I quickened my pace.

Looking down at her, I watched a tear escape the corner of

her eye and roll over her cheekbone. I captured it with my fingertip and brought it to my lips.

Christ, she was beautiful.

The remnants of her red lipstick stained my cock as her lips stretched wide around the base of my shaft. Her pretty cheeks hollowed out as she sucked on the head with each withdrawal.

I stroked her hair. "You're such a good girl. That's it, baby. Suck daddy's cock."

I had never been a *who's your daddy* kind of man, but right now, in this moment, it just felt like a kinky, wrong kind of right. And after all, there was no getting around that I was old enough to be her father, which also gave this entire encounter a sexually taboo edge that added to my pleasure.

Her young innocence to my experience.

Her submission to my dominance.

An explosive combination.

I gripped her hair harder as I wrapped my fingers around the base of my shaft, placing the edge of my hand against my abdomen to prevent me from suffocating her with my cock. I quickened my thrusts as my balls tightened.

Amara gripped my thighs as she tried to pull her head back.

My grip wouldn't let her.

I thrust harder, feeling the squeeze of her throat.

I threw my head back as I came. Shooting my hot seed onto her tongue and down her throat.

Amara choked as she tried to swallow it all.

I released my grip on her hair and picked her up off the floor. I carried her over to the sofa and sat her on my lap. Rubbing circles on her back, I waited for her to catch her breath.

She wiped at the tears on her cheeks while giving me a watery smile.

I tapped the tip of her nose with my finger. "You are a very naughty girl for doing that to me. I was all prepared to be the gentleman and let you go. Now I'm going to take you up to my bed and you'll be lucky if I let you leave anytime this week."

She pushed her tangled hair off her shoulder and laughed. "As tempting as that offer is, it will have to wait. I have to get to work."

I laughed.

She frowned.

I then frowned. "You're not serious?"

"Of course, I'm serious."

"*Dolcezza*, I'm not letting you go to work."

Her eyes widened. "Excuse me? What do you mean you're not *letting* me?"

I placed a proprietary hand on her bare upper thigh, just under the hem of my shirt. "I'm not permitting. Not authorizing. Not allowing. Not—"

She slipped off my lap and stood before me. Hands on her hips. "I don't recall asking for *or needing* your permission. You don't own me."

I rose to my full height and towered over her.

She backed up.

I followed.

Her back connected with the wall.

I placed my forearm against the wall over her head. I then reached with my other hand between her thighs. She grabbed my wrist and tried to dislodge my hand, but I wouldn't be budged. "The moment I tasted this pussy, you became mine for

123

as long as I want you. That means you are my responsibility. I will take care of *all* your needs," I said suggestively as I used my finger to trace the seam of her pussy.

She blinked, then sputtered. "*For as long as you want me?* I've got news for you, *Don Cavalieri,* I don't need you or anyone else. I can take care of myself. So, you can take whatever it is you are so *magnanimously* offering me and shove it."

I moved my hand to gently caress just below her injured eye. "Whether you like it or not, you need me and the protection I offer. Are you forgetting what happened last night? You can cover it up all you like, but it still happened."

She turned her head to the side, breaking my touch. "Rocco and Mario are my problem. I'll handle it. I already have a plan. I'm going to hire a lawyer and get them kicked out of the house. It's my house after all. My mother left it to me."

"That isn't necessary. It's already handled."

"What did you do?"

"I handled it."

"Did you kill them?"

"I wanted to... but no. I *persuaded* them to leave town. They won't be bothering you again."

She leaned against the wall and breathed out a sigh of relief. "Well, see? Then there is no issue. I can return home and to work. You don't need to worry about me anymore."

Fuck. I hated that was true.

And even though just last night I was playing the gallant, saying I would stay away from her and protect her reputation, I didn't think I ever really intended to let her go.

Not until I had had my fill of her.

"Wrong. You're under my protection now. And your only

job will be to keep me happy. In return I'll provide you with everything you need."

"You mean I'll be your whore."

"Don't call yourself that," I ground out.

"Why not? That's what everyone else will call me."

"Not if I have anything to say about it."

Fuck the village gossips.

Fuck their old, traditional, conservative ways.

If money couldn't buy their silence, then what was it good for? I dared anyone to speak out against me or my lifestyle choices. They bit their tongues after what happened with my wife, they would do the same again or face my wrath.

"I'm sorry, Barone. I may be just a poor village girl, but I still have my pride. The answer is no."

Anger and sexual frustration got the better of me.

Why did she always have to fight me?

Why couldn't she understand that it was easier to just give in to my demands?

I would always get what I wanted in the end.

My gaze raked over her face and breasts. "If you think to hold off for a marriage proposal, you are wasting your time. I have no intention of remarrying. I'm offering you pleasure, leisure, and luxury. And when we tire of one another, I will set you up for life. Perhaps an apartment in Rome or Milan if you prefer. I suggest you take me up on my offer."

She slapped me across the face.

Although she was right to do so, I couldn't let her get away with it.

I immediately grabbed her wrist and wrenched her arm

over her head as I pressed my hips into her stomach so she could feel my already hard cock.

Just then there was a pounding on my office door. "Don Cavalieri? Don Cavalieri? You're needed."

I released her and took a step back. Rubbing my fingers over my jaw, I narrowed my gaze on her. "This isn't over. Get upstairs. We will discuss this further when I return."

In my foolish arrogance, I actually expected her to obey me.

I was wrong.

CHAPTER 14

AMARA

M a come si permette?

How *dare* he?

I stumbled and jumped on one foot as I took off my shoe and shook it until the pebble fell out before replacing it and continuing my march down the stony path which led to the village. By the time I got there it would be early afternoon and the piazza would be filled with residents and tourists, but I didn't care. I needed to get as far away from Barone Cavalieri as possible.

Imagine the nerve of that man, suggesting I was angling to become his wife.

Like I was some kind of grasping gold digger!

"Need I remind you. It was *you* who pursued *me*! Not the other way around, buddy!" I shouted to the wind as I waved my arms angrily.

It would be a cold day in hell before I ever kissed... or did anything... with that man again.

I couldn't believe I had actually allowed myself to be swept up in his fantasy.

Actually, almost *slept with* that arrogant, egotistical, self-centered, bossy... argh!

How could I have been so stupid as to think he was some kind of knight in shining armor for rescuing me last night? I was dumb enough to listen to Gabriella go on and on about him. What a great man he would be for any woman lucky enough to catch his eye. How kind and wonderful he was to his staff. What a great father he was to his sons. How he'd still make a great father to more children one day. And wouldn't I love to be *in dolce attesa* myself one day? Blah blah blah. It was all bullshit.

Barone Cavalieri was nothing more than a bully. A mean bully.

How could I have been so stupid?

I'd actually begun to start liking him.

I had even fantasized what it would be like to help him run his business. I dreamed of finally having a job I could be proud of, of being appreciated for my business mind. I allowed myself to imagine him coming into his office and actually *praising* me for organizing his files and offering me a job on the spot. I thought how much fun it would be to work together. Side by side. Sharing those secret moments in the afternoon when our hands would touch as we reached for the same file or when our eyes would meet across a conference table.

A true office romance. Something sweet, like an old American Hollywood film.

Stupid girl.

That only happened in the movies and romance novels.

In real life, the wealthy, powerful man never fell in love with the poor girl from the wrong side of town. Nope.

He just fucked her *for as long as he wanted her...* then he bought her off with a diamond bracelet and an apartment in Rome.

I couldn't believe I had actually fallen for his kisses... had actually gotten on my knees and.... *dio Santo.*

No wonder he'd offered me a whore's bargain.

I had acted like one.

I'd always been so careful not to fall for any boys' tricks, how could I have been so stupid?

But that was just it, wasn't it?

Barone was no boy.

He was a man.

A big, strong, handsome man who intoxicated a girl by making her feel as if she was the only thing in the world worth possessing.

A man who could make a girl go weak in the knees with just a look from those dark eyes of his.

And the way he towered over me, using his brute strength to dominate me, was just so illicitly thrilling.

Let's face it. It may be toxic and all kinds of wrong to say it, but there was just something arousing about a man who didn't take no for an answer. Who wanted you badly enough to toss you over his shoulder and drag you back to his cave to fuck you senseless with his big, heavy cock.

My hand went to my throat at the memory of that same cock pushing past my lips.

Cazzo, andrò dritto in inferno per questi pensieri.

No! No. Stop it.

This kind of thinking was how I'd wound up down on my knees in the first place. I was just lucky I didn't fall far enough into his trap to have sex with him. I could have found myself pregnant and alone. Hush money was cold comfort when you had no husband and a baby to take care of.

Well, it was over.

I would go back to my quiet little life, and he would go back to his. I would simply have to find a different job to supplement my income to avoid ever returning to the villa. It was as simple as that.

Taking a deep breath past the pain in my chest at the thought of never seeing the man I supposedly hated ever again, I focused on putting one foot in front of the other.

I was so focused I didn't hear the horse's hooves until it was almost on top of me.

I turned in time to see Barone's stormy expression as he barreled down on me. He rode on top of a massive black stallion.

I screamed and ran but was no match for the speed of the horse.

Barone leaned low in the saddle and swooped down to snatch me around the waist.

He dragged me up and over his lap.

"Let me go!"

He pulled on the horse's bridle, forcing it to pivot and return in the opposite direction.

"Let me go!"

Barone ignored my screams.

Bracing my palms against his thigh, I pushed my torso up. My tangled hair partially obscured my view, but I could tell we had raced past the villa. He was taking me higher and higher into the mountains. "Stop! Put me down!"

He swatted my ass several times. "Keep quiet."

I had no panties on, and his shirt offered little protection from the stinging heat of his hand. My eyes welled with tears as I endured being bounced on his lap for several more minutes before the horse finally slowed to a walk, then stopped.

The moment it did, I jumped down and tried to run.

Barone was behind me in seconds, snatching me back by the belt around my waist.

I turned on him, claws bared. Before I could scratch at his eyes, he flung me over his shoulder and carried me inside a farmer's cottage.

Despite looking like a humble eighteenth century cottage from the outside, it was actually extremely chic and eclectically decorated on the inside, not that I had much time to look around. Barone marched straight through the open floor plan of the main rooms to the back main bedroom where he flung me onto the center of the bed.

Keeping his eyes trained on me, he kicked the door closed as he reached for his belt buckle.

I sucked in a sharp breath. "What do you think you're doing?"

His gaze roamed over my body as he smirked. "What I should have done the first time I laid eyes on you."

He whipped his belt off.

"You're crazy."

He nodded as he kicked off his boots and pulled his shirt over his head. "Yes, I think I am. And it is you, *dolcezza*, who has made me so."

I skirted back to the edge of the bed and swung my feet over the side. Plastering my back to the wall, I inched toward the large glass doors which led out to the veranda.

He nodded toward the doors. "Go ahead. I can fuck you out there in the wild just as easily as in here on a bed."

Taking my chances, I lunged for the doors.

I didn't make it.

Barone wrapped his arm around my waist and pulled me back onto the bed. Pinning me down, he straddled my hips and yanked at the belt around my waist. "I love my belt on you. I can't wait to use it on your ass."

I huffed. "You wouldn't dare."

His only response was a wink.

Gripping the collar of the shirt I wore, he tore the buttons off it. As I opened my mouth to scream, he flipped me onto my stomach. He wrenched the shirt off my arms and unclasped my bra. He then flipped me onto my back and straddled my hips again.

"I finally get to see you completely naked."

My eyes narrowed as I said through clenched teeth, "I hate you."

He chuckled. "Shall I prove you wrong, *dolcezza?*"

He unzipped his jeans and pulled his cock free.

I stared at the long, hard length with its large mushroom head that was almost purple, it was so turgid with blood.

I sniffed, tears forming in my eyes as I tried to fight my desire for him. "Don't do this, Barone."

He forced his legs between my open thighs and braced himself on his forearms above me. "I'm sorry, *piccola.* I know I should let you go. But I can't."

The head of his cock pressed against my already traitorously wet entrance, and I panicked. I pressed my hands against his chest. "You could have any woman you want. Just forget you ever met me. Please, just let me go."

I knew if he pressed forward, we would both be lost.

For all my bluster about being independent and not wanting him, I knew I could only fight a man like Barone Cavalieri off for so long. He was too charming, too intelligent, too over-whelming, too *everything*. Eventually my heart would give in. And I knew it would be the end of me, because inevitably he would break my heart into a million pieces. Leaving me a shat-tered shell of myself. That's what men like him did to women like me.

If we crossed this line, the only way this ended between us was badly.

Come disse Shakespeare in Romeo e Giulietta - Come il fuoco e la polvere da sparo, che si consumano al primo bacio.

We would consume each other until there was nothing left but ashes.

He looked down at me with dark, unreadable eyes. "I can't do that."

Tears rolled down my cheeks as the truth of his words hit me. I balled my hands into fists and pounded on his chest. He captured my wrists and pulled my arms high over my head. Securing my wrists with one hand, he wrapped his other hand around my throat just under my jaw. "Stop fighting me, Amara. Stop fighting *this*. You won't win."

I stilled my struggles.

He leaned down and pressed his lips to mine. I kept my lips closed.

He squeezed his fingers around my throat. Not enough to cut off my air, just enough to send a message. "Open your mouth for me."

I hesitated.

He leaned down and spoke against my lips. "Do it, baby."

I stopped resisting and opened my mouth.

His tongue swept in to claim mine. Our kiss tasted like my tears.

I groaned as my hips squirmed under his. I knew I was already humiliatingly wet and now the rest of my body was betraying me too.

When he finally broke the kiss, we were both breathing heavily.

He tightened his grip on my wrists. "I'm sorry, *dolcezza.*"

With that, he thrust his full length inside of me.

I let out a short scream from the shocking fullness of it.

Although not a virgin, I was far from experienced and my body was not prepared to take a man of Barone's size, no matter how aroused I may be.

"Take it out! It hurts!" I begged.

He pulled back and thrust in again.

My body burned as it struggled to stretch around his girth. My hips bucked as I tried to push him off me. The zipper from his jeans scraped my inner thigh as he increased the pace of his thrusts.

The moment he released my wrists I attacked him. Raking my nails down his chest.

"That's it, baby. Hurt me back."

He pressed his hand between our bodies to tease my clit.

The pressure caused by the pounding of his cock changed. The pain morphed into a building pleasure.

Barone pulled out, and I immediately missed the feeling of fullness.

He flipped me onto my knees and pulled my hips back to meet his.

He slapped my ass several times before shoving his cock back inside of me.

I screamed again, but this time, not from shock or pain.

Sex with Barone was ruthless, rough, and primal.

Just like I knew it would be.

He fisted his hand in my hair and pulled roughly, bowing my back. "*Caspita!* You're tight."

He then pressed the pad of his thumb against my asshole.

I squeezed it tight in response.

Barone chuckled before he leaned over me and whispered harshly in my ear, "The second I'm done fucking this sweet, tight pussy, I'm fucking this even tighter ass."

A shocked gasp escaped me at the thought of something so dirty and wrong.

Barone reached around my hip and continued to tease my clit until I could no longer resist. My limbs went rigid, and I cried out with an almost unholy scream of pleasure. In that moment I would have handed him my soul. I collapsed forward onto the bed as an orgasmic bliss, a strange sort of euphoria, settled over me, as if I were floating on a cloud. The man wasn't human. This sort of feeling wasn't achieved through basic sex, but then not many men had Barone's domineering and powerful presence .

He continued to thrust deep inside of me several more times before roaring his own release.

He then fell to my side.

We filled the room with the sound of our harsh breathing and the earthy scent of sex and sweat.

I could feel his come trickling out of me. A warning. A condemnation. A regret. Deep down I knew we had crossed a line. He would not let me turn back now. A man like Barone would consider me his now. *His property. His possession. His.* How could I have been so stupid to have fallen into this trap?

As if reading my thoughts, Barone pulled me into his embrace. "Don't, Amara. Blame me. Not yourself."

I traced one of the crimson scratches on his chest. "Well, you got what you wanted. Now will you let me go home?" I asked, hopefully.

Maybe I was wrong.

Maybe he'd let me go.

Maybe all he wanted was a quick fuck, and now he'd lose interest.

He stroked my hair before kissing the top of my head. "No."

CHAPTER 15

AMARA

*H*e leapt off the bed and left the room.

The moment he left, all the heat and energy was sucked out of the room. I was a fragile, empty shell, a stone-cold planet missing the warmth and gravitational pull of his sun. Damn him.

How had I managed to fall so far, so completely, so quickly?

I knew how.

I hadn't fallen.

I was pushed.

Barone walked back into the room, carrying a wet towel.

I turned to my other side, facing away from him. "Go away."

Ignoring my plea, he scooped me up into his arms and settled me onto his lap as he leaned against the carved wooden headboard. He brushed my tearstained cheeks with the warm, wet towel before brushing it over my breasts and stomach, then dipping it between my thighs.

I hissed as he pressed his palm against my sore pussy.

He kissed my forehead as he applied soft, soothing pressure with his fingers and the warm towel.

He then kissed my cheek and moved to the curve of my ear. "Do you want me to kiss your sweet pussy and make it better?"

My thighs clenched around his wrist. Ignoring my body's response to his dirty request, I shook my head no.

Barone placed his hands around my hips and lifted me until I was straddling his hips. "Now be a good girl and reach around me and grip the headboard."

I pushed out my lower lip. "I don't want to. I just want to go home."

I needed to get away from this man. I needed time to think about what had just happened and I couldn't do that with him near me taking up all the air in the room.

He spanked my right ass cheek. "Do as you're told."

"Ow!" I frowned as I rubbed my ass cheek. With a huff, I reached out to the headboard.

Barone slid downward to wedge his sizable shoulders between my outstretched thighs. The motion opened me up in a very vulnerable way. "Barone, I don't like...."

His large hands cupped my ass, lifting me up slightly and pushing me against his mouth.

A cross between a groan and a gurgle fell from my shocked lips.

He didn't just lick my pussy; he *feasted* on it. Using his tongue to swirl and flick my clit until I ground my hips against his lips as I white-knuckled the headboard.

"That's it, baby. Let daddy make it all better."

This sexy, older, domineering man was clearly already doing things for me, but when he referred to himself as daddy in that taboo, gravelly voice it just sent me over the edge. Calling himself daddy just had this protective yet wicked vibe that seemed to sum up our relationship, if you could call it that, to a tee.

I cried out and squeezed my thighs close to his shoulders as wave after wave of increasing pleasure rocked my body. Just as it was cresting, Barone dipped his finger into my arousal and pushed it deep inside my ass.

I rose on my knees, my lips forming a shocked "oh."

He restrained me across the tops of my thighs with his arm and thrust his finger in deeper. When I was pushed back down against his mouth, he used his tongue to gently tease my already sensitive clit to another release while continuing to twist and turn his finger inside of me.

"I want you to come with my finger in your ass. You need to get used to the naughty sensation, *dolcezza.*"

I didn't have to ask why. I knew why. He had already told me of his plans to take me back there. Knowing the size of his cock and how it punished my pussy, there was no way I would ever let him. Not in a million years. It was just one more reason I needed to get as far away as possible from this wicked man.

"I can't," I moaned.

"You will or I'll whip your ass with my leather belt until you do," he growled. The low vibrations of his voice against my cunt was the push I needed. He wrenched a third climax from my resisting body.

He snatched me around the waist and pulled me flat against him. He kissed my open mouth, robbing me of breath. I tasted my release on his lips.

Finally, he slackened his grip on me. I lay sprawled on the bed, boneless.

Barone rose and pulled on his jeans. Leaving them unfastened he kissed my cheek and said, "Rest, *piccola*. I'm going to make us something to eat."

After about twenty minutes, I rose on shaking legs and made my way to the bathroom. Wrapping my tangled hair up in a towel since I had no hair ties, I stepped into a scalding hot shower and tried to wash away Barone's scent. The soap made a nice, thick lather and I ran it all over my arms and legs. As I looked down at my stomach and hips, I could see the faint bruises his fingers had caused. I could wash away the scent of his come and sweat, but not his mark. That would take days, maybe even weeks, to erase.

After drying off, I returned to the bedroom and picked the wrinkled and torn shirt I had borrowed from him earlier up off the floor. Having no other option, I put it back on. He had torn all but one button off in his frenzy to get me naked. That one button was halfway down to my navel. Even though it was useless, I buttoned it anyway.

Gripping the collar closed with my hand, I padded barefoot into the kitchen.

Barone was standing shirtless over the stove. He was the picture of Italian masculinity. All tanned, chiseled chest muscles, thick white hair, trimmed beard, and strong shoulders.

I sat on a stool in front of the marble-topped kitchen island and watched him as he sauteed onions and garlic in a skillet until the onions were translucent. He then added in two handfuls of freshly cut porcini mushrooms. As they cooked down, he turned toward me. He gave me a wink before expertly chopping the fresh parsley on the wood block. He scooped the fragrant herb into his palm and tossed it into the skillet before adding salt. He then picked up a large pepper grinder and ground fresh pepper over the entire dish.

Keeping his back turned to me and his focus on the stove, he said over his shoulder, "*Dolcezza*, pour us some wine. I already opened a bottle."

It was a *Vino Nobile Reserva di Montepulciano* from the Cavalieri winery, of course. I picked up the bottle and poured two generous glasses of the ruby red wine. I took a large gulp, hardly tasting the deep cherry and oak flavor. The wine rushed straight past my empty stomach to my head.

Barone took the skillet off the heat and turned to set the pan on the marble island.

Ignoring his own poured glass, he took my glass from my hand. "Careful, *piccola*. Not so much until you have eaten." He turned the glass and took a sip from where my lips had touched the rim. A strange flutter started in my stomach. It was probably just the wine.

He stirred a small spoonful of butter into the pan of polenta before spooning it into two earthenware bowls and ladling the mushroom ragout on top. As he took the stool next to mine, he pushed one bowl toward me before stretching his arm to the side of the island and reaching into a drawer for two spoons. He passed one to me then gave me another wink and a smile. "*Polenta Pasticciata ai Funghi*, one of the few things I know how to cook well."

I reached for the wineglass again.

He pushed it out of my reach as he raised one eyebrow. "Not until you've taken at least two bites."

I scowled.

He frowned.

Knowing he would win, I spitefully spooned an extra big bite of mushroom and polenta into my mouth. The moment I did my eyes watered. I opened my mouth as I cried out around my food. "Hot! Hot!" I waved my hand in front of my lips.

He held up his cloth napkin. "Spit it out."

Embarrassed, I spit into the napkin. He folded it up and tossed it into the wastebasket

Smirking, he nodded his head toward my bowl. "Now try that again with a normal bite."

I scooped some of the buttery polenta and a small sliver of parsley-covered mushroom onto the tip of my spoon and gently raised it to my mouth. I blew on it for several seconds before slipping it between my lips. I closed my eyes and moaned. It was actually really quite delicious. The earthiness of the mushrooms blended with the minty freshness of the parsley and the acid of the onions and garlic, finishing with the buttery yeastiness of the polenta. It was lovely.

Barone took his own bite and then took another sip from our now shared glass of wine. "I love to make you moan."

My cheeks pinkened.

He watched as I took another bite before he took one of his own. By now my stomach took over. Whereas moments earlier I would have thought I was too nervous to eat, I was now ravenous.

Between bites, Barone said, "I need to head back into the fields, but I'll have Gabriella swing by with some clothes. Later she can take you shopping for anything you'll need."

I blinked. Unsure of what to say.

He looked around the small villa. "This was Enzo's, but he no longer needs it so it's now yours. I had it prepared, so it's fully stocked with food, wine and all the essentials although you may want to purchase whatever toiletries and such you like. Just have Gabriella put it on my accounts."

I lowered my spoon and just stared at him.

He continued, "Later tonight, when I return, I will bring the phone I purchased for you. You will also need an automobile. You are free to choose whichever one of mine you prefer. Just tell Alfonso you have my permission. If you don't see one you like, I'll take you to Rome next week and buy you whatever you want. Perhaps a Fiat would suit you?"

I reached for the wineglass and drained it.

He didn't seem to notice.

"When we are in Rome, I will arrange a private showing with Sebastian Diamanti. We can select several diamonds and other precious jewels to turn into some custom jewelry for you. Perhaps a black diamond to match your beautiful eyes."

I swallowed as I tried to find my voice. "So, I'm just supposed to stay here? Doing nothing?"

He stroked my cheek with the back of his hand. "Of course not."

I let out the breath I had been holding. Perhaps this wasn't as bad as it had sounded. Perhaps he had listened to me when I said I needed to work and wouldn't stand to be just a kept girl-friend living off a man.

"You are free to shop, or take an online course, or perhaps learn a musical instrument. Anything you desire, my little bird."

His little bird.

His little caged bird.

I pushed the bowl of polenta away as I rose. Gripping the shirt firmly closed, I said through clenched teeth, "What I *desire* is to go home. What I *desire* is to work. What I *desire* is my independence!"

He stood so abruptly the stool knocked over onto the floor.

He stalked toward me.

I circled around the island.

He followed.

I turned to run.

He grabbed my upper arm and swung me back to face him. Wrapping his arm around my waist, he pulled me against his body as he circled my throat with his hand. "I tire of having this argument with you, Amara. What I offer is for your own good. In time, you will see that. Your home is no longer safe. I offer you security, protection, and a life of luxury."

A tear slipped down my cheek. "And I only have to be your whore in return."

He shook me. "I will not stand to hear such filthy language from you."

"What filthy language? The truth?"

He forced my body back until he had crowded me against the wall. He then claimed my mouth, pushing his tongue deep inside as he pressed his hips into mine. I whimpered as I struggled in his embrace but could not break free. When he finally relented, I lifted my fingertips to my swollen and bruised lips.

He turned his back on me. "I need to get back to my men. We will discuss this further tonight."

I jumped at the sound of the door slamming shut behind him.

I waited until I heard the pounding of the horse's hooves as he rode away, back to the vineyard.

With shaking hands, I lifted the receiver of the landline and dialed Milana's number.

The moment she answered I said, "It's me. I need you to come get me. And bring some clothes."

CHAPTER 16

AMARA

*T*he moment Milana's metallic orange Fiat 500 beater appeared at the end of the drive, I sprang out of the bushes and pulled on the passenger-side door handle.

"*Madonna santa!* You scared me to death, Amara! What the hell is going on? And what the fuck are you wearing?"

I slunk down low in the seat until I was out of view of the window. "Just drive. Drive!"

She threw her hands up in the air. "Okay! Okay! I'll drive!"

I could hear the limestone rocks ping against her car as she raced down the private lane.

"Don't take the main road. Take the one by Guiseppe's farm," I ordered.

"Fine," she said as she reached into the back seat and grabbed a small black bag. She tossed it onto my lap.

I opened it and pulled out a pair of slim black pants, ballet flats, a black-and-white striped off-the-shoulder sweater, and a red scarf. Keeping my head low, I lifted my hips and pulled on the pants.

"Careful," admonished Milana. "Those are my secondhand Prada pants."

I shrugged out of the torn shirt and pulled the sweater over my head.

Placing a cigarette between her lips, she pushed in the car's cigarette lighter. "Are you going to tell me what the fuck is going on?"

I frowned at her as I used the red scarf to tie my tangled curls back in a low, side ponytail. "Why are you smoking?"

We hadn't smoked since we were in school when we thought it would make us look older and chic. It hadn't.

She kept her eyes on the curving lane as she rummaged in her purse for her lipstick and compact. She handed them to me without looking. "They're not mine. They're Sal's. I grabbed them off the counter after I got your call." She shrugged. "You stressed me out with that freaking call, Amara. I mean, what the hell? You told me to bring clothes! To the Cavalieri villa!"

Sal was her boss at the leather goods store.

The lighter popped out. She lit the cigarette and inhaled.

I grabbed it from her and inhaled as well and promptly choked.

She took the cigarette back. Pinching it between two fingers she gripped the steering wheel with both hands and tried to keep her little car on the bumpy country lane.

I peeked my head out through the window. Breathing a sigh of relief once I realized we were no longer within view of the Cavalieri vineyard, I sat up and pulled down the mirror to check my reflection. I used her compact to cover the fading bruise under my eye.

"Are you going to tell me what the fuck is going on?" She leaned forward and looked at me. "*Porca miseria, Madonna santa!* Why the fuck do you have a black eye?"

The car swerved as she stopped paying attention to the road.

I grabbed the steering wheel. "Keep your eyes on the road." Seeing my opportunity, I snatched the cigarette from her again and took another puff. This one not so big.

She snatched it back and inhaled. "Answers, Amara."

I spit out the smoke in a huff before burying my face in my hand. "I slept with him."

"Who?"

"Barone."

"Barone who?"

"What do you mean, Barone who? How many Barones do we know?"

Her eyes got round. "Barone CAVALIERI! You slept with Barone Cavalieri!"

I groaned and nodded before doubling over and burying my head in my knees.

"Don't get red lipstick on my pants!"

My head sprung back up.

She continued, "So wait. Is he the one who gave you the black eye?"

I shook my head. "No. Fucking Rocco did."

"*Gli spacco il culo.* I'm going to fucking kill him. *Adesso lo uccido!* I swear to God, Amara. I'm done with that bastard. This time I'm going to kill him for hurting you."

"You're too late."

"He's dead?"

"Well, not exactly, but almost. I think. I'm not sure."

"Jesus, Mary and Joseph, Amara, I have a headache trying to keep up with you right now. You're not making any sense. Why do you have a black eye? What the fuck were you wearing just now? And how in the hell did you sleep with Barone Cavalieri?"

The whole sordid affair spilled out of me. Not the details about what happened in the bedroom, I glossed over those parts. I'd have to be stark raving drunk to ever share those details with her.

Milana was so stunned that for once she actually kept quiet until I was done talking.

After several moments of silence, I said, "Say something."

She tapped the center of the steering wheel with her thumb. "Is this why you were avoiding me the last few days?"

I shrugged. "I didn't want you to tell me I was being crazy."

"You are being crazy. I mean, seriously. The man is rich as balls, sexy as fuck, and he wants to spoil the hell out of you. And your response is to run in the other direction. *Those are the actions of a crazy person.* Not to mention, I hear the man is an *absolute beast* in the bedroom."

I groaned. "Milana."

"Seriously, dish the dirt. Is it true? I mean, he tried to hide it by only having flings with women in Rome over the years since —well you know—he drove his wife to suicide over being *a beast in the bedroom,* but that's how kinky he is! The rumors spread across Italy! You know how absolutely *depraved* you'd have to be in bed for rumors to—"

"Milana, if you don't shut the hell up, I'm going to jump out of this car and off a cliff."

She sucked her lips into her mouth. Then mouthed, "I'm sorry."

I sighed. "It's fine."

"You know I'm just teasing because it's my stupid coping mechanism. I'm sorry this happened to you, and I feel stupid and useless that I wasn't there to help last night. I'm a terrible friend."

I laid my head on her shoulder. "Yes, you are."

She laughed and gave me a shove. "Seriously, though. All the money in the world couldn't get me to sleep with Cesare Cavalieri so I respect your decision to run away from Barone. We'll hide you out at my apartment until we decide what to do next."

"Thanks. Can you drop me off at home first? I want to pick up a few things."

"Are you sure it's safe?"

I nodded. "Barone said Rocco and Mario left town."

She drove me to my house, slowing the car as we neared it. We both let out a sigh of relief when we saw the drive was empty. No beat-up *Piaggo Ape*. Distressingly, the front double doors were slightly ajar. I bit my lip. That wasn't necessarily a bad sign. We never locked them. They could have blown open with the wind.

Milana placed a comforting hand on my leg. "Did you want me to come inside with you?"

"No. I'll be fine. You head back to work. Can you come and get me in about an hour?"

"Sure." She leaned over and gave me a kiss on the cheek.

I got out of the car and approached the house.

I listened but could only hear the slow creak of the front doors as they swayed in the gentle breeze.

I turned and gave Milana a reassuring wave. She waved back before throwing her car into reverse and heading back down the road.

I pushed the doors open and was immediately knocked to my knees.

CHAPTER 17

BARONE

"Where the hell have you been?" asked Enzo as he looked up from inspecting a bunch of *Sangiovese Prugnolo Gentile* grapes.

"I had some personal business to attend to."

He nodded. "Right... *personal business.*"

I knew I had been gone far too long, especially with how busy we were right before harvest time. After leaving Amara, I had stopped by the villa to wake up Gabriella and give her instructions to bring clothes by the cottage and to keep Amara company. I'd had to endure her snide remarks for several minutes before I could finally return to the fields, but it was worth it.

I wasn't a fool. I knew I had steamrolled Amara into agreeing to an arrangement with me. I just needed time to convince her it was all for the best. In the meantime, I was certain Gabriella would also plead my case. It was probably a low-down dirty trick to solicit Gabriella's help, but where

Amara was concerned, I was fast learning I wasn't above doing anything to keep her by my side.

"Shut up. How are they looking?" I pulled out my pocketknife and sliced a small bunch off the vine nearest to me. I popped one grape into my mouth. I rolled it around on my tongue before piercing the berry with my teeth, letting the tart juice squirt into the back of my mouth. "Five weeks. Maybe six."

Enzo nodded. "Good. Tommaso agrees. Six weeks at the most."

Tommaso was our third-generation foreman. He had been helping run the harvest since he was practically in his teens.

Harvesting the grapes involved controlled chaos. At harvest time, everyone in the village—men, women, and children—became employees. They all came with their baskets to help us handpick the grapes and enjoy the bountiful feasts we put out at the end of each day in celebration.

Handpicking was backbreaking work which started early and ended late until every grape was off the vine. While some vineyards used machines, we preferred handpicking, not only to honor our ancient winemaking traditions, but also because our variety of grapes didn't pick well by machine. Machines were too harsh, resulting in broken berries and lost revenue.

Besides, wine connoisseurs paid double the price for Montepulciano wines from the Abruzzo region of Italy for a reason—because they could taste the history with each sip.

Cesare rode up between the vines on his chestnut mare, sliding down from the saddle and removing his leather gloves as he approached us. "Did you get my message?"

I patted my back jean pocket. My phone wasn't there. I shook my head. "Phone's probably somewhere on my desk."

"As a paperweight," murmured Enzo under his breath.

My dislike of all things technological was rather notorious.

Cesare sighed. "Don't see the point of you having one if you never answer the damn thing."

I was about to get much better about carrying my phone, now that it was going to be my link to Amara when I was away from her, but my sons didn't need to know what. "What was the message?"

"Benito Ciccone stopped me while I was down in the market. Rocco and Mario doubled back into town last night."

My shoulders stiffened. "And?"

"They started mouthing off to anyone who would listen at the bar how they were going to come up here and teach us a lesson."

I covered my right fist with my left palm. "I don't give a shit about that, what are they saying about Amara?"

Cesare's gaze moved from my eyes to my clenched fist and back. His response was slow and measured. "They tried trashing her, but Amara is well-liked and respected. The people were having none of it and tossed them back out on the street. Benito ran them out of town again. As far as he knows they've stayed away, but he wanted us to be on the alert."

The tension in my shoulders eased. "We'll post some guards around the perimeter of the winery and double security patrols."

Cesare adjusted his stance as he stared me down. "Actually, I've already spoken to Alfonso about taking a few of the men and patrolling around Milana's apartment over the next few days until we have confirmation of Rocco and Mario's whereabouts."

"Now why would we do that?"

Cesare rubbed his jaw. "Because that's where I'm taking Amara. I figure she'd want to be with her close friend."

My jaw clenched. "Out of the question." I pointed at the ground. "She stays here."

"What exactly is going on between the two of you?"

"That's none of your goddamn business."

He stepped up to me. "The fuck it isn't. She's my friend and best friends with the woman I—" He shook his head. "I'm friends with Amara and I will not stand by and watch you hurt her. Now as it stands, the village thinks you're a hero for saving her last night from Rocco, but that's going to change real quick if they think—"

I stepped up chest to chest with him. We were even in height, nose to nose. "If they think what?" I snarled.

"You think we never heard the rumors about Mom? You think we didn't know what you were doing in Rome after she died? If you think I'm going to stand by and watch you trash Amara's reputation just so you can get your rocks off..."

I fisted his shirt in my left hand and drew my right arm back.

Enzo jumped in between us, pulling us apart. "That's enough," he roared.

Cesare reached over Enzo's shoulder to point at me. "I'm taking her with me back to Milana's."

I pointed back. "She's not going anywhere. She's safest here with us."

Cesare shrugged off Enzo's restraining hand. "*You mean here with you.*"

My sons and I were passionate, stubborn men who had

come to blows over many things over the years, but never a woman. I had known it was possible they had heard the whispered rumors about their mother and me, and about her death, but it was never discussed in our household. This was the first time he had even mentioned it. His words were like a spike to my chest, especially since only I and Gabriella knew the awful truth. Still, that didn't change my mind about Amara.

She wasn't leaving my side.

Before I could respond, we both turned to see Gabriella waving her arms as she walked down the path toward us. "Boys! Boys! Come quick!"

Our fight forgotten, we all ran toward Gabriella as she made her way awkwardly through the mud and gravel. I placed my hand on her shoulder. "Gabriella, what is it?"

She bent over and took off her high heels. She was instantly significantly shorter. "Will you look at these heels? They are ruined. God never intended a woman to run in a muddy field with Ferragamo heels on."

"Gabriella!"

She threw her shoe-filled hands up in the air in frustration. "She's gone."

Enzo frowned. "Who's gone?"

"Amara. She's gone. I went to the cottage, but she wasn't there. It's all very mysterious since Barone said she didn't have any clothes on—"

I didn't stay to hear the rest of her sentence.

CHAPTER 18

AMARA

"*A*mara! Amara! Goddammit. Where are you?"

I could hear Barone calling my name but stayed silent.

Seconds later, he burst into the kitchen where I was kneeling on the floor.

He fell to his knees before me and grabbed me by the shoulders. "Are you hurt? Did they hurt you?"

I didn't respond.

His thumbs wiped away the fresh tears on my cheeks. "Baby, please, talk to me. Are you hurt?"

I shook my head, too numb to speak.

Barone gathered me close, pressing my cheek to his heart as his large hand cupped my skull and his arm wrapped around my shoulders. His head turned this way and that, surveying the damage. "Are the bastards in here?"

My voice was rough with tears when I choked out a soft, "No. They're long gone."

He rose, bringing me to my feet, while still holding me close. "Let's get you out of here."

I pulled away. "No."

Reaching out, Barone hugged me around my waist, pulling me close again as he placed a finger under my chin and tilted my head back. "This is non-negotiable, *dolcezza*. This is not about one of your stubborn ideas. Your stepfather and stepbrother were spotted in the piazza late last night. You put yourself in serious jeopardy by coming here alone without my permission."

I bristled at the word *permission*.

Again, I broke away. "I'm not leaving. This is my home and I'm staying."

He gestured with his arms. "They trashed this place. I won't allow it."

It was trashed. It looked like Rocco and Mario had taken a lead pipe to every light fixture, window, and piece of furniture in my mother's humble home. There were fist-sized holes in the walls, doors ripped off their hinges, and what looked suspiciously like a puddle of urine soaking into the sofa cushions. It seemed they wanted to send a final message to me before leaving.

Tears blurred my vision. "This is all your fault. Why couldn't you have just left me alone?"

His brow creased as he took a step toward me.

I stepped back. "I was getting along just fine without you. It was *your gift* that set them off. It was you beating them up and chasing them off that caused them to trash MY HOME before leaving."

He raised his hand as if to reach for me. "*Dolcezza...*"

160

I picked up a broken table leg off the floor and gripped it with both hands, holding it before me like a weapon. "Stop calling me that. I'm not your sweetness. I'm not your anything. I'm just some girl you thought you'd toy with for your own sexual gratification for a few weeks and then discard."

A deep sound close to a growl vibrated in Barone's chest as he circled around the table, trying to close in on me.

I held the table leg higher. "Don't you come any closer. Try to deny it. Try to deny that you had plans to just throw money at me when you were done with me. Just assuming that I would be grateful for the experience. Grateful for being given some time in the Cavalieri sunshine. Given a taste of Cavalieri luxury."

The truth of my words was written on his face. "*Dolcez*—Amara, let me explain. I will not lie, my intentions may have started like that, but—"

My face crumpled. "Don't insult us both by claiming you have somehow fallen in love with me in the span of a few days' acquaintance."

He sighed. "No. I wouldn't do that. I am no more in love with you than you are with me, but I have grown quite fond of you. I do genuinely care for you and want to see you safe. I have wealth. What is the harm in my using it to make you happy? To make your life easier? What is the harm in us enjoying each other's company while this infatuation lasts?"

I could feel a hysterical bubble of self-deprecating laughter rise inside of my chest.

What was the harm, he asked?

Men like him never saw the harm.

They didn't understand what it was like to lose all sense of

161

self, of identity, in the gravitational pull that is a strong, hand-some, charming man. It was wonderful at first. You basked in the warmth of his affection and attention. He made you believe you were the most beautiful, most engaging, sexiest woman in the world.

He made you believe it would never end.

So, you let down your guard.

You fell in love.

And that was when it ended.

You became just a burnt-out star orbiting around his sun, praying for just a little of his attention, for just a little of that warmth he used to show you, a shell of your former self.

I knew because I'd watched it happen to my mother.

And I'd be damned if I let it happen to me.

I had come close. Very close. Dangerously close to forget-ting that lesson until this afternoon.

It was easy to forget when I was around Barone. He was just so strong and domineering and possessive. It would be so easy to lean on his broad shoulders and give in to the comfort and security he offered, but I couldn't. It would be a disaster.

I picked up the bottom half of a broken porcelain vase and stared at it. "The Cavalieri legacy is very important to you, isn't it, Don Cavalieri? Everyone knows and respects the Cavalieris. There is your wealth. Your power. Your vast land. Your ancient lineage. Your winery. Your sons and heirs."

Barone stayed silent. His dark eyes solemn.

I held up the broken vase. "This was part of my legacy. I saved up my money to buy it for my mother when I was a little girl. It was chipped and secondhand, but she loved it. She kept fresh flowers from the garden in it, and it always had pride of place on the sideboard. Even after she died, I kept fresh flowers in it in her memory."

I walked over to the cracked farmhouse kitchen sink which was now on the floor at an odd angle. I pointed to a worn silver spot. "You see that? That's where my mother used to clamp the pasta maker to the sink every Sunday morning." I pointed to the torn cream lace curtains dangling from a broken curtain rod. "And those? We sewed those together from an old, stained wedding dress we found down at the market in a ragbag. The whole time we talked about how one day she would sew me my own splendid wedding gown."

I kicked the broken pasta maker, which laid in pieces among the shattered plates scattered across the terracotta brick floor. "And this was what I was going to use when I made ravioli with my own children. I would pass down my mother's recipe for *Ravioli di Ricotta*. I was going to tell them how she let me mix the spinach, ricotta, and parmesan cheese filling. And how we'd sit at the kitchen table, shoulder to shoulder, making the delicate little pasta pillows together, mother and daughter."

I crossed over to the cabinet where I kept the earthenware jug with the money I had scraped together over the years. The jug was on its side. Empty. I held it up. "I was saving up to open a little business. Nothing fancy. Maybe a bookstore or perhaps a flower and garden shop. Something I could call my own. Something I could work for and be proud of. And now it's gone. The house. My mother's belongings. My money. It may not be a billion-euro winery legacy, but it was *my legacy*, it was all I had and now," my voice caught, "it is all destroyed."

Barone stormed across the room and grabbed me. He cupped my jaw and tilted my head back, staring deeply into my watery eyes. "Goddammit woman, you bring a man to his knees with your beautiful, sad eyes. I've never felt so useless in my entire life." He pushed his fingers into my hair, cradling my scalp. "Tell me. Tell me what you want, and I will give it to you. Name it and it's yours. Tell me how I can take the sadness away. I need to fix this for you."

I blinked the tears back and swallowed. "You want to fix this? Then leave me alone."

He closed his eyes as he kissed my forehead. "Anything but that. I can't leave you alone."

"You mean you won't."

He towered over me as he stared down at me through narrowed eyes. "Have it your way. I *won't* leave you alone. You don't want my money? Fine. I will offer you the job your stubborn pride demands. Your money will be your own, but I will not allow you to refuse my protection. On that I will not bend."

"I don't need your protection. Rocco and Mario are long gone."

"Take it or leave it, Amara."

I lifted my chin. "Fine. But as your *employee*, I won't share your bed, *Don Cavalieri*. As you say, I have my pride."

His upper lip curled as his gaze lowered to my mouth. "No fucking way. I'm making you my personal assistant and your primary duty is to keep me satisfied... *in all things*. In fact, I'm pretty sure you'll be on call twenty-four seven, so I'll need you to live under my roof."

My gaze narrowed in return. "Office manager, I live here, and you keep your hands to yourself."

He stepped forward, pushing his thigh between my legs as

he placed his hand at my lower back. "Office manager, you live under my roof, and we'll see. Final offer, Amara."

I bit my lip.

Barone cursed under his breath.

It was my only warning.

He lifted me by the hips and swung our bodies around to set me on the kitchen countertop. He forced my thighs open as he stepped closer. He then yanked down the off-the-shoulder sweater, exposing my naked breasts. Leaning down, he pulled one nipple deep into his mouth. He grazed the sensitive flesh with his teeth before kissing the column of my neck. He bit my earlobe before harshly whispering, "You haven't accepted the position yet."

Warmth pooled between my legs. "Barone, I—"

His mouth fell on mine, stealing my words. His tongue swept inside. Our kiss tasted like wine and tears. He palmed my breast as he deepened the kiss. I wrapped my legs around his hips. He groaned against my mouth. When he broke away, we were both breathless.

He reached for his belt buckle. "You're not my employee yet, *Signorina Beneventi*. And I have a mind to bend you over and whip your ass raw with my belt for the stunt you just pulled. Don't you dare worry me by running off like that again, or I'll—"

"Get your hands off her!"

Stunned, I looked over Barone's shoulder. Milana was running toward us both.

Before I could stop her, she vaulted onto Barone's back and pummeled him with her fists. "You bastard! I'll kill you!"

I yanked up my sweater and jumped off the counter. Waving my arms, I tried to get her attention. "Milana! Wait! Stop!"

She beat Barone's shoulders with her tiny fists, her legs wrapped around him like a clinging, psychotic monkey. "I'll show you for hitting my friend you piece of shit bastard! *Brutto figlio di puttana bastardo!*"

Barone tilted his torso to the right as he held out his arm, dislodging Milana from his back and catching her before she fell to the floor. He placed her on her feet and stepped back.

Her eyes grew wide as her gaze flew between him and me and back. Her words were muffled as she covered her mouth with her hand. "*Madonna mia!* Don Cavalieri! I am so sorry. I didn't realize it was you. It is so dark in here, I thought it was Amara's stepfather returned to hurt her again."

Barone chuckled as he placed a reassuring hand on Milana's shoulder. "It's all right. You must be Milana."

Milana's cheeks burned a bright pink.

I was glad to see I wasn't the only one affected by Barone's commanding presence.

"Yes, sir."

Did she just *sir* him?

"I'm glad to see Amara has such a champion. You have quite a punch there."

Milana lowered her head. "Thank you, sir."

Again with the *sir!*

"Barone."

Milana looked at me. I shrugged. She looked back at him. "Barone," she whispered, clearly uncomfortable with the whole situation. It was weird to see my confident friend so cowed by his presence, but I wasn't surprised. Barone had that effect on people.

He placed a possessive hand on my lower back. "I was just about to take Amara home."

I shifted away and looped my arm through Milana's. "Actually, I'm going to stay with Milana." At Barone's frown, I hastily added, "For tonight?" I hated that I sounded like I was asking permission, like a little girl asking her daddy for a treat.

Nothing had changed since this afternoon. I still needed time away from him to think about everything that had happened. If anything, I needed it now even more.

Barone turned his intense gaze on Milana. "Where do you live?"

"Just off the piazza. I have an apartment above Sal's leather goods shop."

Barone nodded. "I know Sal. He's a good family man." He seemed to consider it for a moment. "Fine."

I let out the breath I was holding.

Barone leveled his gaze at me. "*For tonight only*," he said meaningfully.

Milana gave me a questioning look. I shot her one back that silently said I'd tell her later.

Barone insisted on waiting while I gathered a few of my things. He then followed Milana's tiny Fiat back to her apartment before roaring off in his big, expensive luxury car.

It wasn't until Milana locked the door of her apartment that I finally allowed myself to collapse onto the sofa and take a deep breath.

Milana collapsed next to me. "Well, that was certainly interesting. Are you going to fill me in?"

"Yes, but first I need a long, hot bath and a glass of cabernet."

She patted my leg. "Done and done. While you're in the bath, I'll grab some blankets and pillows and make you a bed up."

Milana didn't believe in wasting precious wardrobe space with a bed, so in her small apartment, her bedroom was actually her dressing room. She slept on her sofa in the living room which opened off a small kitchen only wide enough for one person. Her appliances consisted of a tiny fridge and a countertop hot plate instead of a stove. There was a tiny balcony, accessible only by climbing through a window, that was just large enough for a cafe table with two chairs, where she ate her meals.

Thankfully, she had a decent-sized bathroom with a practically ancient cast iron soaking tub which I adored. I turned on the hot- and cold-water spigots, pulled the cork stopper off her rose-scented bath salts, and poured a generous portion into the steaming water. I then lit the candles she had strategically placed around the bathroom as I waited for the tub to fill.

Stripping down, I carefully folded Milana's designer pants and sweater and set them aside, then stepped into the tub. I sank into the soothing water and leaned back with a sigh of relief.

Later, I would think about Barone and his offer.

Later, I would think about my body's traitorous response to not only his touch, but his very nearness, and how I would have to master it for my own survival.

Later, I would think about what a mess my life had become.

Later.

Right now, I just wanted to lay back in this tub and forget.

Too bad Barone had other plans.

CHAPTER 19

BARONE

J pulled into the stable behind my villa and turned off the engine.

I reached for the door handle and paused.

No.

I couldn't do it.

I tried.

Well, not really, but that was what I would tell her.

I turned the key. The engine roared back to life. I threw my Maserati Quattroporte into reverse and then drove forward, spinning the tires before heading back toward the center of town. I pulled up before her friend Milana's apartment. Getting out of the car, I headed to the weather-beaten red door to the left of the entrance to the leather store. I rattled the doorknob. It was locked. I turned my head, glancing to the left and right. It was long past dusk on a quiet autumn evening. There was no one in sight. Making a note to send one of my men to make the necessary repairs, I stepped back and kicked the door in.

It opened onto a narrow staircase which I quickly climbed, taking the steps two at a time. They ended at a small landing. There was just one door at the top, and I could hear bossa nova music coming from inside. I rapped my knuckles on the door. After a long pause, I heard a chain being drawn, then a key turning.

Milana opened the door, holding a glass of cabernet. "Don Cavalieri?"

"Where is she?"

"What are you doing here?"

"Where is she?" I demanded. I didn't want to scare her friend, but neither was I in a mood to be thwarted or delayed in my intentions.

Milana pointed behind her. "Back there."

I walked past her.

She quickly followed. "Wait. You can't go in there. She's in the tub. Amara!"

I opened the bathroom door.

Water sloshed over the edge of the chipped white porcelain tub as Amara sat up. Her beautiful breasts glistened in the candlelight. "Barone!"

My cock lengthened down my thigh at the sight of her. "I've changed my mind."

She blinked. I had clearly caught her off guard. "What do you mean?"

I reached down into the water, wrapping one arm behind her back and the other under her knees. I then lifted her out of the tub. Bathwater spilled down my front, drenching my clothes and the floor. "You're coming with me."

Amara screamed, "Put me down!"

I stormed past a stunned Milana. "Absolutely, as soon as I get you home."

Amara held her arm over her breasts as she kicked her legs. "Barone! You're crazy! I'm naked... and wet! Put me down this instant!"

I scanned the small apartment and saw a pile of blankets and a pillow on top of a mat on the floor in front of the sofa. I looked at Milana with questioning eyes. She followed my gaze.

I raised an arrogant eyebrow. "Either way, she's leaving with me."

Milana huffed. "Fine!" She raced over and picked up one of the blankets. She shook it out and draped it over Amara and my shoulders.

"You're helping him?" yelled an outraged Amara.

Milana shrugged and gestured toward me. "Look at the size of him. He's bigger than both of us combined."

I walked out of the apartment and down the stairs, calling over my shoulder, "Tell Sal I'll send someone to fix the door."

I leaned down and opened the car door before depositing a squirming Amara in the passenger seat. Just in case she got any ideas, I whipped her blanket cover off before slamming the door shut. I could hear her angry shouts through the heavy glass as I walked around to the driver's side and got in.

Once I was behind the wheel and the doors were safely locked, I gave her the blanket back. She quickly wrapped it around her wet form.

"You have gone too far this time, Barone. I'll never forgive you for this. How dare you! I can't believe you'd do such a thing. You are without a doubt the most insane, arrogant, egotistical, tyrannical, domineering, arrogant—"

"You said arrogant twice."

"It bears repeating," she said through clenched teeth. "I don't know what you think you'll accomplish with this stunt, but the second you stop this car, I'm marching straight back to Milana's, if I have to do it buck naked!"

I quirked an eyebrow as I cast her a sidelong glance. "We'll see about that."

I pulled my car up to the villa's entrance. The moment I stopped, she sprang out of the car and tried to run. She didn't get far. Limestone rocks were hell on bare feet.

"Ow! Oh. Ow!"

I walked over and bent low, sweeping her up over my shoulder. The blanket draped loosely over her naked form as I carried her inside then directly up the stairs and down the hall to my private suite. Once we were inside the bathroom, I set her down, turned, and locked the door. I slid the brass key on top of the bathroom cabinet, well out of her reach.

She wrapped the blanket more securely around her shoulders. Her cheeks were bright pink from her angry exertions.

Damn, she looked beautiful.

How could I have ever thought, even for a second, that I would get this woman out of my system and simply let her walk out of my life?

I stepped around her and turned on the gold swan's-neck spigot to the massive white marble whirlpool tub that was nestled in an alcove of my bathroom. During the day, the large bay window above it framed a stunning view of the mountains. At the moment, the glass reflected the curves of Amara's ass as the now wet blanket clung to her skin.

"What do you think you're doing?"

I kicked off my work boots. "I thought we'd finish what you started."

She rolled her eyes as she tilted her head to the side and tightened her grasp on the blanket.

I unbuttoned the first few buttons of my now soaked shirt and pulled it over my head.

She nodded toward the fast-filling tub. "You're even crazier than I thought if you think I'm getting in that tub with you."

I reached for my belt buckle.

The corner of my mouth lifted as I watched her gaze focus on my fingers slowly drawing the thick brown leather through the brass metal buckle. I knew what she was thinking... because I was thinking the same damn thing. But that was for later.

I undid my belt and lowered the zipper to my jeans, slipping them and my boxers over my hips. I kicked them aside.

I turned to face Amara. My cock already hard and ready for her.

Her eyes widened as she backed away. "Oh no! I warned you I would not sleep with you as an employee."

I stalked toward her. "Well then, it is my duty, as your potential future employer, to inform you that you have not formally accepted my offer, so you are not my employee, yet."

She bounced up on the pads of her feet. "I accept! I accept!"

I reached for the blanket.

She resisted.

I pulled harder.

She pulled back.

I won.

The blanket fell away. I stepped close, warming her chilled skin with the heat of my body. I traced her collarbone and the swell of her breast with the back of my hand. "I regret to inform you that the Cavalieri Winery offices are currently closed for the evening. We will have to give you our answer in the morning."

I placed my hand around her neck, slowly pulling her close as I leaned my head down. I whispered against her lips, "Give in to me, *dolcezza.*"

"I'm afraid," she whispered back, her breath a light caress against my lips.

I inhaled the rose scent which clung to her skin. I knew she would accept nothing but raw, brutal honesty from me from this point forward. "You should be. I fear you are not wrong. I seem to be a man possessed when it comes to you. One moment I think you are a passing fascination I just need to get out of my system. The next I want to chain you to my side and never let you go. It's as if you have bewitched me, *piccola.*"

"You speak as if I am the one with all the power, when we both know it is you who holds the power over me."

I cupped her jaw. "God help me if you ever learn how wrong you are."

I then claimed her mouth. Holding her close, I lifted her off the floor and carried her across the bathroom. Breaking our kiss, I held her higher and stepped into the tub, sinking into the hot water with her still on my lap.

I shifted her legs until she was straddling my hips. "Lower yourself onto my cock."

After a moment's hesitation, she obeyed. She knelt on her knees and used her slim fingers to guide the head of my cock to her entrance. I leaned my head back and closed my eyes as my cock slowly slipped inside her tight heat.

I had to restrain myself from thrusting deep. Letting her set the pace as she gently settled herself back onto my lap.

I opened my eyes and buried my hands in her hair. "*Brava ragazza.*"

I hissed air through my clenched teeth as she squirmed and adjusted her hips. Time to slow things down and pamper Amara while I teased her a little, so I reached for a cloth and a bar of soap laying nearby. Gathering a rich lather, I set the bar aside and swept the cloth over her neck and down her arm, then over her breasts and her other arm, massaging her tight muscles as my rigid cock stayed deep inside of her.

"Lean forward," I commanded.

She placed her palms on my chest and leaned her head on my shoulder. The movement shifted my cock inside of her, pressing my shaft against the sensitive nub of her clit. She gasped at the contact. Stretching my arms around her, I swept the lathered cloth over her back in long, soothing circles.

When I had finished, I had her sit up again.

With my foot, I turned the tall, curved spigot back on.

Bracing my hands around her hips and on her lower back, I leaned her body all the way back until her hair was under the water spray. The position spread her thighs open even wider. I thrust my hips up and down several times.

Amara moaned.

The fresh hot water swirled and mixed with the cooling water around our bodies.

I brought her back up close to me and poured some shampoo into my hand, gently washing her hair. As I took my time, saturating her curls with lather, she began to squirm and shift on my lap. I knew the feeling of fullness from my cock was affecting her. I leaned her back to rinse her hair. Once again, I teased her by thrusting just enough to bring her close to climax before drawing back.

Amara whimpered as she laid her head on my shoulder.

"What does my baby want?" I asked against her cheek as I ran my fingertips up and down the ridges of her spine.

"I need you to... you know."

"You're going to have to ask me like a good little girl."

She bit her lip as she turned her head and glanced away, her cheeks burning brightly. "I need you to... thrust... harder... like you did before."

I traced her full bottom lip with my wet finger. "You want me to fuck you from behind while I pull your hair?"

If possible, her cheeks burned an even brighter pink. She nodded.

"What do you say?"

I wondered if she would say it. Truth was I would accept anything, even something as slight as a sigh or a moan, but I wanted her to say it. My dark soul wanted to hear her innocent lips say it. I also needed proof I wasn't insane for crossing all bounds of polite society, and truth be told, for breaking more than a few laws, to possess this woman.

Say it, I thought.

Say it.

She licked her lips.

I held my breath.

"Please... *daddy.*"

What little control I had snapped.

I lifted her off my lap and spun her around until she was on her knees, holding the edge of the tub. I twisted the wet rope of her hair in my fist. I closed my fingers around my shaft and guided it to her entrance after using my knees to spread her thighs open as wide as the tub would allow. As the head of my cock slipped barely inside, I placed a hand on her hip and leaned over her now-trembling body.

"Brace yourself, babygirl."

I thrust in deep as I yanked on her hair.

Her tight body clenched around my cock, sending a dark thrill up my shaft and balls.

I pulled back and thrust again and again.

Jesus Christ, I would never get enough of this woman.

Her body rocked back and forth as I pounded into her without mercy.

"Oh, God!" she moaned.

I reached around and teased her clit, feeling the underside of my shaft against my knuckles as it continued to spear relentlessly into her.

Her shoulder blades tensed as her head dropped down. Her fingers clawed at the wet marble edge of the tub as she screamed her release.

My balls tightened, but I ruthlessly clamped down on my release.

I wanted... no... I needed more from her this night.

Reaching for the soap, I pulled free from her tight pussy and lathered my cock.

Amara turned her head to look at me over her shoulder.

Tossing the soap aside, I placed the head of my cock at her puckered entrance.

Her eyes widened as she tried to shift her hips to the left. "No, Barone. Not there," she pleaded.

"I'm sorry, *dolcezza*. If one night is all you are to give me, then I will risk damnation to taste heaven."

Water sloshed around us as I pushed forward, forcing my cock past her body's natural resistance.

Amara cried out.

I flattened my palm on her lower back and watched my soap-lathered shaft disappear between the softly curved cheeks of her ass. I kept my thrusts deep and slow, allowing her body to adjust to my girth, knowing that with pain came pleasure.

"Please," she whimpered, "it hurts."

I rubbed her back. "I know. Do this for me, baby. Do it for daddy."

I reached around and teased her clit. I could feel her thighs clench as her body responded to my touch. We climaxed together.

I then pulled out slowly.

Keeping her on her knees, I spread her ass cheeks wide, enjoying the sight of her tiny hole gaped open from the force of my cock and the small stream of white, creamy come dribbling out of it.

I really was as depraved as the scandalous rumors claimed.

Even more so if they ever found out the real truth behind my wife's death.

CHAPTER 20

MILANA

$\mathcal{I}$ returned from the early morning market to see the outer door to my apartment had been replaced. It was a huge step up from the decrepit wooden door that had looked like it had been pieced together from the wreckage of a Roman ship. In fact, it was almost a little too much. This was Cavalieri, not Naples or Sicily, after all. I hardly thought a steel door with a deadbolt was needed. Half the people in this village barely even bothered to lock their doors at night.

Making a mental note to check in with Sal for the new key, I made my way up the narrow stairs, when I encountered a man kneeling in front of my door. My *open* door.

"What the hell are you doing?"

He rose and turned.

My mouth dropped open when I saw the handsome face of Cesare Cavalieri. "Hello, Milana."

My eyes narrowed. "Get out of here. Now."

His hard gaze traveled slowly over me as he inhaled through

his nose, appearing to be trying to cool his temper. "Not until I've finished."

I stormed past him into my apartment. Dropping my linen grocery bag on the narrow kitchen counter, I returned, propping my hands on my hips. "Why are you here?"

He leaned his shoulder against the doorjamb. I hated how at ease he looked when I was seething inside. "My father said the door needed to be repaired. He was going to send one of the boys, but I..." Again his dark gaze looked me over, lingering on my lips. "*Volunteered*."

I crossed my arms over my chest as I tilted my head. "Only the outer door was broken. Why are you working on *my* door? And how did you even get it open without the key?"

He gave me a charming, crooked smile. "What can I say? *I have skills,* " he said suggestively. "I like what you've done with your hair. It looks cute all short and bouncy like that."

I touched the natural spiral curls of my bobbed, just above shoulder-length hair. I'd cut my long hair a few years ago after leaving school. I loved the chic, fashionable style. Although knowing he liked it made me want to grow it long again just out of spite.

"I want you to leave."

"I'm not finished."

"I don't care. Leave."

He stepped inside. "No."

My heart raced as I backed up. "I don't care what you're doing to my door. I need you to leave. Now."

"Your door had a shitty lock on it. It wasn't safe. I'm not leaving until I finish replacing it with something better. And after that we are going to talk about your *so-called* living arrangements. This place is not acceptable, Milana. It's too small and not secure." He gave my apartment a scathing once-over. "You should have told me this is where you were living. I'm going to move you into one of the Cavalieri properties first thing tomorrow."

I ticked off the items on the tips of my fingers. "First, I liked my shitty lock just the way it was. Second, I didn't ask you to replace it. I'd never ask *you* for anything. And third, *when fucking hell freezes over will I ever move into a Cavalieri property!*"

He rubbed his jaw as he looked at me. "We'll see about that. It's over, Milana. You understand me? Whatever bullshit excuse you have used to keep me at arm's length these last few years. I'm done."

I gave him a dismissive wave of my hand. "Yeah? Heaven forbid someone treat one of the great Cavalieri men as if they weren't God's gift to women. What's the matter, Cesare? Can't accept the fact that I'm not clamoring to be one of your groupies?"

He reached behind him and closed the door, trapping us inside.

The air in my lungs seized.

I couldn't take a deep breath.

He stepped closer as his hands rested on his belt buckle. "That's it. My patience is at an end. We are going to clear up whatever craziness you have worked up in that beautifully insane little mind of yours, right here, right now."

Stepping back, I stumbled over the edge of my throw rug. "No. We're not. Get out."

He held out a hand to steady me when I stumbled, and I

flinched. His gaze narrowed as his jaw hardened. It was too much to hope he had missed the reaction.

"What the fuck, Milana?" he ground out.

Panicking, I snatched up an empty Murano glass bowl I kept on a nearby table and held it over my head. "Get out, Cesare! Now!"

He needed to leave.

The walls were closing in on me.

The edges of my vision were blackening.

I was back there.

Trapped in the nightmare.

In the darkness.

I could feel their hands on me.

Pushing me.

I could hear their laughter as the door slammed shut, locking me inside.

It was all just a big joke to them, but not to me.

Never to me.

My palms itched like they had that day, after hours of banging on the door, shouting for help.

But no one came.

For hours and hours and hours.

And it was all his fault.

Cesare's fault.

He put them up to it.

He betrayed me.

My entire body trembled.

Cesare frowned. He raised up both hands, palms out, like one would if approaching a wild animal. All the anger drained from his voice, replaced by concern. "Baby, what's wrong?

Tell me."

My lips thinned. "I'm not your baby."

My body was shaking so badly, I could no longer hold on to the bowl. It dropped from my hand and shattered on the floor. Tears sprang to my eyes. I hated showing weakness in front of anyone, but especially in front of *him*.

I bent to pick up the shards.

Cesare wrapped his arm around my waist and pulled me back. "Don't, you'll cut yourself."

I didn't like to be touched.

Ever.

My vision went black.

This time, I became a wild animal.

I screamed and kicked and clawed.

Fighting with all my will to get free from his grasp.

"Fuck! Milana! Stop! Baby, I don't want to hurt you!"

I leaned down and sunk my teeth into his hand, relishing his yelp of pain.

"That's it," he growled.

Using brute strength, he lifted and pressed me against the wall. He then wedged his knee between my legs. Because he was so much taller than me, I was practically riding his thigh. He grabbed my wrists and stretched my arms high over my head.

We were both breathing heavily from the struggle.

He leaned down close to me until we were nose to nose. "Milana, stop."

I spit in his face.

He transferred my slim wrists into one of his own and wiped his face before he wrapped his hand around my throat.

Without saying another word, his mouth crashed down onto mine.

It wasn't a kiss.

It was a punishment.

A claiming.

A possession.

The moment he ended the kiss, I broke free. I ran out of the apartment and down the stairs. I didn't stop running until I had reached the crowds in the piazza. I walked around for hours, not daring to return until dusk.

When I did there was a small envelope taped to my door. Inside was a shiny new set of keys, and a handwritten note in a heavy, masculine scrawl.

This isn't over.

- C

CHAPTER 21

AMARA

"Wake up, lazybones, or we will miss our train."

I rubbed my eyes as I sat up in bed. My mouth opened with a shocked gasp as the blanket fell away and my naked breasts were on full display. I slinked down in Barone's massive bed, mortified to have been found naked in it.

Gabriella walked over to the heavy curtains concealing the veranda doors and spread them open wide, letting in the sunshine. She clapped her hands as she walked to the next set of curtains. "*Su! Su! Su! Dobbiamo sbrigarci!* If I have to be up at this ungodly hour, so do you."

As usual, she was impeccably dressed. She was wearing a zebra print Dolce & Gabbana pencil skirt with a black lace peek-a-boo seam up the side and a slim-fitting black sweater with red pumps and bright red lipstick. Her thick black curls, not showing even a hint of gray of course, were tamed in a chic chignon highlighting her thick, silver hoop earrings, which matched her platinum and diamond bracelets. She was the very epitome of Italian style.

"Gabriella, I know you must be wondering—"

She waved her hand dismissively. "Posh, darling. What is there to wonder? Barone is a virile, handsome man with needs. You are a beautiful young girl. This is Italy, after all. What is life for if it's not meant to be lived to its fullest? Fuck whomever you please. Now get up, we have shopping to do!"

I pushed my tangled hair away from my face. "Shopping?"

She leaned over the bureau and checked her already perfect lipstick in the mirror. She met my gaze in the reflection as she gave me a wink. "In Rome."

I hugged the covers more closely to my chest. "No, absolutely not. There has been a mistake. I know what this looks like, but it's not that. I mean it is that, but it's no longer that. Not anymore, I mean." I let out a frustrated sigh as I beat the bedcovers with my fist. "I made it very clear to Barone that last night was the last time. I'm his employee now, and I won't be accepting any inappropriate gifts."

She came to sit on the edge of the bed, close to my side. She lifted both sides of my hair. "I always see your hair down in a tangled mess. I mean it's beautiful, but still a mess. Do you ever wear it up? We should probably get you a nice trim while we are there. I'll call Ignazio and tell him to fit you in. He usually books months in advance, but for me I'm sure he'll make an exception."

I clasped her hands in mine and leaned in close. "Gabriella, I need you to listen to me. I'm not going to Rome. I don't need any clothes. I have my own clothes."

She laughed as she stood. "Don't need any clothes? What a

strange thing to say. Darling, a woman always needs more clothes. There is no such thing as too many clothes."

I huffed. "Fine. Then I don't need Barone to buy me any clothes."

She pressed her hand to her chest and laughed. "Really, it's like you slip into another language at times. Not wanting a man to buy you things? Whoever heard of such a silly notion?"

"Gabriella!"

She sighed. "I am just teasing. Barone said you may fight me on this, something about you being oddly stubborn and prideful. He told me to tell you as the new office manager of Cavalieri Winery you will be part of the face of the company and therefore will be expected to display an image of luxury. The clothes we are buying today will be owned by the company, not you, and should be considered"—she gave a dramatic shudder before continuing—"part of your uniform."

I leaned against the headboard and smiled. I couldn't help how I was begrudgingly charmed by the man. I mean, he was of course being manipulative and pushy and his usual arrogant self. Even so, it was kind of sweet. I reluctantly admired his clever end-run around any objections I may have.

There was a soft knock on the door. Gabriella opened it and stepped aside for a maid to enter with a breakfast tray. She set it on the edge of the bed and left with a nod to us both. Gabriella handed me the *caffè lungo* and picked up the smaller espresso for herself. I looked on the tray and saw a platter of warm, buttery *cornetti* and a jar of plum jam.

Gabriella followed my gaze. "Those are for you. Barone says they are your favorite."

I did not know how he knew what I liked to drink and eat in

the morning, but it was hard not to feel touched by the gesture even as a chilling fear crept over me. I was already fighting an attraction to the over-the-top, arrogant, domineering, commanding, controlling version of Barone. What would happen if he also became charming, thoughtful, and considerate? I would be doomed.

Gabriella broke into my musings. She drank her espresso in one gulp and replaced the cup on its saucer with a clink. "Now get a move on or we will miss the train to Rome. I have appointments set up with personal shoppers at all the best stores, but we must go. *Adesso. Doccia!*"

I slipped the blanket out from under the breakfast tray and wrapped it around my body as I ran into the bathroom.

While I was naked in the shower, Gabriella burst into the room. She scoffed when I objected. "Don't be so modest. You have a stunning body. Really, darling. Those breasts! What I wouldn't do to have my twenty-year-old breasts back."

She was holding up two stunning dresses. "I'm going to put you in Gucci. I just haven't decided on the green with the classic bamboo animal print purse or the chartreuse with the yellow python belt bag. It depends on which one of these I'll be the most angry to see you look better in than me. Then I'll give you the other one." She laughed.

"We will of course dress you mostly in classic Valentino and Versace, but it will make them angry to see you in Gucci, and they'll fight harder to get you as a client. We are also meeting Arabella Diamanti for lunch. You are going to adore her. She's my favorite of all the Diamantis. Sebastian's too serious for his own good and Rafaello's too charming by half for his, but Arabella is an absolute darling. Her mother on the other hand is crazy as fuck, but what can you do. Afterward we are going to the Diamanti vault at their headquarters for you to pick out a few of their couture pieces. Sebastian will arrange to have them delivered by armed carrier to the villa later."

My head swam. This was a lot of information to take in so early in the morning. Washing the soap from my face, I asked, "Why would Valentino and Versace fight for me as a client?"

"In case it has escaped your notice, except for meetings and specific events, Barone and his sons dress more like farmhands than the insanely rich landowners they happen to be."

I turned my shoulders to hide my smile. I happened to like the rugged way Barone dressed. There was something about the way he filled out a pair of jeans and the sound his heavy boots made when he stomped toward me. There were also his work-honed muscles and sun-kissed skin. If it wasn't for the gray hair, you'd think he was a man half his age. That certainly was true about his sex drive. I clenched my thighs as I forced myself to stop thinking about him.

Gabriella continued, "There will be a great deal of excitement finally to have a beautiful young female employee of Cavalieri Winery at these events. What designer wouldn't want their designs showcased on such a stage?"

This all sounded very suspect to me. It wasn't like Cavalieri Winery didn't have other female employees, but I hadn't seen any in the office at the villa headquarters so far, so I couldn't argue.

In the end, Gabriella chose the bright green, A-line Gucci dress for me. She paired it with a bold gold necklace and an animal print handbag with the classic Gucci dark bamboo handle. Alfonso drove us to the train station, and we just made the train to Rome.

Traveling on the commuter train with Gabriella was a fascinatingly entertaining experience. The woman was the living embodiment of *La Dolce Vita*. I had noticed Alfonso lugging a large wicker basket with him when he escorted us to our seats on the train, which he set on the seats across from us. The moment the wheels were set into motion, Gabriella unbuckled the leather straps and flipped the lid open. Inside were four large silver thermal flasks, stacks of tiny white porcelain espresso cups, and several long baskets filled with a cornucopia of pastries: sugar-covered and jam-filled *bomboloni*, gooey honey-topped *castagnole*, cheese-filled *focaccia*, ribbons of crispy powdered sugar-covered *chiacchiere*, and delicate *sfogliatella* filled with custard and black cherries. It was like *Carnivale* had come early.

Gabriella grabbed a flask and stood up. She raised it high. *"Venite, amiche mie. Mangiamo e godiamoci la vita!"*

The train full of already animatedly chatting business commuters burst into cheers.

Gabriella handed me the flask and reached for two espresso cups. "Amara, darling, will you pour?"

I unscrewed the lid to the flask and enjoyed the rich, earthy scent of roasted coffee beans as steam rose from the narrow opening. I steadied my hand to the rhythmic motion of the train and poured two cups of espresso. Gabriella handed them to two eager women and grabbed two more cups. Two gentlemen nodded their heads and politely asked if they could pass the pastries.

"*Ma certo! Certo! Prendetene tutti un boccone!*" responded Gabriella as she waved her hand over the basket.

We continued to pour cups of steaming espresso as everyone ate, drank, laughed, and even at one point burst into a rousing rendition of *Funicul, Funiculà*. Now it is known that Italians are a warm-hearted people who often will become fast friends over a standard train work commute while chatting about the latest football match or their mother's recipe for *Risotto All'Agnello E Finocchietto*, but this was something beyond anything I had ever experienced.

By the time we disembarked at the Roma Termini train station, I was pretty sure I had agreed to two Sunday dinners and had promised to meet at least three "good boy" grandsons of marrying age.

"Gabriella, we are forgetting the basket," I advised as we left the train, preparing to collect the empty espresso cups scattered about.

"It's my gift to the porters." Gabriella handed the porter standing nearby a wad of bills with a wink. "Here's a little extra for the cleanup." She called to me over her shoulder as she put on her dark designer sunglasses. "Come, darling. We have shopping to do."

The moment we emerged from the terminal, two gentlemen dressed in black suits with white shirts and slim black ties approached us. They both bowed their heads in greeting. "Signora De Luca. Signorina Beneventi." The one who spoke placed his hand over his heart. "My name is Pietro, and this is Nunzio. Sebastian Diamanti has sent us to drive you about the city, with his compliments. The car is just this way."

Gabriella raised her arm and allowed Pietro to kiss the back of her hand as she looked the young man over from head to toe. "How very *accommodating* of him. Lead the way, gentlemen."

The idea of being driven about Rome in style would have been much more exciting if I hadn't noticed the dangerous looking sidearms which peeked out from under both men's jackets.

CHAPTER 22

AMARA

*D*espite the busy, chaotic streets of Rome, there seemed to be this invisible barrier placed around Sebastian Diamanti's car. As if everyone somehow knew to keep away. Nunzio moved ahead to open the back door of the white-and-silver Maserati Levante. After we slipped inside, I couldn't help caressing the luxurious leather and silk seats and running my fingertips over the smooth coolness of the polished wood accents.

Gabriella leaned forward. "We are going to start along the Via Condotti at Valentino, then make our way along the Via del Babuino and finish around the Via Borgognona."

Pietro nodded. "Very good, Signora." He pulled into traffic, and we sped away.

A woman dressed in the designer's iconic hue, Rosso Valentino red, greeted us the moment we crossed the threshold of the glamorous store. Her dirty blonde hair was pulled back into a severe bun at the base of her neck, and she wore a choker of massive pearls. Her long, elegant fingers clasped Gabriella's hands as she leaned in to press her cheek to each of Gabriella's. *"Ciao, Bella. Sei bellissima come sempre."*

Gabriella stepped to the side after greeting her friend warmly and looped her arm through mine, pulling me forward. I had been hanging back slightly behind her out of trepidation.

"Thank you, Maria Rosa. This is Barone Cavalieri's protégé, Signorina Amara Beneventi."

Maria Rosa grabbed my hands. Hers were pale and cool, gripping mine with surprising strength. She pressed her cheek to mine as well. *"Ciao*, Amara. It is a great pleasure to meet such a close, *personal* friend of Barone's."

I bristled slightly, casting a dark glance at Gabriella as I wondered just exactly what Maria Rosa had been told about my relationship with Barone. Gabriella batted her thick, false eyelashes, feigning complete innocence.

Maria Rosa interrupted my thoughts. "Shall we continue somewhere private?"

She snapped her fingers, and attendants appeared out of nowhere. Some offered to hold our purses, others offered espresso or caffe, still others offered champagne. If none of that was to our satisfaction, they offered to send out to any of the surrounding restaurants for something more to our taste.

They ushered us into a private suite where I was asked to stand on a pedestal surrounded by mirrors as they took my measurements.

Maria Rosa's lips thinned. "I see you are wearing Gucci." She raised an eyebrow before turning to engage in a heated, whispered conversation with a gentleman in the corner.

I looked over at Gabriella. She mouthed, "Told you," before

winking.

After that it was wave after wave of colorful fabrics and designs. Dresses for work, for dinner engagements, for cocktail parties, for formal balls. Blouses, slacks, matching jackets, belts, bags, scarves. It was all a blur. And of course, there were no price tags, so I could only imagine how much all of this was costing.

I tried twice to stem the tide, and both times was met with shocked disgust. The first time was when I whispered a question to someone who I thought would be a sympathetic attendant, asking them how much a particular dress was. The entire room stopped in stunned silence as everyone turned to Gabriella for guidance. She just laughed and told them all I was jesting before sending me a warning glare. The second time was when I tried to say I didn't think I needed three ball gowns. Again, they turned to Gabriella who waved off my objection.

After that I gave up.

If I thought Barone was difficult to say no to, Gabriella was impossible.

The next few hours were a blur of stores; Armani for accessories, Prada for some casual ensembles, Ferragamo for shoes, and Dolce & Gabbana for handbags.

Gabriella had repeatedly assured me it was all just my imagination that we were buying an entire wardrobe for me and that it only *seemed* that way because of all the options. She claimed she was only selecting a few items from each store for me, but I didn't believe her for a hot second. Either way, I was determined to only wear the bare minimum of outfits and only at work, leaving the rest untouched, just in case.

"We have one more place to stop before we meet with

Arabella for lunch," said Gabriella as she handed Nunzio a few of our purchases. A small army of seamstresses would alter most items and finish in time for them to be loaded onto the train back to Cavalieri. We walked into the unfamiliar designer's shop, and they greeted Gabriella with the same warm familiarity I'd witnessed everywhere today.

"Hello, Armand. I thought I would swing by in case those slacks I purchased last week were ready," said Gabriella.

Armand snapped his fingers and instructed an attendant to check. While we waited, he chatted animatedly with Gabriella about some yacht party they had both attended recently.

I had wandered deeper into the store, gazing at the elaborate designs, when I overheard two female attendants talking.

"That's the sister-in-law of Barone Cavalieri. Gina over at Dolce says she's buying out the stores up and down the Via Condotti, for his future fiancée."

The other girl pouted. "Some girls have all the luck. Is she beautiful?"

The girl frowned. "Of course, she's beautiful, it's Barone Cavalieri. You think he'd be marrying a cow?"

The first attendant picked up a silk scarf and delicately folded it. "Have you heard the rumor he murdered his first wife in bed by strangling her?"

The other girl leaned over the display of alligator leather belts. "No! Was it, like, an accidental kink thing? Like, maybe he likes it rough and took it a little too far one night?" She bit her lower lip as her cheeks pinkened.

The other girl's eyes lit up with unholy delight. "Maybe he likes to choke them as he fucks them, and he squeezed too hard and killed her."

I raised my fingertips to my throat, remembering the feel of Barone's hand wrapped around my neck.

How often had he done so before kissing me?

How often had he overpowered me?

How often had he held me down with the force of his weight?

And we'd only had sex twice!

"Amara!" called Gabriella. "Let's go."

"Coming."

I scurried past the display case which had hidden me from view. Casting a glance over my shoulder, I saw the two attendants exchange a worried look as they realized they had been overheard.

Nunzio held open the door, and we climbed into the car and drove to All'Oro where we were meeting Arabella for lunch.

Gabriella chatted for several minutes before touching my knee. "You are quiet. Am I tiring you out?"

I thought about asking her about Barone's late wife. Somehow, I thought if anyone knew the truth it would be her. I opened my mouth to ask but closed it. I gave her a close-lipped smile. "That must be it. I'm not used to being fussed over like this."

It wasn't any of my business. I had made it clear to Barone that I only wanted a professional relationship with him. I had no intention of marrying the man so whether he murdered his late wife was of no consequence to me.

I stared out the tinted car window. Fuck. I couldn't even make myself believe that lie.

* * *

WE DESCENDED the flight of stairs into the somber interior of the Tailor Suite of All'Oro. Crossing the dark wood parquet floor, we were ushered to a private booth with lush turquoise velour chairs. The table was lit by a solitary brass pin light suspended from a rod attached to the wall.

We had barely looked at the menus before the force of nature that was Arabella Diamanti arrived.

Everyone in Italy knew Arabella Diamanti, the infamous little sister of Sebastian Diamanti. She was the quintessential socialite. No event was considered a success unless she was in attendance. Her exploits and scandals were legendary, and fodder for the fashion magazines as well as the tabloids.

She seemed to light up the dim interior with energy and light. Dressed in a bright fuchsia and lime green Versace logo orchid midi dress and black modo jacket which she'd paired with thigh-high black velvet boots, it was no wonder all eyes in the restaurant turned to her as she entered.

"Gabriella! *Ciao, bella.* I'm sorry I'm so dreadfully late." She leaned down and gave Gabriella an affectionate kiss on each cheek.

She then turned her startlingly vivid silver eyes on me. "You must be Amara!"

I held out my hand in greeting. "Hello," I said shyly.

She threw her hands into the air. "Don't be silly, sweetie! Stand up, let me look at you." She grabbed my hand and drew me out of my chair. She lifted my arm high and spun me around before clasping her warm hands on my cheeks and giving me a quick kiss on the lips. "Oh my, you are stunning!"

She turned to Gabriella. "Don't hate me for saying so, sweetie, but I can't imagine why you lent this creature your green Gucci. She looks far better in it than you. You know you have to give it to her now."

I blushed at the compliment.

We both sat.

Gabriella narrowed her eyes at Arabella. "Just for that I'm going to scuff those Jimmy Choos I borrowed of yours."

Arabella pressed the back of her hand to her forehead and pretended to faint. "Sacrilege."

Although to my knowledge not related, and despite having at least a thirty-year age difference, the two women could have been sisters, or at least mother and daughter.

Arabella ordered a bottle of *Bottega Pink Gold Prosecco Rose Brut*. When the metallic pink bottle arrived, she insisted on opening it herself with a flourish. We all cried out with delight when the white foamy spray shot up and out before several servers raced forward with crystal flutes and cloth napkins.

After filling our glasses, she raised hers. "A toast—to Barone finally finding happiness."

My smile faltered. "Oh, I think there's been a miscommunication. We're not together. Not like that. I'm just his new employee."

Arabella frowned as she looked at Gabriella. "You told me—"

Gabriella shrugged dismissively. "I can't be held responsible for anything I say after midnight or my third glass of wine."

We stopped talking as three servers surrounded the table. As if given a silent cue, each placed a plate of raviolini pasta stuffed with mascarpone cheese with duck ragout and a red wine reduction in front of us at the precise same moment.

After taking a few bites of the amazing dish, I took a sip of prosecco and turned to Arabella. "I'm the new office manager for Cavalieri Winery. Barone and I are... well, we are... we're just —" My cheeks heated as I struggled to come up with a believable truth or even a decent lie. The truth was, I had no idea what we were or how to define us.

She smiled indulgently. "I'm sure you're going to be fabulous. That place could use some fresh ideas."

* * *

Hours later, when we were on the train back to Cavalieri, I turned to Gabriella. "What did you really tell Arabella about me and Barone?"

She sighed. "Would it be the worst thing in the world to marry Barone? He's rich and handsome. What more could a girl ask for?"

I stared at my lap for a few moments. "Love."

She patted my knee. "Aw, to be so foolishly young and naïve again," she said wistfully.

My brow creased. "What's that supposed to mean? You don't believe in love?"

"On the contrary, darling, I think love is the most important thing in life. I try to fall in love at least once every few months."

"So what did you mean when you said I was being foolish and naïve, if not to imply it was silly to believe in love?"

Our train slowed as we prepared to pull into the Cavalieri Porta Nuova train station.

Gabriella rose and turned to look down at me. "I think it's foolish and naïve of you to not realize you already have his love."

CHAPTER 23

AMARA

*B*arone Cavalieri did not love me.

Barone Cavalieri did not freaking love me.

Cavolo! Barone Cavalieri couldn't possibly fucking love me.

Alfonso insisted on tucking a blanket over Gabriella's lap despite the heated leather seats before he would load our purchases into the trunk. It was the first time all day I had seen Gabriella actually take an order instead of giving one. If I wasn't so distracted by my thoughts of Barone, I would almost have thought she was blushing as Alfonso leaned over her to tuck the blanket around her slim hips and admonish her for being too thin.

As Alfonso took his seat behind the wheel, he adjusted his ever-present cap and peered at us through the mirror. "I see you girls had fun in Roma today."

Again, Gabriella blushed and giggled. She *giggled.*

I let the two continue their good-natured banter while I stared out at the familiar, twinkling lights of Cavalieri as we

201

followed the worn, narrow cobblestone road winding its way between the ancient buildings. Before long, the town slipped into the distance as we crept higher into the mountains toward the winery and Barone's villa.

All too soon, we were pulling into the circular drive. The open-flame wrought iron gas lamps on either side of the arched doorway cast a warm light in greeting. Barone himself opened the door. He was dressed casually in a pair of gray trousers and an untucked white linen shirt. Several buttons were undone at the collar, showing off his tanned chest. The cuffs were rolled up, displaying his watch and leather and sterling silver bracelets. His feet were bare. He looked so effortlessly stylish and handsome my heart skipped a beat. I mean, damn. Even the man's feet were sexy.

Barone Cavalieri did not freaking love me.

Barone Cavalieri couldn't possibly fucking love me.

He opened my door for me as Alfonso opened Gabriella's.

He smiled warmly, the flames from the gaslights reflecting in his black diamond eyes. "Did you have a nice time?"

Before I could respond, Gabriella had circled around the car and snatched the glass of cabernet from his hand. She drained the contents. "Of course, it's impossible not to have a nice time in Rome, darling." She raised the empty glass high over her head as she turned and walked into the house. "This is delicious. Is there more?"

Barone kept his intense gaze on me as he called out, "Yes, I just opened the bottle. It's on the counter in the kitchen."

He raised his hand as if to caress my cheek.

I held my breath.

He paused.

His hand a mere inch from touching me.

Time stopped.

We were so close, I could practically feel the heat from his body warm mine against the chill of the night.

He lowered his hand.

I had to blink to stop tears from forming in my eyes from the crushing disappointment that enveloped me. I inhaled a shaky breath. This was my fault. I meant, this was my decision. I had made it very clear to him; I wanted a professional relationship moving forward. He was only abiding by my wishes.

So why did it hurt so much?

Barone cleared his throat as he broke his gaze and stared off into the distance. "Would you like to come inside and have a glass of wine?"

I didn't trust myself to speak, so I just nodded.

As I turned to enter the villa, I could have sworn I felt the slight brush of his hand against my lower back, but it was gone so quickly I couldn't be certain.

We crossed the spacious open entryway to the back where the kitchen spanned the width of the villa. Gabriella had already poured herself a generous glass of wine.

Barone opened a cabinet and, pulling down two more glasses, poured us each one.

He then picked up two white linen cloths with navy blue stripes and opened the stainless steel oven. He pulled out a deep pan with handles. The aroma was heavenly.

I leaned over the counter and took a peek. "It smells wonderful. What is that?"

"*Pesce Spada Con La Salsa Di Limone E Zafferano*," answered Barone.

Swordfish with lemon and saffron sauce. I was impressed. "Did you make it?"

He laughed. "No, Rosa, my chef, put it in the oven before she left. Can I fix you both a plate?"

Gabriella looked between the two of us. She then walked over to Barone and leaned up on her toes to give him a kiss on the cheek. "Tempting, but no. I'm exhausted and I'm catching the dreadfully early train to Sorrento to meet up with Lucrezia tomorrow. Can you have a car and driver waiting for me at the station, as usual?"

"Of course. Are you staying long? Should I leave instructions to open the villa there?"

"The one on the cliff overlooking the sea with the pretty lemon grove?"

He nodded.

She patted him on the cheek. "Yes, please. You do spoil me."

I wondered what it would be like to have a man spoil me like that. To have luxury cars and seaside villas at my disposal. It was a dangerous thought since that was precisely what Barone had offered to me. I had turned it down for my own good... and out of pride. Nevertheless, it was an intriguing, if traitorous, thought.

Gabriella turned and gave me a kiss on the cheek as well. She examined us both again. "You two have fun. Don't do anything I wouldn't do." She then whispered in my ear, "And that's a *very* short list."

I blushed as I glanced up to see if Barone had heard.

Judging by the grin he was trying to hide behind his wineglass, he had.

There was a long, awkward silence after Gabriella left. I bit my lip as I looked around the vast, empty kitchen. "Perhaps I should go."

"Nonsense. You haven't eaten and there is plenty."

"I don't know."

He placed a hand over his heart. "Don't make me eat alone with only me to keep myself company. I'm a terrible conversationalist."

I tucked a lock of hair behind my ear as I relented. "Okay, maybe a quick bite."

Barone let me know where the silverware was, and I set two places for us at the long, natural wood-edge table while he dished up two plates of swordfish. He also brought over two small plates of *segato di zucchini e pistacchi tostate*. The zucchini was expertly latticed, then drizzled with extra virgin olive oil and dusted with toasted pistachio and pine nuts, fresh basil, chives, and sea salt.

He sat at the table's head, and I sat to his right.

He raised his wineglass. "To my new office manager."

I clinked his glass.

He kept his eyes focused on me over the lip of his glass as he drank.

I picked up my fork and gently pushed the pistachios to the side.

Barone frowned. "Do you not like the food? I can make you something else."

Embarrassed at being caught, my cheeks burned. "Oh no. It's lovely. I just don't like pistachios. I'm sorry! I'm sure they taste great. I just don't like them."

Barone winked. "Your secret is safe with me. In fact, I'll trade you. Your pistachios for my pine nuts."

"Deal!"

Barone lifted my plate and expertly separated off all the pistachios and gave me all his pine nuts. When he returned my plate, I picked up one remaining pistachio. "Missed one."

He opened his mouth.

I laughed and tossed it between his lips. He closed his mouth and chewed as he gave me another wink.

It was such a simple yet intimate exchange.

We fell into a companionable silence, each of us sampling the delicious fish with its delicate lemon and saffron sauce.

After several bites, I reached for my wine. Taking a sip, I then teased him. "Aren't we breaking some unwritten rule by drinking red wine with fish?"

He rubbed his beard and seemed to contemplate the problem for a moment. "I won't tell if you won't."

I quirked my lips to the side as I pretended to ponder the situation as well. I shook my head. "I don't know. This is pretty salacious stuff. The great Barone Cavalieri, billionaire wine-maker to the elite, violating one of the quintessential wine connoisseur rules?" I raised a hand to my chest and pretended to be shocked. "I mean imagine the scandal if word got out?"

"Brat," he teased as he took another sip of wine.

I continued with our little game. "You'd be branded a fraud for sure."

Barone played along. "My entire fortune would collapse."

I nodded sagely. "No doubt."

Baron leaned in close, his gaze falling to my mouth. "I would be destitute. Probably reduced to having to share a bed with some kind stranger willing to take me in."

I swallowed as the air thickened between us. "I don't know.

Not many people are willing to do something for nothing nowadays."

His gaze rose to mine, then back to my mouth and lower. "Perhaps I could offer something in trade, a... *service*... of some kind."

My breathing quickened and became shallow. I licked my lips.

There was a low, dark rumble deep from inside Barone's chest.

I was playing with fire, and yet I couldn't help myself. "That depends... Do you have any skills?"

The thin thread we were stretching between us snapped.

Barone leapt from his chair. With a sweep of his arm, he sent the plates, silverware, and wineglasses crashing to the floor. He wrapped his hands around my waist and lifted me onto the kitchen table.

I braced my hands against his shoulders. "Barone, I—"

He shoved his hands into my hair, wrenching my head back. "Shut up, Amara."

His mouth claimed mine as his hips pressed between my thighs. His tongue pushed between my lips, dueling with mine, stealing the breath from my lungs. The inner skin of my lips was cut against the sharp edges of my teeth from the pressure of his mouth. The bristled hair from his beard scraped the soft skin of my chin as he twisted his head from left to right, devouring me.

Fisting one hand in my hair, he moved the other down my front to squeeze my breast before grasping the hem of my borrowed dress. He wrenched it upward, shoving his fingers inside the silk of my panties, feeling for my humiliatingly wet arousal.

I tilted my head to the side, gasping in great gulps of air. "Barone, please, wait."

He lowered the zipper of his trousers. "Fuck waiting, Amara. I want inside you."

He reached for my hips and pulled. My body slid along the table until my ass cheeks were on the edge. He then pressed the flat of his palm against the center of my chest, forcing me to lie back. Pulling his erect cock free, he pushed my panties to the side and positioned the head of his cock at my entrance.

Leaning over my body, he wrapped his hand around my throat.

And every cell in my body froze in fear.

The sales attendant's words about his dead wife came back to haunt me.

Maybe he likes to choke them as he fucks them, and he squeezed too hard and killed her.

I screamed.

Barone frowned. "Amara, what the fuck?"

I screamed again as I scrambled backward, yanking down the hem of my Gucci dress.

Barone held up his hands. "*Dolcezza*, what's wrong?"

My eyes were wide with terror as my body trembled. I drew my knees up to my chest, trying to curl up into a ball on top of the table.

Barone tucked his cock back into his trousers. With a curse, he turned and opened a lower cabinet in the kitchen. He pulled out a bottle of whiskey, unscrewed the cap, and took a large gulp straight from the bottle. He pulled in several deep breaths and looked as if he were going to say something. Instead, he stopped, shook his head, and took another deep drink from the whiskey bottle.

He wiped his mouth with the back of his hand and stared at me.

Finally, he spoke. "You're driving me motherfucking crazy, you know that, Amara?"

He slammed the bottle down on the counter.

I jumped at the harsh sound of glass hitting polished stone and hugged my knees closer to my chest.

He glared at me before running a frustrated hand through his silver locks. He paced a few feet away and then turned and stormed toward me. He gripped the nearest high-backed kitchen chair so hard, his knuckles were white. "Jesus Christ, what the fuck do you want from me? I'm only a man. You can't keep fighting me like this, baby."

That got me angry.

No longer caring about my fear, I leaned up on my knees and pointed at him. "This isn't my fault! You are the one who keeps forcing us together. If you'd just let me go—"

"Not going to happen," he growled.

"Why not?"

"Because I said so." He pointed to the floor. "I want you here, so here is where you are fucking staying."

My eyes narrowed. "And your word is law."

"You're goddamn right it is."

"Is that how you got away with murdering your wife?"

I gasped as my hands flew to cover my mouth. I didn't mean to say it. I shouldn't have said it. It just slipped out.

Barone stilled.

Neither of us spoke or moved.

The silence in the room was deafening.

The look of betrayal and sadness on Barone's face shattered my heart into a million pieces. In that very moment, I knew he couldn't possibly have done what the village had gossiped about and accused him of all these years. How could I have believed it for even a second, let alone said it out loud? Barone could be arrogant and domineering and overbearing, but at his heart he was an honorable, caring man. I knew that to my core. And I had just hurt him, deeply.

"Barone, I—"

"Get out."

"Please—"

"*Fuori!*"

He grabbed me by the upper arm and dragged me off the table. He then pulled me across the room and out the front door. I had to run to keep up with his long steps as he marched me to the stables where he yelled for Alfonso. The moment the man came into view, Barone practically threw me at him. "See that she gets to Enzo's cottage safely." Turning, he disappeared into the darkness without another word.

I cried the entire short distance to the cottage.

It had been an amazing day, filled with adventure and luxury beyond my wildest dreams and yet my favorite part had been sharing that simple meal in that quiet kitchen with Barone. And I had ruined it.

I hugged a pillow to my stomach as I swiped at the tears on my cheeks. I knew I was wrinkling Gabriella's Gucci dress and should probably change out of it, but I couldn't seem to care at that moment. I just wanted to turn back time and take back what I'd said, take back the pain I saw reflected in Barone's eyes, pain I had caused. Why? Why had I said such an awful thing? Why had I repeated that terrible, scandalous rumor when I knew it probably wasn't true? How could I have been so stupid?

Just then, I heard the cottage door open.

I raced out of the bedroom, hoping it was Barone.

Hoping for a chance to apologize.

It shocked me to see Cesare marching in with a screaming Milana, dressed only in her lingerie, draped over his shoulder.

He tossed her onto the center of the sofa then leaned down, caging her in with his arms. He was nose to nose with her when he snarled, "Stay," before turning and leaving without saying another word, slamming the door shut in his wake.

I looked at Milana, the closed door, and back at Milana again. "What the hell is going on?"

Milana grabbed a pillow, clutched it to her face, and screamed into it, before turning to me with narrowed eyes. "I fucking hate him."

CHAPTER 24

AMARA

*M*ilana and I received two notes yesterday.

One from Barone and one from Cesare.

Both had said to be ready at eight a.m. on Monday to start our new jobs.

Apparently, despite the awful thing I'd said, Barone still wanted me as his new office manager.

And Cesare had arranged for Milana to train as his office assistant at the Cavalieri property management offices. Milana had of course refused and tried to show up at her old job at the leather shop as usual, only to be told by Sal that she didn't have a job. Not to be bested, she had spent the rest of the weekend going from shop to shop, asking about any open positions, only to be told the same thing repeatedly.

She was spoken for by Cesare Cavalieri, and they wouldn't hire her.

To make matters worse, they had changed the locks on her apartment. Again.

They completely locked her out. All her belongings had been packed up by unseen hands and delivered to Enzo's old cottage while we were both in the village.

Milana had practically been spitting nails she was so pissed when she saw the stacked boxes and all her clothes neatly hanging up in the closet of one of the bedrooms.

I tried to put a positive spin on things. "Look at it this way. We get to live together in this beautiful cottage."

She huffed. "That's not the point and you know it."

I sighed. "I know."

She turned and glared at me. "As soon as we've saved up enough money, you and I are out of here. Got it?"

I nodded emphatically. I couldn't agree with her more. It was hard not to feel like both of our lives had been steamrolled by these Cavalieri men.

* * *

Now it was Monday morning, and we were both making the best of the situation.

Milana more than me.

Nothing rallied her better than the sight of designer clothes.

She flipped through the padded silk hangers filled with Valentino, Versace, Prada, and Gucci designs. "Seriously, you bought *all* of these?"

"Technically, Gabriella bought all of them, but with his money."

"I will never forgive you for not bringing me along."

I hugged her shoulders from behind as I met her gaze in the wardrobe mirror. "I know. I feel really guilty about that. My only defense is that I had absolutely no idea it was going to be like that. Plus, you know I have no intention of keeping any of these."

She shook her head, taking a few steps away from me and holding up a black-and-red Prada dress as she studied her reflection in the other mirror. "You're insane. The man has more money than God. He has no wife and no daughters. Who else is he going to spend his money on, but his mistress?"

I threw a decorative pillow from the bed at her. "Fuck you. I'm not his mistress."

She shrugged. "Whatever you say."

"I'm not."

She threw the pillow back at me. "Fine. You're not his mistress. I still say you should keep the clothes."

I played with the blue-and-gold fringe of the throw pillow now on my lap. "Don't tempt me. I'm trying to do the right thing here."

She waved her hand dismissively at me. "Since when did doing the right thing ever get anyone anywhere? Men like Barone Cavalieri have money because their ancestors *didn't* do the right thing. Trust me on that. It hardly seems fair that they should hold us to a higher standard."

I frowned. "Stop making good points."

"Only if you stop making stupid ones. Now pick out something fabulous to wear on your first day."

I gestured to the clothes I had laid out on the other side of the bed. "I already have."

She groaned and stomped over to the bed and picked up the black skirt. "Really, Amara?"

"What?"

"Prada black pencil skirt and a white blouse? Could you get more boring?"

"The emerald-green-and-gold Gucci neck scarf will give it some color."

"Why?" she whined.

"I looked it up online and as far as I can tell these are the least expensive items out of the whole wardrobe. Plus, they are the most serviceable. We have to stick to my plan to wear as few items as possible." Then to deflect her attention from me, I asked, "What are you going to wear?"

Since we were relatively the same size, I had agreed to give Milana access to the clothes I bought with Gabriella, within reason.

Her lips twisted in an evil smile. She reached into the wardrobe and pulled out a conservative, long-sleeved black Valentino gown that reached just below the knee and a large-brimmed hat with a gauze veil.

I looked from her to the gown and back. "I don't understand. We only bought that in case I needed to accompany Barone to the funeral of a business associate as his assistant."

Her dark eyes lit up with fiendish delight and she cackled. "Exactly."

I groaned. "Why do you insist on being so mean to poor Cesare? We were all friends once."

Her body stiffened as her eyes narrowed. Her lips thinned and she gave me the same response she always did when I dared to broach the subject. "He knows what he did." She then yanked the dress off its hanger so aggressively I cringed, listening for the sound of ripped stitching. "I'll be in the shower."

I climbed off the bed and adjusted the belt around my worn

silk robe. Just like Milana, my meager belongings had also magically appeared at the cottage. My poor excuse for a wardrobe looked rather shabby next to the elegant designer attire Barone purchased, but it was what it was.

I padded barefoot into the kitchen, intending to fix myself a *caffè lungo*.

"*Buongiorno*."

Barone stood there in the middle of the kitchen.

Stood there looking all... *him*.

All big and sexy and masculine with his tousled hair, silver beard, and tanned skin. Standing there in his jeans, black blazer, hunter green shirt, loosely arranged gray scarf, and work boots, as if he wasn't the billionaire owner of a winery.

I froze.

Is that how you got away with murdering your wife?

My harsh, unforgivable words from last night crashed around my brain like a metal ping-pong ball.

Is that how you got away with murdering your wife?

To the man who had been overbearing and arrogant, but also protective and generous and kind to me.

Is that how you got away with murdering your wife?

To the man who had given me a job that represented a chance to better myself and perhaps save enough money to open my own business one day.

Is that how you got away with murdering your wife?

To the man I was seriously suspecting I was growing to love....

I twisted the belt of my robe around my index finger so tightly I cut off the circulation. I didn't know what to say. I wanted to turn and run but I couldn't make my feet move. I want to apologize but I couldn't make my lips move. My brain wouldn't form the words. I just stood there, like an idiot. Caught in the trap of my own humiliating stupidity and cruelty.

Barone stepped toward me.

His large hands closed over mine.

Without saying a word, he gently unwrapped the silk tie from around my tortured finger. He then lifted my hand up to his lips and kissed it. I met his gaze. His dark eyes were warm and inviting, not cold and unforgiving.

My own filled with tears. My lower lip trembled. I sniffed.

Before I could say a word, he wrapped his hand around my neck and pulled me into his chest.

I wrapped my arms around his middle as his strong arms held me close.

He kissed the top of my head.

My words were muffled against his shirt. "I'm so sorry. I didn't mean it."

And I truly meant it. I never should have repeated such silly village gossip. Not only because Barone was a kind man, but because I also considered myself a school friend of Cesare's and to a lesser extent Enzo's. It was a disservice to all of them to repeat something so nasty about his wife and their mother.

It was none of my business how she died.

Regardless of if I had doubts, who was I to question her death? I was a nobody. Just because the man had slept with me a couple of times and bought me clothes, I didn't have the right to go digging around in his past like that, even if I were developing feelings for him. It was not like I would let it lead anywhere.

We were too different from one another, from two different worlds.

Besides, I was now his employee, not his mistress.

He cupped the back of my head and leaned back to capture my gaze. "We will not speak of it again. Understood?"

I nodded.

"Good girl."

He stepped back and turned toward the espresso machine. He made me my *caffè lungo* and made himself an espresso. He gestured with a nod of his head toward a basket covered in a white linen napkin. "Rosa insisted I bring you pastries for your first day."

I smiled as I bit into the still warm cornetto. I really was getting spoiled. Usually, breakfast was a piece of toast with butter. Cornetti had been a special treat since I was a child, but usually something I received only rarely on holidays. I guessed it was a perk of being rich and having a live-in cook.

"Thank you."

He looked at the clock above the kitchen cabinets. "We had better hurry before you are late. I hear your boss is a real asshole," he said with a wink.

I swallowed those last sweet creamy drops of my coffee. "You don't have to wait for me."

"I'm driving you in."

"I can walk. It's barely a kilometer from here to the villa offices."

He rose to his full height and towered over me. "I don't like the idea of you walking. Now go get ready for work."

I didn't want to seem obstinate or difficult especially after we just reconciled but I couldn't let this go. "Barone, this doesn't make sense. What are you going to do? Leave the villa each morning and pick me up, just to drive back to the villa?"

He stared down at me, saying nothing.

I put my hands on my hips. "I told you I didn't want any special treatment."

He inhaled a deep, slow breath through his nostrils as he looked upward as if praying for patience. He pressed his palms together and rested them against the center of his chest. "What do you want from me, *dolcezza*? I wanted you to stay at the villa. You said no. I offered to buy you a car. You said no. So now here we are. You are not at the villa, and you have no automobile. So yes, I will drive you each morning. *Now. Go. Get. Ready.*"

I stamped my foot. "I will not get ready until you leave and let me get to work on my own like all your other employees."

His brow lowered as he stepped toward me.

I realized too late I had crossed yet another line with him.

I raised up my hand as I backed up. "Barone... be reasonable."

His hands curled into fists as he growled. Literally growled.

I circled around the kitchen island as I pointed at him. "You promised to treat me like a regular employee." I pulled a high-backed chair into his path.

He pushed it out of the way. "No. I promised not to bend you over my desk and *fuck you* every chance I got."

I gasped as I dragged another chair into his path. "This is so unfair. All I'm asking for is a chance to prove myself."

He pushed that chair out of the way and advanced on me.

My back hit the wall.

He flattened his hands on either side of my head as he leaned down. "And I'm giving you that chance... as long as you follow my rules."

I crossed my arms over my chest and thrust my chin out. "And what exactly are *your rules?*"

"Rule number one is I drive you to and from work each day."

"And the other rules?"

His gaze traveled to my mouth and back. "I'll let you know."

I let out an outraged shriek as I stamped my foot. I was acting like a petulant child, but I didn't care. "That's not fair."

"Life isn't fair. Now are you going to go get ready or do I need to make other plans for our morning?" he asked suggestively.

Every fiber of my being did not want to give in to him. I huffed as I tapped my foot. "I'm thinking."

Barone raised one eyebrow.

It was my only warning.

He swooped down and lifted me onto his shoulder.

I pounded him on his back with my fists. "Put me down!"

He marched out of the kitchen and down the hall toward the bedrooms.

"Fine! Fine! I give in! I'll get ready!"

He gave my ass a stinging slap.

"Ow!"

"And you agree to my rules?"

"How can I when you won't tell me what they are?"

He spanked me again.

"Ow! Fine! Yes! Yes! I'll agree to your stupid rules!"

Barone kicked the bathroom door open.

Milana shouted in surprise.

I leaned up and looked over my shoulder. Thankfully, she was already dressed in her funeral attire.

She placed her hands on her hips. "Don't you Cavalieri men ever knock?"

Barone fired back, "Not when it's our property."

Milana's eyes narrowed. "Very well. I'll just go back to my apartment," she challenged.

Barone wasn't the slightest bit put off. "Try it and see what happens."

"Whatever," she huffed before squeezing past us.

It was terrifying to see how even my fiery friend was no match against the daunting and domineering Barone.

Barone set me down on my feet and called out to Milana. "Cesare is coming to pick you up and take you to work. Something about not trusting that run-down, unreliable, piece of shit you call a car."

She settled the large-brimmed black hat on her head and drew the thick gauze veil down over her face. "First off, tell him to fuck off. I happen to like my car. And second, he can try, but I won't be here when he arrives."

I wasn't going to point out to her that her car was still back in the village, several kilometers down the mountain. Their staff had brought all the rest of her belongings, but not her car. Probably because we couldn't get it started over the weekend. Again. And had to abandon it behind Mario's Butcher Shop. Again.

I stood back and watched, wondering if Milana would fare any better than I had in this argument.

Barone chuckled. "He thought you might say that." He reached into his pocket and pulled out a set of automobile keys and tossed them to Milana. He then nodded toward the window. "It's yours. It's parked outside."

Milana marched to the window and wrenched the curtains back. "It's a brand-new red Fiat," she deadpanned.

I looked between Milana and Barone. Completely unsure what was going to happen next. On the one hand, I knew Milana had always wanted a new red Fiat. On the other, I knew her unbridled hatred of Cesare. She turned sharply to face us, shoulders squared. Taking a deep breath, she looped the thin strap of her purse over her forearm. Then in a crisp, elegant voice, she said, "If you two will excuse me, I have a car to key."

My mouth dropped open as I slid my foot back, slinking deeper into the safety of the bathroom, unsure how Barone was going to react to my friend's reception of his son's gift.

Barone turned his heated gaze on me. He raised one eyebrow. "Try that with my car, and employee or not, you won't sit for a week."

I nodded furiously in response.

"You have precisely the time it takes for me to make and drink an espresso. If you are not ready by then, we give up this insane idea of you working and spend the day in my bed."

I gave him a shove over the threshold and slammed the door shut as I raced to the vanity to finish putting on my makeup.

My new career was off to a terrible start.

As I steadied my hand and outlined my lips, I consoled myself. Everything was going to be fine.

Barone was known to spend most of his time engaging in physical labor with his men, out among the grapevines. It wasn't like he was going to spend all day in the office making me nervous.

CHAPTER 25

AMARA

*B*arone spent all day in the office making me nervous.

We arrived, and the villa was strangely quiet. Barone explained that Rosa and most of the staff had headed into the village for market day.

"We are alone?" I asked, my voice coming out in a high-pitched squeak as I followed him down the corridor leading to his office.

He stopped and turned.

I didn't stop in time and barreled straight into him.

He steadied me with his warm hands on my shoulders.

I had to tilt my head back to meet his sardonic gaze.

His lips twitched. "Is that a problem, *Signorina Beneventi?*"

My eyes narrowed. He was baiting me. I lifted my chin. "Of course not, *Don Cavalieri.*"

He nodded. "Good."

He turned sharply and continued down the hall.

I closed my eyes and sent up a prayer to the Madonna as the warmth of his touch and the spicy scent of his cologne lingered.

This whole employee-employer thing was going to be harder than I thought.

Barone turned into his office.

I followed but lingered in the doorway.

He crossed to stand behind his desk. It had barely been a day or two and already there were several messy stacks of files and loose papers piled up on the desktop after I had spent hours clearing away the previous piles. Barone picked up a piece of paper and studied it.

I interlaced my fingers as I waited impatiently for instructions.

Before I could ask him, Barone turned to the windows and opened one of the sashes holding a large pane of glass. He shouted down, "Vito! Vito! *Vito! Vito! Cosa è questa storia dell'ordine dei barili? È tutto sbagliato! Di' a Julius di togliersi la testa dal culo e di rimediare o lo prendo a calci nel culo!*" Barone crumpled the sheet of paper and threw it down to Vito.

Vito shouted up, "*Hai intenzione di prenderlo a calci nel culo prima o dopo avergli tirato fuori la testa dal culo? Desidero solo trasmettere un messaggio corretto, Don Cavalieri.*"

Barone leaned back and tossed him a rude gesture as he laughed. "*Vaffanculo, Vito. Vai a cercare Julius e trova una soluzione che se no ci ritroviamo con un casino tra le mani quando arriverà il momento della raccolta.*"

"*Subito, capo.*"

It was entertaining to see the informal way Barone engaged with his employees. Few men could easily move between the worlds of the field laborer and the boardroom billionaire like

Barone seemed to. He looked as much at ease in a pair of jeans as he did in an Armani suit. It was what made him so charming, and so dangerous.

Barone slid the window back into place and turned to face me.

I gestured behind me. "I should probably find my desk."

Barone frowned. "What are you talking about?"

I returned his frown. "My desk? Where I'll be working from."

He swept his arm out in front of him. "This is your desk."

I put my hands on my hips. "No. That's your desk."

"And now it's our desk."

Our desk.

As in our shared desk.

Our shared space.

As in working together.

Working closely together.

Oh, hell no.

I raised my arm and pointed my finger. "You said you were going to take me seriously."

"I am taking you seriously. The last time you were in here, you were a miracle worker when it came to organizing all these files. Do it again."

I swept my gaze over him, studying his face, trying to see if he was teasing me or not.

There was no hint of sarcasm or amusement. A pleasant warmth spread in my chest. It really was nice to be appreciated for something you did. "You really mean it?"

He leveled a hard look at me. "If there is one thing you

should have learned by now, Amara, it's that I mean every word I say."

I blinked. It was difficult to know if that statement was meant as a promise, a threat, or a warning.

Deciding it was best to take it as all three, I scurried around him and snatched up the first stack. "I better get to work."

For the next several hours, we worked in companionable silence as I organized the files and Barone signed off on invoices and took the occasional phone call.

I was actually foolish enough to think this whole situation might work.

Then it happened.

I made the mistake of becoming too complacent.

Of getting too close.

It was after we had eaten a pleasant lunch of *polpo, patate, capperi e olive.* Barone had grilled the octopus tentacles until they were brown and crisp on the edges, while I pitted and prepared the Taggiasca olives before tossing them with the salted capers and fingerling potatoes.

Barone brought our plates onto the veranda and placed them on a rustic wooden table under the shade of a linden tree, angering several wild canaries that scattered into the bright azure sky. He opened a bottle of Ligurian white *Colli di Luni Vermentino 'Il Maggiore* from Ottaviano Lambruschi and poured us each a glass.

Lifting his own, he said, "To my new employee, may she prove to have many hidden talents." He winked before taking a long sip from his glass.

My belly flipped at the double entendre.

Stay strong.

I needed to stay strong.

To remember the lessons my mother's wretched life taught me.

A career with Cavalieri Winery was worth more in the long run than warming the owner's bed in the short-term until he got bored and moved on.

I glanced over at Barone's handsome face.

Especially if that owner was charming, handsome, an amazing kisser, incredible in bed, domineering, and arrogant in a way that infuriated your feminist side, but which made your primal female side just melt so you were certain you'd eventually get your heart shattered into a million tiny little pieces.

I gave him a tight, close-lipped smile that I hoped gave nothing of my true inner thoughts away, before sipping my wine.

I then watched as his strong hand gripped a lemon half and squeezed it over my plate.

Why?

Why did even *that* have to be sexy as hell?

I took a deeper gulp of my wine.

Barone lifted the glass out of my hand. "No more wine for you, *piccola*, until you eat something." He pulled my plate toward him and cut up one of the octopus tentacles into smaller pieces. He then pushed the plate back toward me. "Eat."

I forked a piece of octopus into my mouth, chewing on the salty, smoky, tangy dish as I watched Barone enjoy his meal. I swallowed and took a sip of water. "Do you always have lunch with your employees?"

Laugh lines etched the tanned skin around his dark eyes. "In this you have no argument with me, Amara. If it were not market day, Rosa and perhaps some of the other staff would be here with us. Other times I eat outside with the men."

I pulled my lips between my teeth to keep my lower lip from pouting. It was what I wanted and kept demanding, to be treated equally. So why was I so disappointed to learn that our lunch together wasn't something special?

I shivered. The cold chill of the shade and my own confused emotions were getting the better of me.

Barone rose, shrugged out of his blazer, and wrapped it around my shoulders.

I objected. "No. I'm fine."

Barone sat back down. "Keep it on," he ordered as I tried to shrug it off.

I stilled.

He sipped his wine and then gestured toward me with the glass still in his hand. "Tomorrow we will eat inside. It is probably getting too cold out here for you."

"No. It is so nice. It was just a chill."

He put down his fork and studied my face. "You probably haven't fully recovered from your ordeal. I should have been more considerate." After a moment, he reached out his hand and cupped my jaw. The caress of his thumb was gentle along my cheekbone. "At least your bruise has finally faded."

I lowered my gaze. "I know I never really properly thanked you for what you did."

Barone dropped his hand and returned to his meal, spearing a piece of octopus so hard the fork clattered loudly against the plate. "I don't want your thanks, Amara. Far from it. It was the least I could do after not doing enough to keep you safe."

"I wasn't your responsibility."

He dropped his fork and swiped his linen napkin over his mouth before tossing it over his half-eaten plate. He rose, shoving his chair back. "And on that we must disagree."

I folded my napkin and placed it next to my plate. My stomach clenched, souring what little food I had eaten. I had ruined our nice lunch. "I don't understand."

"Someday, you will. Come, let's get back to work."

Silently, I helped him clear our plates. Leaving them in the sink for Rosa.

When we returned to the office, I reluctantly shrugged out of his blazer and draped it over an empty hanger on the coat rack. I could feel Barone's intense gaze on me as I did so.

I had a very difficult time focusing on work for the rest of the afternoon.

* * *

THE SUN WAS HANGING low behind the mountain, casting a fiery orange glow across the sky by the time I had finally worked my way through the mess of files and papers which had accumulated on Barone's desk in the span of only a few days.

Barone was on the phone with one of Cavalieri Winery's long-standing distributors. "I agree with you Antonio, but if you want to keep my business you are going to have to push into more markets, my friend. Your orders have become stagnant in the last few years. I will need to see a twenty percent increase in volume if you want to remain among my select distributors."

The distributor was clearly agitated. I could hear him complain through the receiver. "Now, Don Cavalieri, be reasonable. There is only so much room in the market for wines of your elevated caliber."

I ducked under the slightly tangled black rubber phone cord to reach for the last stack of files on Barone's desk. I had been playing an odd game of phone cord limbo all day. Apparently, Barone was notorious for hating mobile phones, and most forms of technology for that matter. Which I found deeply hypocritical given how pissed off he got when I'd refused to accept the mobile phone he'd offered me.

Barone changed direction, pacing to the left. The cord rubbed against my lower back.

Barone's deep voice continued to hold Antonio accountable. "Our current vintage with its fruity yet peppery finish is very drinkable and should be popular with restaurants that need the balance of a distinctive savory-sweet wine that ages well on their menus, which is why I expect to see an increase in demand, Antonio."

He circled around the desk just as I bent low to reach for the files.

I tried to scurry out of his way, but the phone cord was wrapped around my waist.

Barone was now directly behind me, his body towering over mine.

I froze.

He was so close I could feel the deep, vibrating rumbles in his chest as he responded to Antonio's final plea. "That's your problem, Antonio, not mine. I have a more *pressing* issue to attend to. *Arrivederci.*"

I licked my dry lips as the silence in the room stretched.

The cloth of his shirt rustling softly, Barone kept the phone receiver clasped in one hand while reaching around in front of me with the other.

I swayed slightly on my feet as I tried to force myself to breathe.

His right hand brushed my hip as he passed the receiver to his left hand, untangling the cord from around my waist.

He then leaned forward, the length of his body brushing mine as he hung the phone up.

The entire room was charged with sexual energy. You could practically see sparks of blue lightning fracture and glow around us as if Barone truly was the Roman god Jupiter, commanding nature, and me, to bend to his will.

I stiffened my limbs to stop them from trembling.

I heard Barone inhale slowly, as if taking in my scent... like a predator.

He then sighed softly, before darkly commanding, "Turn around, Amara."

I started at the sound of his voice.

I closed my eyes as I white-knuckled the edge of the desk. I was certain it was the only reason I was still upright. If he knew how badly I wanted to turn around. How desperately I wanted to forget my pride and my principles, and all the lessons my mother's life taught me, and just believe there would be no consequences tomorrow. I didn't want to be this way. I wished I could just fall into his arms with abandon. I wished I could believe those feelings of warmth, safety, and protection I felt each time he held me close were real, but they were just illusions. Soon the cold would return.

"I can't."

The tips of his fingers gently skimmed the exposed skin on

the top of my shoulder as he brushed my hair back. He leaned in close to my ear. "Baby, why are you doing this to us?"

Tears blurred my vision. My voice cracked as I spoke. "You promised."

I wasn't being fair.

After today, I knew I wasn't strong enough to resist him. He was too charming, too intelligent, too protective... too everything I'd ever wanted... for me to hold out for long. My heart was in danger. My only defense would be to unfairly keep him to his promise to treat me like an employee.

He had to be the one to save me from myself.

But what happened when the very person you needed to save you was the same person who would destroy you to get what they wanted?

"Madonna santa." Barone wrapped his strong hands around my narrow waist and spun me violently around to face him. He drove his hands into my hair, pressing his palms against each side of my face. He leaned his body into mine, pushing me against the edge of the desk. The hard press of his cock against my stomach was both a threat and a different promise. His sharp gaze searched my eyes before falling to my mouth. "Fuck my promise. Why must you insist on this charade? I want nothing more than to pamper and protect you. *I want to take care of you.* Why won't you let me?"

Tears scalded my cheeks. "It's not that simple."

He leaned his forehead against mine. "Yes, *dolcezza*. It is. It is that simple, if only you'd let it be."

His lips hovered over mine.

We breathed the same warm air.

He increased the pressure of his hands holding my face as he groaned. "Give in to me, *piccola*. Before you force me to take what I know we both want."

I curled my fingers, crumpling the fabric of his shirt in my fists. "Please, Barone, don't do this."

I knew if he forced the issue, he would find my body aroused and ready for him. My body, but not my mind. And if I gave in so soon after being presented with a real chance at an independent future, I would be lost. I would never forgive myself.

"I'm sorry, babygirl."

I cried out as Baron flipped me around and bent my body over the desk. He twisted his fist in my long hair, holding me in place. His callous-roughened hand brushed my thigh as he yanked my skirt up high.

A discreet knock sounded on the office door. A man called through it. "Don Cavalieri. It is Benito Ciccone. I need your assistance. It's urgent."

CHAPTER 26

BARONE

*I*n that precise moment, I wasn't certain whether I should thank Benito or murder him.

Amara took advantage of the distraction to slip out from under my grasp. She stood before me on the other side of the desk, as if placing the large piece of furniture between us would somehow protect her from me.

She swiped the tears from her cheeks as she jutted out her chin. Those big, beautifully sad eyes stared at me with silent accusation.

I refused to feel guilty. She was far too young to know what was best for her own good.

I was what was fucking best for her and the sooner she realized that the better.

Keeping my narrowed gaze trained on her, I called out, "Enter."

Benito opened the door and stepped inside the office but stayed near the threshold. His fingers skimmed over the brim of his hat, twirling it around and around as he spoke. "I'm very sorry to interrupt, Don Cavalieri."

"You said it was urgent."

Benito's gaze moved from Amara to me and back. "Yes."

Amara cleared her throat. Her brow furrowed. "Have my stepfather and stepbrother returned?"

Benito lifted a hand as he shook his head. "Oh no, Signorina. I'm sorry, I did not mean to distress you. We have not heard a word about those dirty dogs." He nodded. "Begging your pardon."

She shrugged. "I would have used worse language."

Benito reached into his shirt pocket and pulled out a hand-rolled cigarette. He lit a match using the bottom of his shoe. "I doubt they will return." He nodded toward me. "Your man scared them off for good, to be sure."

Amara straightened her shoulders. "He's not my man. He's my boss."

I clenched my right hand into a fist. "Amara," I said in a low, warning tone.

She stepped behind Benito. "I'll leave you two to your business."

Before she could leave, I called out, "Do not leave the villa."

She turned. "But I—"

I raised an eyebrow. "Do not leave the villa."

She sighed. "Yes, Barone."

After she left the office, I sat down in the chair behind my desk and nodded for Benito to take a seat. "What is so urgent, my friend?"

"It is a... delicate matter."

"You can speak freely."

He adjusted his seat. Then he snubbed out his half-smoked cigarette and lit another one. After taking several puffs, he finally spoke. "It involves the Morettis and the Agnellos."

I leaned forward and placed my forearms on the desk. That was a delicate matter. As the new wife of my eldest son, Renata Moretti was now Renata Cavalieri and therefore part of my family. Given that connection, anything her extended family did reflected on ours.

And that included getting into bed with a notorious mafia family from Rome, the Agnellos.

"What do you know?"

"Not much. There's a son, Dante. Recently returned from America with a number of ideas for expansion. Apparently, Bruno Moretti needs money, so he's offered the use of his warehouses in Cavalieri as a base of operations, for a substantial fee, of course. I got word that their first shipment of drugs is arriving tonight. There is a skeleton crew of Agnello's men holed up at the warehouse now waiting for it."

I rubbed my eyes. There wasn't a single businessman or mafia family on the west coast of Italy who wasn't aware of my policy regarding mafia involvement in a legitimate business enterprise. Once you let them in, it was like a cancer for any foreign investment. I didn't give a shit what they did in the dark, but in my territory, you stayed the fuck away from the light.

"Who knows?"

Benito took a long drag from his cigarette. "No one. I have not called this in to the home office yet. Bruno being your son's new father-in-law and the Agnellos obviously trying to make an entry into Cavalieri, I thought perhaps we might want to handle this... internally."

I rose. "You thought correctly. Go find Alfonso. Tell him to unlock the armory and then leave. We'll take it from here."

Benito put his hat on, nodded, and gave me a wave over his shoulder as he left. "I was never here."

I went to find Amara.

She was sitting in the parlor.

The moment I entered she shot to her feet.

"I want to go home."

I clenched my jaw. I hated how she continued to refer to that damn cottage as her home. I never should have taken her there. I should have chained her to my bed here at the villa when I'd had the chance. Maybe then she wouldn't be fighting the fact that she was mine now, and that this was happening between us regardless of her career plans.

"I can't take you home just yet, I have some business to attend to."

"It's fine. Alfonso can drive me."

"I need him with me."

"Then I'll walk."

"Absolutely not. It's not safe. Trust me on this. You're staying at the villa, Amara. End of discussion."

She crossed her arms. "Am I allowed to know why?"

I stepped close and kissed her on the forehead. "No. Now go upstairs and take a bubble bath. I will be *home* as soon as possible," I said, deliberately emphasizing the word "home."

Her narrowed gaze proved she didn't miss the effort.

By the time I changed and stepped outside, Enzo and Cesare had arrived.

I checked the magazine on the Benelli M4 Tactical Titanium Cerakote semi-automatic shotgun Alfonso handed me as Enzo approached.

Dammit. This was a conversation I sincerely hoped I would never have to have. I knew Enzo marrying that bitch was going to bite us in the ass. The moment he found out she was pregnant, there was no talking him out of it. He was determined. Even if there was only a sliver of a chance that the baby could be his, he would not let it be born illegitimately. And I had to respect him for that.

I laid my hand on his shoulder. "I'm sorry, son. We're going to have to make a choice for the good of the family. Renata can either be trusted... or she can't. Do you know if she's involved in this shit?"

He rubbed the back of his neck. "*Porca troia*. What a fucking mess."

Cesare joined us. He handed each of us a Tanfoglio Defiant Stock Master handgun. "Is she still *in dolce attesa*? Or has that finally been proven a lie?"

Enzo leaned his back against the Defender X Land Rover. He interlaced his fingers as he stared down at his hands. "She won't give me enough details to know for certain, but she's supposed to be at least five months along."

Cesare nodded toward me, brow furrowed. "Aren't women supposed to show more by that time?"

I raised an eyebrow. "Do I look like a fucking midwife? Your mother was old-fashioned. They did not exactly include me in the details of her pregnancies. She preferred to spend most of them staying *dai tuoi nonni* instead of the villa. Let's just say I was there at the beginning and in time to light the cigars at your births."

Gravel crunched under his boots as Alfonso approached. "Ready when you are, boss."

I nodded before turning to my sons. "It doesn't matter if she's involved or not. We can't do anything until after the pregnancy, for the safety of the baby. Enzo made his decision, and we'll support him in it. We do nothing about Renata until after she gives birth, but this needs to be handled tonight. It would be too dangerous to wait."

Cesare nodded. "Agreed."

Enzo stood. "And Bruno?"

"He'll have to wait too. We can't risk him saying something to Renata. We'll cut the business off tonight and assume that will be the end of it for now. Then, after the baby is born, I'll lay down the law with your new father-in-law."

As we got into the waiting vehicles, I glanced up at the villa. Amara was watching from one of the windows.

* * *

It was dark by the time we rolled up near the warehouse, which was just out of view of the village train station.

Cesare walked up to my right. "They should be inside. What's the plan? Should we surround the building and surprise them by storming the back entrance?"

I frowned. "Don't be ridiculous. We are all gentlemen here. We're going through the front door."

My sons, Alfonso, and I strolled up to the front entrance of Bruno's warehouse. I tried the rusted handle of the weather-beaten door. It was locked. I stepped back and nodded toward Enzo, who was the best shot out of all of us. Gripping his hand-gun, he barely took time to aim before he fired a bullet straight through the lock.

The door crashed open, sending a cloud of dust and debris into the air.

By the time we crossed the threshold, five men who had been lounging about the warehouse were on their feet with guns drawn.

One of them stepped forward. "Who the fuck are you?"

Cesare looked around the dilapidated, rusted steel structure which was filled with dusty metal train cargo containers. "Love what you've done with the place."

Enzo rested his Benelli on his hip. "It has that cozy criminal chic feel that's so popular right now."

Cesare waved his hand in front of his nose. "For me it's also that certain something in the air. What is that?"

Enzo tilted his head to the right. "I believe it's a pungent mixture of petrol, urine, and... wait... yes... just a hint of vomit."

I crossed my arms over my chest. "Boys, be nice. We are guests, after all."

The one who spoke first took two steps closer and raised his gun, leveling it at my head. "If you don't get out of here, I'm going to put a bullet through your dumb skull."

Cesare leaned forward. "I don't mean to quibble, but when threatening someone, it is important to get the small details right, for the full effect. I think you mean you're going to put a bullet in his dumb brain. Since, technically, a skull is bone, and you can't gauge the intelligence of bone."

"Excellent point, brother," offered Enzo.

I widened my stance. "As much as I would enjoy standing around this cold, rat-infested warehouse debating semantics, surprisingly enough, I have better plans for my evening. I'll get to the point. You get the fuck out of my territory and don't return, and I won't kill you."

The man stepped within an arm's length of me. "It's you who'll be dying tonight, old man."

Cesare sucked air through his teeth.

Enzo gave out a low whistle.

Even the usually silent Alfonso snorted.

I raised an eyebrow. "Old man?"

With my right forearm, I knocked his gun arm off aim. I then slid my hand down his arm, disarming him. At the same time, I pivoted my body to the side and punched up with my left elbow, breaking his nose. The man fell to his knees as his hands clutched his face, a gush of crimson blood spurting through his fingers.

I flipped the man's cheap Chiappa M9 handgun in my hand and fired at the second man as he approached, gun drawn, taking him out at the kneecap. He fell to the dirty, cement floor, screaming.

The other three men dropped their guns and ran.

"My nose! My nose! You broke my nose!"

Enzo grimaced. "Bit of a whiner, isn't he?"

I circled around the leader. "Gather all the drugs and guns, while I have a chat with our host." I crossed back in front. Careful to avoid the pool of blood, I crouched down on my haunches. "I'm going to need you to pay very close attention to me."

The man whimpered as he clutched at his nose.

I grabbed him by the hair and wrenched his head back. "Are you listening?"

"I'm listening. I'm listening."

"No one. And I mean, no one. Does dirty business in my territory. So, you tell your boss to find another way, you understand me?"

"Dante isn't going to like this."

"Then you tell Dante to come talk to Barone Cavalieri. And if you know what's good for you, you won't mention a word of this to Bruno Moretti. Tell him the deal fell through. You got it?"

The man bobbed his head up and down.

"Good. Now go collect your trash and get the fuck out of here."

I stood.

We watched as the man hobbled over to his friend with the bullet wound and dragged him up by the arm.

Enzo handed Alfonso his armory guns. "I'll drop the Agnello guns and drugs we collected off at Benito's station before heading home."

I laid a hand on his shoulder. "We'll figure this out, as a family."

He placed his hand over mine and nodded then walked away.

Alfonso caught my look and nodded. He followed Enzo.

Cesare slung the Benelli shotgun over his shoulder as we watched Enzo leave the warehouse, followed by a silent Alfonso. "Poor bastard. He always did have terrible taste in women."

I patted my youngest son on the back. "You obviously haven't seen that cute little red Fiat you just bought."

He groaned and threw his head back to stare at the ceiling. "What did she do to it?"

Before I could respond, he raised up a palm. "Better yet, don't tell me. I have to head to London tomorrow morning for a few weeks and it's probably best I don't know."

"Now you're learning, son."

CHAPTER 27

BARONE

The kitchen was warm and inviting, filled with the scent of simmering Bolognese when I returned.

Amara was standing over the pot, adding the cream. She didn't turn around as I entered.

I poured myself a glass of wine from the open bottle on the counter and watched her.

There was always something quintessentially life affirming about watching a beautiful woman cooking, but with Amara it went even deeper. It felt *right*.

This wasn't about fucking. This wasn't lust.

This was about appreciating her for who she was and loving the idea of having her in my home, cooking a meal for me in my kitchen. I didn't want to capture this moment so I could savor it in the future. I wanted this moment to become so common, so mundane, so ordinary that I came close to taking it for granted. I wanted to cook every meal with her. I wanted to go to sleep at night with her snuggled up at my side and wake up in the morning with her still sleeping, nestled safe and warm in my bed.

But at the same time, I knew I had no right to want those things.

A woman like Amara deserved a family, children, a home.

Things I was not prepared to give her.

Especially with my past. If the truth were ever to come out about my late wife...

But damn, if anyone could change my mind about that, it would be Amara.

Until then, I would be the man she needed and keep my promise.

I set my wineglass aside and approached her from behind.

She continued to slowly stir the Bolognese.

I wrapped my arms around her waist. Fuck, it felt good just to hold her close.

She stiffened, but after a moment her muscles relaxed. "I sent Rosa home. If I am going to be your prisoner, I might as well be useful and make dinner."

She really was adorable when she was mad.

I leaned my chin on her shoulder. "There was a dangerous situation in the village that required my help. It has been resolved. After we eat, I'll take you back to the cottage."

She lowered the spoon and turned in my arms. "Really?"

God, she was beautiful.

I caressed her cheek. "Unless you would prefer to stay here... with me."

She lowered her gaze.

I leaned in and kissed her forehead. "It's okay, *dolcezza.*"

She leaned her head against my chest. I closed my arms around her and hugged her close. Her voice was muffled against my shirt. "I keep making you angry. I don't mean to."

I stroked her hair. How could I make her understand?

I picked her up in my arms and walked over to one of the kitchen chairs. I sat down, settling her on my lap. Cupping the side of her head, I pressed it down on my shoulder and breathed deeply, filling my nose with the fresh, clean scent of her. Banishing the ugly scent of blood and filth from earlier.

I leaned back in the chair and caressed her back, speaking softly to her as if I were telling her a bedtime story.

"It's like I've found a sweet little bird with a broken wing. And all I want to do is protect her and keep her safe so her wing will heal, but to do that I must put her in a cage."

I tilted my head to the side and brushed her hair away from her face so I could look into her eyes. "Now the problem with that is, my sweet little bird is a wild creature. She doesn't understand that this cage is for her own protection. That she will be warm and safe and have everything she could ever want or need. And that it will give her time to heal. All she knows is that it is a cage. So, she beats her wings against the bars, demanding to be free and fly."

I ran a fingertip down the center of her nose. "What would you do if you were me, *piccola*? Would you let the bird fly? Knowing she is wounded and unprotected? Or would you fight to keep her safe? Knowing it is for her own good?"

She stared at me for a full minute with those dark, beautifully sad eyes of hers. "I don't know."

I leaned down and gave her a gentle kiss on the mouth

before tightening my arms around her. "Neither do I, *dolcezza*. Neither do I."

I was lying.

I knew my answer.

CHAPTER 28

BARONE

I kept my promise for three weeks.

Three tortuous weeks.

During those three unbearable weeks, she added insult to injury by becoming indispensable to my business.

My family had been running this winery for generations and frankly, I wasn't sure how we'd survived, let alone thrived, without her.

Wineries were labor-intensive businesses, so most of our resources went to that, not toward office staff. We could actually run our business with very few administrative staff since our job was to make quality wine and get it to the distributors. After that it was their job to transport it to the various restaurants, hotels, and shops around the world and handle all the promos and marketing for the most part.

Or so I thought.

In the first few days, Amara completely streamlined our filing system.

In the next few days, she updated us to a different inventory software that vastly improved how we ordered supplies, eliminating waste.

And by the end of the first week, we had social media accounts on Twitter, Facebook, Snapchat, Instagram and TikTok, whatever the fuck that was.

She went through our archives and posted a steady stream of old sepia-tinted photos of my ancestors in the fields working the vines or standing in front of massive oak barrels holding up glasses of wine. I particularly enjoyed the pictures she found of the women in our family proudly displaying overflowing bowls of pasta and platters of fruits and stewed vegetables as we fed the workers at harvest time.

All the things that showed the history of Cavalieri wines.

By the end of her second week, we had our first-ever website and our distributors were already increasing their usual order size, saying they were hearing from their clients who were specifically requesting more Cavalieri wines.

By the end of her third week, I found myself agreeing to consider a new label design, our first in over thirty years, and reviewing bar graphs she created to chart the rising demand of certain wines as related to web and social media traffic, whatever the fuck *that* meant.

In less than a month, Amara had taken an ancient family business, one of the first and most successful wineries in Italy, a multi-billion-euro business, and put it on track to make some very seriously ridiculous money, all by putting a fresher, more vibrant spin on our business outreach.

Was I focused on how she was going to make me an even more obscenely rich man? No.

Was I thinking about all the new employment and business opportunities this was going to open up for the village, my staff, and beyond? No.

Was I pondering how this type of innovative forward thinking would continue to secure the Cavalieri legacy well into the twenty-first century and beyond for my family and my heirs? Not in the least.

I'm thinking about her ass.

And her beautiful mouth.

And how her lips look, stretched around my cock.

And the cute moaning sound she makes when I thrust deep inside of her.

I really was the worst kind of absolute, selfish, arrogant bastard.

Amara was a beautiful, intelligent woman with an outstanding mind for business and all I could think about was how badly I wanted to fire her, so I could fuck her.

Much to my severe discomfort, Amara had kept me to my promise to keep my hands off her once she was my employee. And for three long weeks, I had kept my word, but it was getting harder and harder, each day. *Literally.*

I didn't trust myself anymore.

I was very close to snapping.

Everything about her set me off. The sound of her voice. The smell of her perfume. Those damn designer outfits I insisted she buy that hugged her curves like a second skin. Even though she insisted on wearing only the same two or three outfits out of the fifty I bought her.

Every morning I joined her for coffee and pastries before driving her to our office in the villa, and every evening I drove her back. I usually wound up staying and we'd cook dinner together and talk late into the evening.

I'd never spent this much time with a woman without fucking her in my life... not even my late wife.

What was truly alarming was how much I was enjoying Amara's company.

I looked forward to seeing her smile each morning and learning what she had planned for us for dinner each evening.

I was quickly learning it wasn't extravagant gifts that made her happy, but thoughtful gestures.

I could still remember the way her beautiful face lit up with joy the day she walked into my office and saw that I had rearranged the furniture so she could have her own desk near the window next to mine. Truth be told it was a selfish move.

The villa was a large one, and I was worried she was getting ready to ask me to use one of the empty rooms as her office. It would have deprived me of one of my new favorite pastimes, watching her work. She made the cutest little faces when she concentrated on some new software program or spreadsheet. She'd scrunch up her brow and wrinkle her nose as she leaned in closer to the screen until she got it right.

I also preferred to keep my eye on her since she had quickly charmed her way into the hearts of all my men. Who suddenly had all sorts of stupid reasons to visit my office since I'd brought her on staff.

It was mid-morning and Rosa had just brought in a small silver tray decorated with a delicate lace overlay, carrying two espresso cups and a plate of biscotti. She beamed when Amara thanked her warmly and complimented her on the elegant display. All I got was a dismissive wave of Rosa's hand when I commented that previously I was lucky if I received a luke-warm cup of espresso left for me on the kitchen counter, let alone having biscotti personally delivered to my desk.

The tip of Amara's tongue swept a crumb of biscotti from the corner of her mouth. "Maybe if you complimented Rosa more often, like I do, she'd be nicer to you."

I hadn't heard a word Amara said. My entire focus was on that cute pink tongue of hers and what it would feel like on the sensitive head of my cock. I cleared my throat as I adjusted my seat. "Rosa's just mad because I told her she added too much sugar and not enough bay leaves to the *fichi giulebbati* the other night," I grumbled as I downed my espresso in one gulp and tossed the cup back onto its white porcelain saucer with a clatter.

Amara laughed before taking a sip of hers. "As she should be. Her poached figs were perfect, and you were just being churlish because I refused to stay the night."

It had become our sadomasochistic ritual on the nights we worked late and had dinner at the villa instead of the cottage. We would have an amazing dinner filled with food, wine, and conversation and at the end, I would try to convince her to spend the night with me, and she would turn me down flat.

If this continued, I was going to start taking it personally.

A man only had so much patience, and mine was quickly coming to an end.

There was a soft knock on the door.

One of my men entered, swiping the cloth cap off his head. "Excuse me, Don Cavalieri."

"What is it, Rolando?"

He nodded toward Amara with his head and then headed

toward her desk. He leaned in close as he showed her his phone. "Signorina Beneventi, I took this photo that I thought you might like for the twitter."

My eyes narrowed.

Rolando was leaning over Amara's shoulder. He had a perfect view down her blouse of her beautiful black-lace-covered breasts.

I knew because I had already pulled that move myself this morning. Twice.

I shot out of my chair.

Storming over to her desk, I grabbed Rolando by the back of his shirt. "That's enough."

"But, Don Cavalieri, I was just—"

"I know what you were just—"

I lifted him so high the toes of his boots dragged along the marble tile as I carried him toward the door. "Tell the others I have had enough of this bullshit. The next man who comes to this office better have a legitimate reason, or he's fucking fired."

I tossed Rolando over the threshold and slammed the door shut.

I turned to see Amara staring at me with her hands on her hips. "Was that necessary?"

My brows snapped together. "Very."

"I'm encouraging the men to take photos while they're out in the fields. It adds to the authenticity of our social media feed."

"I don't give a hot fucking damn about our social media feed. I've had enough of my men traipsing into this office just to look at your tits."

Her lips thinned. She stiffly rearranged some files on her desk. As she gathered the stacks and sharply slammed the edges of the folders on the surface to straighten them, she said, "I'm not even going to dignify that with a response." She arranged the stack of files on the edge of her desk and lifted a leather portfolio. Leveling her hard gaze on me, she jutted out her chin. "Security phoned. Mr. Fattoria has passed the gate. He will be here in a few moments. We are due to meet him in the old office to sign the paperwork."

I looked down at my jeans. "I need to change into a suit. Wait for me here. I don't want you in a room alone with that man. We'll go down together."

Her lips thinned. "Isn't it part of my job to greet your business associates?"

Having had enough of her back talk, I marched across the office and grabbed her by that impertinent chin of hers with its adorable little cleft. "Listen to me, *piccola*. Giacomo Fattoria is an arrogant sonofabitch who thinks that women are just playthings put on this earth to amuse him."

She grumbled under her breath, "Sounds like someone I know."

I chose to ignore her and continued, "I will not have you alone in an isolated, underground room with him. Is that understood? Now wait here. I will change and we will greet him together."

I RETURNED several minutes later to find her gone.

CHAPTER 29

BARONE

*L*ike a man possessed, I raced through the winding corridors to the ancient office we used for formal business and tastings. The moment I burst through the doors, I could tell something had happened.

My baby's face was ashen white, and there was a button missing from her blouse.

Her lipstick was smeared.

I pointed my finger at Giacomo. "I'm going to rip your goddamn throat out."

"Barone, no!"

I seized Giacomo by the lapels of his suit and yanked him toward me.

"What the fuck, Barone? She's just some office slut!"

I curled my right hand into a fist, pulled my arm back and slammed it forward into his eye socket.

Giacomo fell backward, hitting my desk. Several bottles of

wine teetered then smashed onto the floor, sending bloodred wine and green glass scattering across the stone.

Giacomo bent his head low and charged, catching me in the middle.

We both flew backward. Crashing into a small table.

I grabbed him by the hair, wrenched his torso upright, and gave him a strong uppercut that sent him reeling backward.

Amara flew at me. Hanging onto my arm, she pleaded, "Please, Barone. It was just a misunderstanding."

I shrugged her off.

Pulling off my tie, I waited for Giacomo to stagger to his feet.

When he finally did so, he swiped at the blood pooling from his cut lip with the back of his hand. "Are you seriously going to do this, my friend? Are you going to ruin a million-euro deal and a long friendship over some pussy?"

I saw red.

No one.

And I mean, no one.

Referred to my Amara like that.

I pummeled him with my fists. Crushing his eye socket bone, then breaking his jaw.

The only reason the man was still alive was due to Enzo and Cesare who, hearing the commotion, ran into the office and pulled me off him in time.

I shrugged off their restraining hands. "Get him out of my fucking sight. I want him off my land. Now!"

Enzo and Cesare each put a shoulder under Giacomo's arms and dragged the half-conscious, bloody mess of a man out of my office.

I then turned my rage on Amara.

She cowered in the corner.

My chest rose and fell with my heavy breathing. The fight had done nothing to cool the heat in my blood. "I gave you a direct order."

She swallowed. "I didn't think—"

"You're goddamn right, you didn't think," I snarled as my chest heaved. "Do you have any idea? Any fucking idea what could have happened had I not arrived in time?"

"I know! I'm sorry!"

I shrugged out of my torn suit jacket, pacing the room like a caged tiger. "I told you to wait for me. What part of 'wait for me' was unclear?" Dammit. I didn't want to take my anger out on her, but if she had only listened to me, none of this would have happened. It was her own stubbornness which had put her in a dangerous situation. *Again.*

She twisted her hands before her. "I was just trying to do my job."

I stopped dead in my tracks.

I was so motherfucking tired of hearing about her job.

The job I was stupid enough to give her.

The job that had cock-blocked me from day one.

The job that allowed my men to ogle what was fucking mine.

The job that gave her independence from me.

The job. The job. The fucking job.

Something inside of me snapped.

Without saying a word, I stormed across the room and grabbed her by the upper arm, dragging her out of the office and through the corridors and up the stairs which led to the villa. When we reached the main floor, she stumbled and slipped on the sleek marble tile. Undeterred, I bent down and twisted a fistful of the back of her blouse in my hand and dragged her along the floor on her ass until we reached the stairwell to the bedroom level. Honestly, the way I was feeling right now, she was lucky I wasn't dragging her by her hair like a fucking caveman.

I pulled her upright by her blouse. "Get your ass up those stairs."

She turned to face me. "I think we need to discuss this in your office."

I leaned down until my nose practically touched hers. "Trust me, babygirl. You don't want anyone else to overhear what I have planned. Now march up those stairs."

Her eyes widened. She walked up a few of the stairs but turned again and tried to face me. "Barone, this is very unprofessional of you. As your employee—"

"You're fired."

Her mouth dropped open. "What?"

"You're fired."

"You can't fire me!"

I walked up the stairs, forcing her to walk up them backward. "Well, I just fucking did."

"Oh yeah, well then I quit," she threatened as she gripped the banister to steady herself as she took each step up.

"Good! We're agreed then." I continued to force her to walk backward up the stairs. "No more job."

"I'll pack up my things and be gone immediately. I'll find another job. A better job!"

"Good luck, babygirl. No one will hire you. I'll see to that."

She sucked in a shocked gasp. "You'd blackball me?"

"In a heartbeat. You won't find a job to so much as scrub toilets from here to Rome."

We had reached the top of the stairs. I stalked toward her, pushing her backward down the hallway toward my bedroom.

"This isn't fair!"

"Life isn't fair."

"I hate you."

"No, you don't."

"If you think now that you've fired me I'll sleep with you, you're crazy."

My lips lifted in a sneer as we crossed the threshold of my bedroom. I slammed the doors shut behind me and locked them. "Wrong again, *dolcezza.*"

Her head swiveled to the right and left, only just now realizing her surroundings.

And the danger she was in.

My gaze swept over her. "Take your clothes off."

She inhaled sharply. "*Vaffanculo!*"

One eyebrow rose as I loosened my tie. "Is that an invitation, my sweet?"

I pulled my tie free from my collar and tossed it aside. I then slowly unbuttoned my shirt as I kicked off my shoes. Amara watched me with rapt horror. Her eyes focused on my bloody knuckles as I pulled the tails of my shirt free from my trousers before shrugging it off.

Three weeks.

Three long, torturous weeks.

And I was about to make up for every fucking minute of them.

"I'm not going to tell you again. Take off your clothes,

Amara, or I'm going to tear every fucking stitch off your body," I threatened.

Her lower lip trembled. "What are you going to do?"

I took a step toward her.

She backed up.

A growl rumbled low in my chest.

This time when I stepped close, she stayed still.

I lifted her chin with my finger, tilting her head back. I looked deeply into her beautiful dark eyes. Those sad eyes which had so fascinated me from the moment I first met her. I stroked her bottom lip with the side of my thumb. "Everything," I whispered harshly before claiming her mouth.

I reeled back with disgust. "You taste of him. Your skin smells of his cologne."

Before she could respond, I fisted her hair at the base of her neck and spun her around to march her in front of me into the bathroom. Once inside, I reached into the shower and turned the spray on to the hottest setting. I then turned to her.

She threw up her arms defensively. I swatted them aside. Placing my fingers inside the collar of her blouse, I tore downward. Shredding it. Amara screamed and turned to run. I wrapped my arm around her waist from behind. As she kicked out with her feet, I used my free hand to undo the button and lower the zipper to her trousers. I pushed them off her hips and down her legs. They caught on her high heels but fortunately her own kicking freed them both. Soon she was in her bare feet and only her panties and bra. By then the water was hot.

Still in my own trousers, I lifted her struggling form and hauled her into the glass-enclosed shower.

She gasped the moment the steaming water hit her exposed skin.

Brushing the wet hair out of her eyes, drops of water spit from her lips as she yelled, "You can't do this to me!"

She tried to turn to leave.

I raised my arm and blocked her exit, then leaned down and nipped at her earlobe. "Oh, yes I can."

Pinning her between my arms, I unhooked her bra and tossed it over the glass wall of the shower.

She covered her bare breasts with her arms as she backed up into a corner of the large, cobalt-blue-tiled shower. Keeping my gaze trained on her, I lowered the zipper to my trousers. I pulled the sodden fabric off my hips and down my legs, kicking it to the side. Naked, I fisted my erect cock as I observed her trembling form.

"Get on your knees."

A sob escaped her lips.

I was unmoved.

"I'm done playing the gentleman, Amara. *Fucking done.* We play by my rules from now on. And trust me when I say this. *You have absolutely no choice in the matter.* Do you understand me?"

She slowly nodded.

"*Brava ragazza.* Now get on your knees."

Flattening her palm on the wet tile, she slowly lowered to her knees before me.

I squeezed my fingers around my shaft as I inched it closer to her lips. "Now open your mouth."

She opened her lips.

"Wider," I growled.

She closed her eyes and obeyed.

I shoved my cock deep inside her mouth with no warning.

Her shoulders jerked as she gagged.

I pulled back, then pressed in again. Relishing in the feel of her tongue as it swept the sensitive underside of my cock. The back of her throat tightened around the head as I forced it deep.

Her small hands pushed against the tops of my thighs.

I wrapped my hand around the back of her head, holding her in place as I thrust my hips back and forth, using her mouth.

She whimpered, but still I showed no mercy.

The sharp edges of her teeth scraped my flesh as I increased my pace. Her big eyes pleaded with me as her body jerked and shook with her suppressed coughs.

Already worked up from weeks of denying myself, I came quickly and fiercely.

Filling her mouth with my come.

I pulled free, wanting to see her tongue coated in my seed.

I cupped my hand under her jaw and tilted her head back. Black mascara was streaked under her eyes. Her thick black hair was plastered in sodden curls over her shoulders and breasts. Her lips were swollen from my assault. She looked beautiful.

"Swallow," I commanded.

She tried to lower her eyes.

"Eyes on me," I snapped.

I watched as her throat contracted and she swallowed every drop of my warm, salty come.

My cock was already hard again.

I grabbed her hair and pulled her to her feet. I pressed her against the shower wall and claimed her mouth again. Sweeping my tongue inside, I kissed her deeply. When I finally let her breathe, I whispered against her mouth, "Now you no longer taste like him. You taste like mine and only mine."

She sniffed as she placed her hands on my chest. "I didn't want him to kiss me. Please, Barone. You have to believe me. I just turned around, and he was there."

I stroked her cheek with the back of my hand. "I know, baby. I know, but this is why I ordered you not to go down there without me."

She nodded forlornly.

"And why you need to be punished."

"Punished. Haven't I already been punished?"

"Oh, my poor *piccola*, I haven't even begun to punish you."

I took a step back. "Get the cloth and soap."

She did as she was told.

"Now lather up the cloth. I want you to wash every inch of your body. I want that bastard's scent off you."

I leaned against the shower wall and stroked my cock as I watched her run the soapy cloth over her shoulders and arms, then her breasts and over her stomach.

"That's it, baby. Wash that dirty body for me."

She pressed the cloth between her legs and moaned.

I smiled. I knew she was loving this as much as she was hating it. My little *dolcezza* hated to admit it, but she liked it when I was rough with her... and it had been way, way too long.

She ran the cloth down each of her sleek legs and back up.

"Put the cloth aside and get your hands nice and soapy."

She kept her eyes on me as she followed my instructions.

When her hands were covered in a nice creamy foam, I said, "Turn around and face the wall."

She hesitated for a moment and then obeyed.

"Push your hips out."

She did as she was told.

"Now I want you to bring your right hand back and press it between your ass cheeks."

She glanced at me over her shoulder.

I raised a single eyebrow. "Do as you're told, Amara."

Her right arm swept around her hip. She slipped her hand between her cheeks.

"*Brava ragazza.* Press your finger against your little puckered hole."

Amara groaned with humiliation as she pressed her forehead against the shower tiles.

I watched as her hand shifted between the two globes of her ass.

"Now switch hands. Use your left hand to get that tiny asshole of yours nice and soapy for daddy."

She whimpered. "Please, Barone. I don't enjoy doing that. It hurts."

I pushed her wet hair to the side, exposing more of her back. I ran the tips of my fingers down her spine, feeling her body tremble. "That's the point, *piccola*. It wouldn't be a punishment if it didn't hurt. Now do as I command."

Her left arm reached behind her and pushed between her ass cheeks.

I gripped her cheeks and stretched them open. "That's it. Swirl your finger around your little hole."

I watched as her soap-covered index finger swirled around

her own little asshole, getting it ready for my cock. My shaft became so engorged it was painfully hard.

"Now brace yourself against the wall."

I picked up the cloth from the shower niche where she had discarded it, held it over the cleft of her ass, and squeezed, watching as a sudsy stream of water fell onto her lower back and swished down between her cheeks. I dropped the cloth and fisted my cock.

Using my free hand, I pressed my palm down on her ass, forcing her to bend lower, pushing her hips toward me. I placed the head of my cock against her back hole and thrust forward.

Her body resisted. I pushed harder. The small ridges around her puckered hole smoothed out as the pink skin turned white. Her reluctant ass slowly swallowed my cock. It was a glorious sight.

Amara cried out in pain as her fingers clawed at the wet tiles.

I gripped her hip in one hand as my other hand tangled in her wet hair.

I pushed my hips forward, going in deeper, stretching her open.

"*Dio Santo*! Oh no. It hurts!"

I pulled back. Then thrust forward. Pulled back. Then thrust forward. I did this again and again, slowly and relentlessly opening her hole with my girth. Using her body for my pleasure. I tightened my grip on her hip as I looked down to see my shaft disappear deeper and deeper into her ass.

"Where's daddy's cock, baby?"

Amara's only response was a small whimper.

I swatted her ass.

"Answer me."

"In my ass," she squealed.

I pulled out until only the head remained inside. "And why is daddy's cock in your ass?"

She rolled her head from side to side against the shower tile. "I don't know," she sniffed.

I spanked her ass again. A bright red handprint appeared on her wet skin. "Try again."

Her body shook. "Because I was a bad girl."

I thrust in deep, straight to my balls. Her sweet body tightened around my shaft.

"Ow! Ow! Ow!" she moaned.

"That's right. Because you were a bad girl and disobeyed daddy."

I thrust several more times as I reached around and pinched her nipple. "Are you ever going to do that again?"

"No," she whimpered. "I swear."

"*Brava ragazza*. Now beg me to come in your ass."

"Please, daddy. Come in my ass."

CHAPTER 30

AMARA

The moment he came he swept me up into his arms and carried me out of the shower and into the bedroom. Holding me around the waist, he swung my body around until my legs were wrapped around his hips. With his free hand, he pulled the covers back and laid me down in the center of his warm bed. After stepping back into the bathroom for a moment, he returned, settling the weight of his body on top of me.

His hands gripped the sides of my face. "Jesus Christ, baby, you're going to be the death of me."

He kissed me hard, his lips crushing mine. His hand caressed down over my throat to cup my breast, then he pinched my nipple. With feverish urgency he sucked my nipple into his mouth, using his teeth to nip and bite. My back arched off the bed as my fingers gripped the sheets.

He wedged his thigh between mine.

"I need you again," he rasped against the curve of my breast.

"This time I need to feel the heat of your pussy around my cock."

I gripped his wet hair as I pushed my breast deeper into his mouth. "Yes," I breathed.

He licked the underside curve of my left breast before tracing a line of kisses down over my stomach, then the top of my thigh, then my inner thigh. "But first I want to taste this sweet cunt."

His tongue pushed between my pussy lips. Using the tip to flick my clit. My hips shot off the bed as I cried out. It had been so long. Too long. An eternity. I had tried so hard to hold him off. All for my stubborn pride. But now I could no more hold him back than I could stop the sun from rising.

I wanted it all.

The pain.

The pleasure.

The torment.

The ecstasy.

I wanted it all.

Everything.

All of it.

All of him.

He gripped my thighs as he wedged his shoulders under them, raising me up. His tongue flicked my clit harder and faster. I gripped his hair as I moved my hips. My feet pressed against his lower back.

He shifted his hand to press two fingers inside of me. Then three. The rough hair of his beard teased the sensitive skin of my pussy lips. He moved his mouth lower. My mouth opened on a gasp and my cheeks burned with humiliated pleasure when he lapped the tip of his tongue over my puckered asshole, tasting himself on my skin.

He shifted again, increasing the rhythm of his tongue over my clit. The increased pace, the feel of his thrusting fingers, the memory of the swipe of his tongue over my still sore asshole... it was all too much. My orgasm felt as if it was violently torn from my body. The moment it crested, Barone flipped me over onto my stomach, wrenched my hips upward, and plowed into me from behind.

He fucked me so forcefully my body fell forward. The top of my head almost struck the headboard.

He grabbed my hair and pulled me back.

Using his grip on my hair, he kept my body in place as he pounded into me over and over again. Bruising my pussy with his cock. It felt as if the weight of his thick shaft being forced inside of me was pressing against my internal organs, forcing the air from my lungs. With his free hand, he penetrated my ass with his thumb.

It was violent and brutal and overwhelming.

This wasn't lovemaking.

This wasn't sex.

This was fucking.

Punishing. Soul-shaking. Fucking.

My mouth opened on a silent scream.

Barone released my hair and wrapped his arm around my hips, pushing his fingers between my legs to ease my already swollen and sensitive clit.

I reached up to grip the headboard, trying to hold on for dear life.

My entire body shook with the force of his thrusts.

His voice was a harsh, dark growl. "Who's my dirty little girl?"

I threw my head back, letting a guttural, primal groan escape my lips.

His voice. Those words. It was just so dirty, sexy wrong.

I came again. This time I clenched my thighs tightly, locking his hand between my legs.

Barone pulled his thumb from my ass and spanked me several times before thrusting in deep. His body tensed for several seconds before collapsing on top of mine.

He rolled off of me onto his back and pulled me into his embrace.

Neither of us said anything.

The room was filled with the sound of our harsh, erratic breathing.

Several minutes later, Barone rose and left the room.

I curled up tight under the covers and tried to process what had just happened.

Sometime later, he returned. He gently picked me up and carried me back into the bathroom.

By now the sun had set behind the mountain, dusk having fallen. The view from the windows surrounding the massive double tub was of a fiery orange and purple sky. Barone stepped over the tub's edge and lowered us into the warm, sudsy water. Keeping me on his lap, he leaned back and sighed as I rested my head on his shoulder, letting the warm water ease my aching muscles.

He smoothed his palm over my back in small, soothing circles. "You and I need to come to an understanding, *dolcezza.*"

I swallowed. "I'm sorry I didn't listen to your warning earlier. I promise I will be more careful next time."

And I really was sorry. He was absolutely right to be angry with me. It had been a stupid thing to do. He had warned me not to be alone with that man and I had stubbornly disobeyed him. The moment we crossed the threshold into Barone's office, Giacomo had been all over me. Pressing his disgusting mouth on mine and clawing at my breast. Calling me a slut and telling me he would pay me double whatever Barone was paying me. I'd wanted to throw up. If Barone hadn't arrived in time, I didn't know what would have happened.

He looked down at me as I looked up at him. "There won't be a next time."

I pushed my palms against his chest and sat up in the water. "Please, Barone. Please don't do this. For the first time in my life, I'm doing something important. Something I can be proud of. Please don't take that away from me. I'll do anything you say. Just please let me keep my job."

He peeled a wet tendril of hair off my cheek. "Why is this so important to you? Name anything you want or need and it's yours. You don't need to work. Why won't you just let me spoil you? Why must you cause such trouble between us?"

I traced an imaginary design with the tip of my index finger over the hair on his chest. I didn't want to answer. I didn't want to explain. Frankly, I didn't think I should have to explain. Why couldn't he just accept that I didn't want his money? If things were reversed, no one would question why a man wouldn't want a woman's money. I sighed. Knowing things were not like that in Italy and there was no way Barone was going to let me off without getting an answer. "My mother relied on men and all it got her was widowed and practically destitute at a young age with a baby to support and, later, a string of black eyes and broken bones." I looked him directly in the eye as I stuck out my chin. "That will not happen to me."

He wrapped his hand around the side of my neck. "You need to understand, babygirl, that no matter what happens between us, you will always be under my protection. Always. *That is a promise I will never break.* No man will hurt you that way and live, and I will see that you will never want for anything."

I looked over his shoulder.

The sun had set. The darkness outside allowed my reflection to be seen clearly in the glass. I looked like one of those actresses playing the wanton you used to see in those old Italian films. The black-and-white ones where the women's dresses were always falling off their shoulders. Where their hair was always a teased, tangled mess and everyone smoked cigarettes as if they were inhaling the breath of the gods. Where the women spoke passionately about love and easily moved from lover to lover like a bee from flower to flower until the final reel where they appeared sad and broken by life's disappointments, staring blankly at an old Roman water fountain while remembering with bitterness the rash decisions of their youth.

Barone touched my cheek, bringing me back to the present. "There it is again."

I blinked. "What?"

He stared at me thoughtfully. "The sadness in your eyes."

I lowered my gaze. "I don't know what you mean."

He ran the backs of his fingers over the top of my right breast. "Yes, you do." He inhaled, then exhaled slowly. "What I wouldn't give to be the man to take that sadness from your dark, beautiful eyes, *dolcezza.*"

I pressed my advantage. "Let me keep my job."

He chuckled. "I know when I'm beaten."

I squealed with delight. The water splashed around us as I rose up to straddle him. I wrapped my arms around his neck and kissed him on both cheeks and then the lips. "Thank you, Barone. Truly, thank you. You won't regret this."

He smirked. "Before you say that, there are conditions."

I frowned, narrowing my eyes. "What conditions?"

"You live here at the villa... and share my bed."

I opened my mouth.

"Before you object, this is non-negotiable. You have already proven yourself to be an intelligent woman who has earned her place on my staff through merit. Your pride should be satisfied at this point. I'm through pretending I don't want to bend you over my desk and fuck you every chance I get."

"Only if you agree to keep it strictly professional during business hours."

"Agreed."

"Fine. What else?"

"You start wearing all those damn clothes Gabriella made me buy. I'm tired of seeing you in the same three boring outfits. I know what you are trying to do and I'm sick of it. I bought those clothes to see them on your body."

I rolled my eyes. "Fine. Anything else?"

"Probably. I'll let you know later."

I could feel his cock harden between my legs. I wiggled on his lap. I leaned down and gently bit his earlobe before whispering in his ear, "Am I still fired?"

He grabbed my ass with his massive hands. "Until tomorrow morning, yes."

Knowing how much the taboo dirty talk drove him crazy during sex, I gave him a coy look from under my lashes, licked my lips, and said, "Okay, *daddy*."

He spent the rest of the night making the most of my *unemployed* hours.

CHAPTER 31

AMARA

*T*wo weeks later.

"WHY CAN'T I just go to the cottage and spend the night with Milana?"

True to his word, Barone was undeterred in insisting that I move into the villa with him. I was sure I would be anxious and overthinking the whole scenario if I had had so much as a moment to myself to think, but with the harvest fast approaching, the Cavalieri offices had been a hive of non-stop activity the last two weeks.

We had fallen into a comfortable routine of sending Rosa home early each night so that we could cook dinner together. As it turned out, the one time we weren't stubbornly fighting with each other was when we were cooking together. He would then carry me up to his bed and use my body in such shameful and overwhelmingly vigorous ways that I often fell into an exhausted sleep, too tired to think about my feelings or what our relationship meant or the future.

There were a few times when he genuinely frightened me with the strength and violence of his ardor, especially when he wrapped his hands around my throat or used silk ties to bind my wrists and ankles. He liked it when I fought him, so occasionally things went a little too far before Barone realized I was no longer aroused by his actions but alarmed and scared.

It was during those times that the rumors about his dead wife swirled around in my head like the calls of an ominous raven portending doom.

But then Barone would enclose me in his strong arms, kiss my forehead and call me his babygirl, and I would feel protected and safe again.

Making it that much easier to chase the shadows of doubt and fear away.

I leaned in closer and stared at my reflection in the mirror as I thickened the line of black eyeliner over my right eye. "I feel like I haven't seen Milana in weeks. It would be nice to have a girl's night to catch up."

As luck would have it, Milana was actually taking to her new job quite well. Turned out she had a knack for real estate and property development.

And even luckier, there had been no bloodshed yet.

Cesare had been called to London the first few weeks she worked in his office, and then Milan afterward.

So she had been spending her days learning the business from his cousin, Matteo.

His very handsome, eligible bachelor cousin, Matteo.

A fact that had been driving Cesare mad with jealousy.

Milana had been sending me screenshots of all the angry text messages she was receiving from Cesare, because she of course refused to answer the phone whenever he called, warning her to keep her distance from his cousin.

I had been looking forward to ditching this dinner with Barone tonight in favor of hearing more of the juicy details of Milana's stories in person over a bottle of wine and a bowl of wonderfully fattening risotto. Words could not express how much I didn't want to go to this dinner tonight. It would be torture. Enzo was going to be there with Renata who I just knew would not miss an opportunity to sink her teeth into me every chance she got.

No one in the village thought Enzo had been remotely serious about Renata. She was a cold-hearted social climber who only cared about money and getting as far away as possible from our village. At twenty-seven, she was several years older than me, so we were never friends, not that we ever would have been. My family was far too poor for me to be considered one of the *chosen ones* of her inner circle. Still, we were all shocked when Enzo not only proposed, but insisted on a quick wedding.

With Cesare still stuck in Milan dealing with the infamous Italian bureaucratic red tape over his latest land development project, there would be no buffer.

Barone came up behind me. Wearing an olive wool fawn covert coat with a cream cashmere sweater and a hunter-green-and-blue silk scarf, he looked incredibly dashing in that casually stylish way only Italian men could pull off. He curled his hands over my shoulders and kissed the top of my head. "You are staying for dinner because it is a Cavalieri family tradition, and I want you there."

I sighed. "But I'm not family. I'm just your employ—"

Barone's jaw hardened as his dark eyes turned to hard black diamonds. "I swear to God, Amara, if you dare to once again say to me you are just an employee, I will take off my belt and whip your bare ass. Right here, right now. And I don't give a damn if our guests are waiting downstairs."

I sucked my lips between my teeth and lowered my eyes as I nodded, unable to meet his stern gaze in the mirror.

"Good. I'll see you downstairs."

"Okay," I whispered.

I didn't take a full breath until he had left the bedroom.

What. The. Fuck.

I wrapped my arms around my stomach and squeezed, as if I could somehow physically suppress the unease I was feeling deep inside. It was getting harder and harder to navigate Barone's mercurial moods. One day he was reminding me this was all just temporary and we would eventually go our separate ways, and the next he was insisting I attend a traditional dinner the family always had in the days before the harvest began. One night he was leaving me panting and wanting while he raced into the next room to get a condom because he didn't want me to get pregnant, and the next he was riding me bareback, too frenzied to bother with protection.

One day I'd imagine a future filled with children and laughter with the man. Then later at night I'd wonder if he was going to strangle the life out of me while he fucked my throat with his cock.

This was not a healthy relationship. It was toxic.

Despite all my best efforts to avoid doing so, it seemed I was following the same destructive path as my mother. Choosing a man who was all wrong for me. The only difference was I was choosing a man with insane amounts of money, not one who was dirt poor like the men my mother chose. That didn't make me smarter, it just made the man I chose more dangerous.

I rose on shaking legs and crossed to the wardrobe. I pulled the silver-and-pink baroque pattern Versace dress that Barone had chosen for me to wear this evening off its black silk padded hanger. It was elegant, with demure long sleeves, a high collar, and keyhole cutouts.

Slipping it over my head, I steadied myself and slid my feet into pale pink wedge Gucci ankle boots adorned with dangling silver padlocks on their sides. I added my lipstick, some tissues, and a compact to the matching pink Versace Medusa purse I would carry downstairs, even though we weren't leaving the villa.

I stared at my reflection. I'd pulled my long black hair back in a tight, high ponytail with the ends curled. I had kept the jewelry simple with silver hoop earrings and a large fake pink diamond cocktail ring I had gotten years ago from a trip to Rome. I looked very retro seventies chic.

Taking a deep breath, I left the bedroom to join Barone for what was probably going to be one of the longest, worst nights of my life.

CHAPTER 32

AMARA

"*O*h, Amara, I see you're dressed to go to the store, would you be a dear and pick me up a pack of cigarettes while you are there?" asked Renata with feigned sugary sweetness the moment I reached the lower level.

She had swept into view from the parlor area wearing a gorgeous, long, black velvet Valentino gown and positively dripping in diamonds. Holy fuck, was that an actual fucking tiara tucked into her upswept curls? I resisted the urge to roll my eyes.

I bit back a sarcastic response and kept silent.

And so, it begins.

Enzo came up from behind Renata, dressed more suitably for the intimate family occasion in a gray houndstooth blazer over a black cashmere roll neck and gray wool trousers. The outfit made his startling green eyes, the one feature he had gotten from his mother, really pop. They made him stand out from his father and brother, who had the more typical Italian dark eyes. His only flash of wealth was the glimpse of a Rolex on his wrist. Like his father, and to the usual mortification of Renata, Enzo could usually be found in a pair of jeans and cargo shirt with rolled-up sleeves, working side by side with his laborers. For all their wealth, the Cavalieri men were still salt of the earth men who liked to get their hands dirty.

"Renata, you are mistaken. Amara is dining with us this evening. Besides, I've warned you to stop smoking. It's not good for the baby." He handed me a glass of wine. "*Buonasera*, Amara. *Sei bellissima.*"

I set my purse to the side on the hallway table and nodded toward Enzo in greeting as I took the offered glass. "Thank you, Enzo. You look very handsome as well." I raised the glass in a toast. "And congratulations to you both on your recent wedding, it was a beautiful affair."

Renata tilted her head to the side as she narrowed her eyes. She gave a small, shrill laugh. "Funny, I can't seem to recall you being on the guest list. Were you the guest of one of the elderly gentlemen, perhaps?"

Wow, a double barb.

Uninvited and a whore escort.

She had really honed her skills since our school days.

I forced my lips into a stiff smile. "Actually, I was one of the catering servers."

Renata gave me a limp-wristed wave. "Oh my gosh, that's right. You're still doing that job thing. That's so cute. I love that for you."

We could hear Barone's deep voice speaking to the servants as he approached from the other room.

The moment Enzo turned away to join his father, Renata

sunk her claws in. "Anyone can lure a rich man into their bed, but only a special select few have the beauty and breeding necessary to get them to the altar."

She raised her left hand casually to caress her collarbone, ensuring that I saw the enormous diamond engagement ring and diamond encrusted wedding band on her ring finger before turning to join her husband. I fidgeted with the fake pink diamond on my own finger.

I drained my prosecco and set it on the empty tray of a passing servant with a wan smile.

As I walked into the parlor, Barone beckoned me. "Amara, I'd like you to meet Matteo. He's my nephew. My brother's son."

Barone placed a comforting hand on my lower back, making me feel welcomed and wanted. I leaned into his side. I so badly wanted to turn and stick out my tongue at Renata but decided against it.

Matteo clasped my hand in his and then covered both our hands with his free hand. He smiled warmly in greeting. "I finally get to meet the infamous Amara."

I could see why Cesare was so concerned about Milana spending time with this man. He was quite handsome. He shared the same rugged features as Barone and his sons. He was clearly a Cavalieri through and through.

I exchanged a glance with Barone. "What do you mean?"

He released our hands and placed a hand over his heart. "Your friend Milana has been regaling our office with tales of your exploits together. Did you both really sneak onto the convent grounds at night to go skinny dipping in their court-yard fountain?"

Barone looked down at me with one eyebrow raised. "I

believe I would definitely like to hear the answer to that question, *piccola.*"

My cheeks flamed. I was going to kill Milana for telling that story. I cleared my throat. "You're Barone's nephew? What does your father do?"

Matteo leaned in close. "Nice deflection. As I am a gentleman, I will allow it, but I will need an answer to my question later," he said with a conspiratorial wink. "My father is Benedict Cavalieri. He didn't take to the wine business as well as my uncle, so he oversees the family properties in the north where we raise champion horses."

Barone gave my waist a squeeze. "Believe it or not, *dolcezza,* I'm the more *civilized* one of the two brothers."

I accepted an offered glass of *Vino Nobile di Montepulciano d'Abruzzo dei Cavalieri* wine from a passing servant as I glanced between the two of them. "Now, I find that impossible to believe."

Matteo laughed in agreement with Barone.

I shook my head as I waved them off. "No. No. Absolutely not. You are both just teasing me. I refuse to believe you. Matteo, your father would have to be living in a cave surviving on berries and raw meat to be more uncivilized than this man here," I teased as I affectionately patted Barone in the center of his chest.

Barone stroked a finger under my chin and whispered hotly in my ear, "I didn't hear any complaints earlier today when I pushed you to your knees under my desk and pulled your hair while I forced you to swallow my cock."

I choked on my sip of wine, quickly covering my mouth as I

lowered my head, wishing I hadn't worn my hair up so I could cover my flaming cheeks.

Barone rubbed and patted my back. "Wrong pipe," he said dismissively as if he hadn't just uttered the most scandalously filthy thing to me in the middle of a family party. "She has a tiny, tight throat. She chokes easily."

My cheeks burned hotter at the double entendre.

I could tell by the sly look Matteo shot us both that we were not fooling him for one second.

Renata slithered up to our small group. "My, my, you have to tell me what is so amusing. I know it can't be something Amara said."

Before anyone could respond, dinner was announced.

Renata pushed her hand through Barone's arm. "Will you escort me into dinner, *father?*"

I bristled.

The seductive way she said "father" came very close to the dirty, sexy way he used *daddy* with me in the bedroom. A flash of white-hot, irrational, jealous anger shot through me. Had Barone slept with Renata? No. He would never have done such a thing to his son. Still....

Barone disengaged her hand. He nodded toward Enzo who was approaching us. "I believe that honor belongs to your husband, Renata."

He then turned his attention to me, escorting me into the dining room.

The dining room was ablaze with candlelight from several tall, silver candelabra strategically placed down the center of the long, oak table which had been covered in ancient lace, probably hand stitched by the nimble fingers of a Cavalieri wife centuries earlier.

The *ora per primo* was already served in heaping platters down the center of the table, alongside serving dishes filled with *fiori di zucchine ripiene con ricotta e sughetto di pomodorini, stracciatella alla romana, spaghetti cacio e pepe, and paccheri tricolore.*

I went back to say hello to Rosa and help her platter up the first course. I then returned through the kitchen archway, carrying a large silver platter of *peperoni ripiene di farro e tonno.*

Barone hurried over to take the heavy platter of roasted red peppers and tuna from me and place it in the center of the already over-flowing table.

Renata scowled at us both. "Really, Amara. You look like a common servant. Brush the flour off your dress and come sit down."

I sighed. "Yes, Renata."

Barone was chatting with Rosa about the second course as Renata assumed the position as hostess and directed everyone where to sit. Since she was the wife of his eldest son and Barone was not married, it seemed proper for her to do so.

After all, I was only the woman sharing his bed. Still, it made me wish Gabriella wasn't currently living it up with her latest lover on the Amalfi Coast. If she were here, I knew she'd be setting Renata back on her heels.

Renata made sure she was seated to Barone's right, almost as if she were his wife, and Enzo to his left. With Matteo and me down at the lower end of the table.

When Barone turned his attention back to the dining room,

he frowned as he captured my gaze. I could see he was not happy with Renata's choice of seating arrangement.

Before he said anything, I gave my head a small shake. Whether or not he liked it, it wasn't appropriate for me to be seated at his side and it would only make an already tense and awkward evening worse if he were to make a fuss.

Pulling his heavy, high-backed chair out with more force than necessary, Barone sat down.

The additional servants he had brought in for the occasion raced around our small gathering to fill our wineglasses with the best the Cavalieri cellars offered, as was tradition.

Barone raised his glass. "I raise a glass to those who came before us, and to those who will come after us. May Cavalieri blood, sweat, and tears water these lands for many generations to come. To the upcoming harvest, may its bounty secure and enrich the Cavalieri legacy, *alla nostra salute!*"

We all raised our glasses and drank.

Matteo raised his glass again. "To family. May we always be welcome at each other's table. And may our children's laughter be the song of ages."

I caught Renata staring unabashedly straight at Barone.

Alarmed, my gaze flashed to Barone.

He was staring intently at me, as if no one else in the room existed.

I swallowed.

He slowly nodded, raised his glass, and took a long sip, as if he were toasting me and me alone.

On a toast about the future and children.

Renata followed his gaze. She glared daggers at me. Averting my gaze, I lifted my wineglass and drank deeply. If this evening got any more awkward, I was going to get seriously drunk.

Lifting her overly filled, puffy lips in a sneer, she stood and raised her glass. "I would also like to make a toast."

Enzo returned his attention to her. "You really shouldn't be drinking, *dearest*."

The endearment was curt and forced.

"Don't tell me what to do, *darling*."

Ditto for her endearment, as well.

Seems like the gossip about their wedding was on the mark.

She turned to Barone. "To my father...."

I noticed she left off the *in-law* part.

"My wonderful *papà*...."

My fingernails dug into the varnish of the table. This really was laying it on a bit thick.

"I am so happy you welcomed me into your family as your dutiful daughter. I'm proud to be a Cavalieri and..." she then stroked her barely showing belly, "even more proud to bear a son to carry on the next generation."

Bear *a* son.

That was an odd choice of words.

Not give him a grandson but bear a son.

She was careful not to say bear *him* a son but still. Tears pricked behind my eyelids as every nerve in my body seemed to crystallize into tiny, broken shards of glass. This was just Renata fucking with me.

It had to be.

She continued, "I would also like to commend you for welcoming not only family, but loyal staff to your table, as if they are also a true part of the Cavalieri family. It shows your generous spirit and your—"

Ouch.

Enzo rose and crossed around behind Barone. He snatched the glass from Renata's hand. "That's enough, wife. Sit your ass down."

"How dare you embarrass me in front of strangers!"

Enzo placed his hands on her chair and leaned down. "I'll do a great deal more than embarrass you, if you don't start behaving."

There was a long moment of tense silence as we waited to see who would essentially blink first.

I sprang up from my chair. "Who wants some zucchini blossoms? They are delicious. I snuck one back in the kitchen while I was helping Rosa." I reached for the slotted spoon. It clattered against the clay platter when my shaking hand dropped it.

Barone rose and stood behind me. His large frame dwarfed mine. He reached around me and placed his calming hand over my trembling one. When he spoke, his breath moved the curls near my cheek. "Let me help you, *dolcezza.*"

Renata slammed her wineglass down on the table so hard red wine sloshed over the side, staining the white lace underneath.

This was all too much. While no one had been violent, the tension in the room was too reminiscent of countless childhood mealtimes, where I had to keep quiet and still for fear of angering the man my mother was with and causing a fight.

Enough. I stepped out of Barone's arms. "I need a little air."

Barone glared at Renata. "I will go with you."

I held up my hand. "That's all right. I'll be fine. I just need a moment of fresh air."

I headed through the French glass doors which flanked one side of the dining room onto the stone veranda. I paced down the length of it until I was cloaked in the shadows, staring back at the pale, glowing light cast by the candlelight through the white gauze curtains from the dining room doors at the far end.

I placed my palms on the stone balustrade, relishing the firm, chilling hardness. It was grounding. I needed to get a grip. My thoughts were spiraling out of control. This was like one of those nights you saw in indie art films where old friends got together, and after a few bottles of wine and a well-placed thunderstorm, old secrets and forgotten grudges came to the fore and before you knew it, everyone was fighting, and someone got murdered. Then morning came and everyone packed up their belongings and drove away as if nothing happened.

Everything was fine.

It was just the heat of the room, my empty stomach, and the wine.

Renata was just getting inside of my head, twisting things about, and causing trouble just like she used to do in school. She was always stirring up gossip and inventing drama for her own amusement. She didn't care who she hurt as long as she was entertained by the carnage.

"Are you okay, sweetie?"

Speak of the devil.

I pasted a fake smile on my face. "Fine. It was just a little warm in there."

She nodded sagely. "It was probably that polyester fabric you are wearing. Those fake fabrics don't breathe."

I desperately wanted to fire back that I happened to be wearing a Versace dress that Barone bought me but didn't want to give her any more firepower.

"Really, I'm fine. You should go back in. I don't want to take you away from your husband."

"Well, it's more taking away from my duties as Barone's hostess. As the highest ranking Cavalieri female in the household, I have a responsibility to take care of him, but as his guest and a member of his staff, you are my responsibility too," she said with a pseudo-sympathetic tilt of her head.

I wondered how much pressure one needed to twist a human head off its spine.

It was hard to speak through my clenched jaw. "I appreciate your concern, but as I said, I'm fine."

She placed her left hand on her chest, once again displaying, to dazzling effect, her large wedding ring. "I'm so glad. I was worried you had finally learned the truth about Barone and his late wife and were upset."

Don't take the bait.

Don't take the bait.

Dammit, don't take the bait.

Turing to face her, I asked, "What about Barone and his wife?"

She looked me over with her snake-like eyes. "Well, I'm sure you've heard the rumors that he killed her."

"That's just gossip."

She looked over her shoulder before leaning in close. "It's actually true."

I frowned as beads of sweat broke out on my brow. "What?"

"Enzo told me. He overheard his father and Gabriella talking about it one day years ago when he was still a teenager. Barone doesn't know that he knows."

I gripped the stone balustrade as my vision blurred. Without even thinking, I whispered out loud, "Barone really killed his wife?"

"Of course, he did. Don't tell me you haven't noticed his famous temper... and peculiar appetites in bed," she said suggestively. She then leaned a hip against the balustrade and stretched her arm out along its length. She tapped one perfectly manicured nail against the stone. "You can believe me, of course, because I'm a Cavalieri now. *I know all the family secrets.* I'm only telling you this because we are close friends, and I worry about your safety."

I was barely listening to her.

Barone killed his wife.

CHAPTER 33

BARONE

I looked up, expecting to see Amara.

I was disappointed to see Renata at the door to my private study instead.

Since, unfortunately, none of us had shown much of an appetite for food, I had gone there in search of a few cigars for myself, Enzo, and Matteo.

"Where is Amara? Is she okay?" I asked as I selected three cigars and closed the lid on the humidor, replacing it on the bookshelf.

Renata entered the study and closed the door behind her. "She's fine. She was not feeling well and said she wanted to lie down."

Immediately concerned, I dropped the cigars on a nearby side table. "I had better go check on her."

Renata crossed to me and placed a hand on the center of my chest. "She would be mortified if you did. Female troubles. It seems she bled on that dress you bought her. Quite a bit actually. Ruined it. It was a real mess, so she went upstairs out of embarrassment. Really, Barone, you should have been more considerate of the girl."

Christ. I had no idea it was her time of the month. Was that the reason she'd been encouraging me to fuck her mouth this afternoon and not her pussy? Fuck, she should have said something. I ran a hand through my hair. I was no better than a fucking animal rutting with the poor girl every chance I got. No wonder she felt the need to hide her discomfort. It was probably why she had tried to get out of this damn, disastrous dinner.

My poor *piccola* probably wanted nothing more than to curl up with a hot-water bottle and cup of tea, and here I had made her squeeze into a designer dress and entertain my son's horrid bitch of a wife. I was a selfish bastard.

Renata played with the buttons on my blazer. "Women like her lack breeding and etiquette. They were not raised to persevere and rise above their own discomfort and disgusting bodily fluids to fulfill their duties as wife, mother, and hostess... *as I was.*"

She inched closer to me and placed both her hands on my chest.

I looked down at her still rather slim frame. According to Enzo she should be over six months pregnant by now. She was either lying about the timing of her pregnancy or it was an unhealthy one. Enzo had shared with me his concern at her continued habit of drinking, smoking, and dieting, despite her condition. Apparently, she was actually trying *not* to gain weight, complaining about how she would not let a baby ruin her figure.

She licked her lips suggestively. "If I had known you wanted a younger woman to warm your bed, Barone, I would have been more than willing to oblige. I still could, you know. Enzo would never have to know. I should have married you, not him. Together we could be an amazing power couple. I would make you the perfect trophy wife. All your friends would be envious of my beauty. I would make all their wives jealous. Wouldn't you like that, Barone? I know things too. *Kinky things.* I would keep you very happy in bed. I know you like the weird stuff." She lowered her eyes and glanced up at me through her lashes in a miserably pathetic attempt to look coy. "I would let you put your cock *anywhere* you like."

I grabbed both her wrists and pulled them off me. I walked her backward until she collided with the bookcase. She gasped, keeping her lips open in an exaggerated and obvious way. She then moaned and recited in a stiff and stilted fashion, "Yes, Barone, yes. Treat me rough. Manhandle me. Fuck me hard."

Jesus Christ.

It was like listening to a nun recite a porn script.

I curled my hands into fists and reminded myself that it would be very, very bad to hit a pregnant woman, let alone my son's wife. Taking a deep breath, I leveled a cold, hard gaze on Renata. "I want you to listen carefully to me. If you ever, *ever*, approach me with this bullshit again, I will make sure Enzo divorces you and throws you out onto the streets like the traitorous bitch alley cat you are. Do you understand me?"

Renata straightened. "Are you rejecting me?"

"You're goddamn right I am. And next time you come into my house you had better show Amara the respect she deserves, or you won't be welcome. I don't give a shit whose wife you are.

And I'm not your father or your *papà*. It's 'Don Cavalieri' to you."

"You can't talk to me like this. I'm your son's wife. I'm bearing your grandson. It's *you* who disrespected *me* tonight. Parading *your whore* in front of your respectable family. Having her wear that stupid plastic diamond ring as if it could compare to being a wife and having the real thing," she sneered as she raised her hand and pointed at the obscene diamond she'd insisted my son buy her.

"You've got a lot of fucking nerve calling my sweet Amara the whore when we all know you're bearing a bastard my son agreed to claim because he's an honorable man."

First, she threw herself at me, and now she was baiting me into a fight.

What the fuck is going on?

This isn't a seduction.

It's a fucking shakedown.

My gaze traveled over her. "It was you, wasn't it? Not your father?"

The deal with Dante Agnello to give a mafia family a foothold in Abruzzo and especially the rich areas owned by me. I had marveled at the outrageous arrogance of Bruno Moretti to risk my wrath by making such a deal when there were very few businessmen in Italy not aware of my feelings on the subject. It hadn't been Bruno. It was his daughter.

Her upper lip curled. She picked up one of the cigars I had discarded and ran the length just under her nose. "*Papà* was afraid to anger the great and powerful Don Cavalieri." She picked up the silver cigar cutters and snipped the end with a decisive snap. "He lacked vision." It was hard not to see the parallels to her cutting off her own father's balls. "I told him I was family now. There would be nothing you could do."

"My son married you. He gives you whatever you want. You have more than enough money. Why would you be a party to bringing something so cancerous and ruthless into our village?"

She placed the cigar in her mouth and picked up the lighter. She lit the flame, holding it under the tobacco, warming it from the heat. She then inhaled deeply. She blew out a cloud of smoke. "There's no such thing as *enough* money."

Amara.

Amara.

Amara.

Figlio di puttana. I'd been a fool. A goddamn fool. I had a caring, intelligent, hardworking woman, the kind of woman who helped build the Cavalieri legacy, and all this time I'd been what? *Pissed* because I couldn't turn her into the kind of woman I now see before me. The kind who refused to work and only valued money and the objects it bought her.

I owed my sweet babygirl an apology.

She was a treasure.

One I planned to hold on to.

I was done letting the past dictate my future.

But first, I needed to deal with Renata. "Well, I will not let that happen. The deal is off. I've made that clear to Dante's men."

She blew another cloud of smoke as she leaned against my desk. "The deal is back on. And you will not interfere or that precious whore of yours is going to meet with a very unfortunate accident."

I took a step toward her as I raised my fist, never so angry at a woman in my entire life.

Her eyes lit up as she cackled. "Go ahead and hit me. You might as well. I'm going to tell your *honorable* son you hit me, anyway. You see, if I'm to succeed, I'm going to need Enzo more on my side." She casually snubbed out the cigar. Then she stared me straight in the eye as she reached up and tore the sleeve on her dress. "I'm going to tell him you tried to attack me, too... *his pregnant wife.*"

She ran her bloodred fingernails over her cheek, scratching her own skin.

CHAPTER 34

BARONE

J backed away from her in disgust.

She tilted her head back and laughed again. The noise shrill and chilling. "What are you going to do now, *Don Cavalieri?* I'm the one with all the power. And Enzo is going to—"

Enzo walked into the study followed by Matteo.

I could tell from his gaze he missed nothing.

Not my clenched fists or Renata's scratched face and torn gown.

I loved my son.

I trusted my son, and I knew deep in my bones that my son trusted me.

Just as I knew I didn't deserve that trust. Never had.

I knew he didn't love his wife, but that didn't mean he wouldn't defend her. I had raised my sons to protect women from the very violence she was accusing me of.

And hell, if I were truly honest with myself, her description wasn't that far off from how beastly I had been with Amara at times. On more than one occasion, the reins of civility had snapped when I was around her. There was no way the staff hadn't noticed the torn gowns, panties, and shirts in the waste-basket after our sexual encounters. Combine that with the past scandalous rumors about my late wife and this all looked very damning.

Enzo's stance was deceptively relaxed, but I could see the tension in his arms and shoulders. "What is Enzo going to do, darling?"

Renata fell dramatically into his arms. "Thank God, you are here." She grabbed the lapels of his blazer and sobbed. "He was like an animal. He said he's always desired me and now that I was your wife his jealousy knew no bounds. I fought him off the best I could. I knew I had to for the sake of you... *and our precious baby.*"

Porca miseria.

I pinched the bridge of my nose as I crossed the room, twisted the brass key to the liquor cabinet, and pulled out the silver tray which held the whiskey decanter and several glasses. I placed the tray on my desk and pulled the stopper off the crystal decanter. I lifted it and nodded toward my son and nephew. They both nodded back. I splashed a generous portion of whiskey over all three glasses, getting as much on the tray as I did in the glasses.

Meanwhile, Enzo placed a finger under Renata's chin and leaned his head back. He frowned. "You're slipping, my dear. Your own claws clearly made these scratches. Tsk. Tsk. Tsk. Very sloppy of you. You're usually so careful about this sort of detail." He looked over her head at me. "Her attention to detail is usually the only thing that makes her lies and drama so amusing."

Matteo chuckled as he accepted the glass of whiskey I was holding out to him. "Now, Enzo, I think you are being a bit harsh on the girl. She managed to drum up some realistic looking tears."

Renata was not one to give up easily. Wrenching herself away from Enzo she pointed at me. "Are you seriously going to take the word of a *murderer* over your wife? The man who murdered your own mother in cold blood?"

Vaffanculo.

She really was a manipulative bitch.

I raised the whiskey glass to my lips. "You're going to have to try harder than that, Renata. My son is hardly one to believe trivial village gossip."

She turned her venomous gaze on me. Her lips thinned as she narrowed her eyes. She clapped her hands on her hips and sauntered confidently toward me. "Except we all know it isn't a rumor, is it, *Don Cavalieri*? Enzo told me the truth."

My gaze snapped to Enzo. I searched his face for signs of the truth. Was this just another twist of the knife by Renata? He couldn't know. He would have told me. It had been fifteen years. *Fifteen years.* My son would have told me he knew the truth. No. It wasn't possible. There had been rumors. I had always known there would be rumors, but no one had ever gotten close to the truth.

Enzo snatched her by the upper arm. "That's enough, Renata," he growled through clenched teeth.

I stilled.

My hand gripped the crystal glass so hard, I was surprised it didn't shatter. The hair rose on the back of my neck as I held my breath, willing my face to remain cold and impassive. This could still just be another one of her tricks.

She smirked. "Not so high and mighty now, are we?" She turned to Enzo. "Go on. Why don't you tell him you know? Tell him you know all about how he murdered your mother!"

I winced.

To hear those words.

To know the truth of them.

It was almost more than I could bear.

The guilt from that fateful decision all those years ago had been weighing especially heavily on me these last few months since meeting Amara. It was as if the prospect of finally being truly happy and maybe even finding love had brought all the shame and unforgivable guilt of my actions that night to the fore.

And now knowing that my son, my beloved son, may have known all along....

Enzo looked at me. He had his mother's eyes, a bright forest green. God forgive me, I've hated those eyes at times. It was as if she were staring back at me from the grave. "*Papà*...."

I swallowed. "Enzo, my son, I can explain—"

Renata laughed. "*Enzo, my son, I can explain,*" she mimicked. "Oh, I'm sure you can. And I'm sure he will forgive you, because he worships his father." She then tilted her head and squinted her eyes, tapping her chin as if deep in thought. "But I wonder if Amara will be so forgiving?"

Something deep inside my chest turned into crystalized fear, then shattered.

She had spewed this poison in Amara's ear.

Dear God.

Renata bent over laughing. "You should see your face right now. And over a low-class whore like Amara Beneventi? Really?"

Enzo grabbed Renata by the shoulders and turned her away from me. He shoved her into Matteo's arms. "Get her away from me. I can't stand the sight of her. Take her home, Matteo. See that she stays there and talks to no one until I return."

Matteo nodded. "You got it, *cugino*." He nodded in my direction. "Uncle."

I nodded back.

Matteo dragged a kicking and screaming Renata out of the room.

I drained the contents of my glass and poured another one.

Neither of us said anything for several moments.

I stared down at the amber liquid in my glass. "How long have you known?"

Enzo took a deep breath. "Almost from the beginning. I heard you sobbing the night of her funeral. Aunt Gabriella was consoling you. She was saying repeatedly how it was the right thing to do. How it was what my mother wanted." He took another shaky breath and reached for the whiskey I had poured him earlier. He took a long swallow and continued. "How she wouldn't have wanted her sons to see her like a living corpse. That she wanted us to remember her as their loving, vibrant mother. How in the end you were there for her when it counted the most."

I rubbed at my tear-filled eyes and cleared my throat before speaking. "Why did you never...."

He shook his head. "I may have been just a kid, *Papà*, but I wasn't stupid. I could guess why you did it. And I knew there would be consequences if we ever spoke of it, so I kept my mouth shut. I ignored all the hurtful gossip, because I knew if I fought back people might ask questions."

"Does Cesare know?"

I knew my sons were extremely close. There was very little chance Enzo had kept this from his brother all these years.

Enzo nodded solemnly. "He didn't at first. I told him a few years later. There were some boys at school teasing him about the rumors, so I explained the truth to him."

I clenched my jaw as I swiped at my eyes again. Almost unable to form the words. "And did he—"

Enzo placed a hand on my shoulder. "He understood. Just like I've always understood. You did what you had to do out of mercy. What she *asked* you to do."

I put my hand around the back of his neck and clasped him to my chest, hugging him close.

He patted my back. "I love you, *Papà*."

I leaned back and cupped my hands around his face. "I love you, son. I'm sorry I never told you the truth all these years."

He shook his head. "I'm sorry I betrayed you by telling Renata. There is no excuse. I told her years ago, back when I thought she was different. I was going through some shit, and it slipped out one drunken night. I should have known she would use it one day as a weapon. But don't worry. No matter what it takes, I'll make sure she keeps her mouth shut."

I studied my son's strained expression. "You know I never shared your mother's deeply religious views. Your happiness is more important to me than any church doctrine. There is no shame in divorce, son."

He took another long sip of whiskey before muttering, "I'm being punished for marrying the wrong sister."

I frowned. "What?"

He gave me a dismissive gesture. "Nothing. You should talk to Amara. Undo the damage Renata has caused this evening."

Amara.

My dolcezza.

She was probably planning her escape from me at this very moment.

I kicked back the last of the whiskey in my glass and clasped him on the shoulder. "We will talk again. Together. As a family. When your brother gets back."

Enzo nodded. "But please, after the harvest."

I laughed. "Yes, after the harvest."

"Go, make things right with Amara. She is good for you, *Papà.*"

I raised an eyebrow. "You know the woman drives me to distraction. She never listens. Is always disobeying me. Stubborn to a fault. If I were to say the sky is blue, she'd insist it was purple. Always insisting on earning her own way. I don't think we've gotten through a single day without fighting. And she's forever trying to run away from me."

Enzo patted me on the back. "Like I said, she's good for you."

I winked at him. "I couldn't agree with you more. Now, I must go. With my luck, she's probably shimmied halfway down the outside drainpipe with a suitcase in tow by now."

CHAPTER 35

BARONE

*H*er suitcase was already packed.

It was a tiny, beat-up brown thing that looked like it had been through at least two world wars. Held together by duct tape and dreams.

Bracing myself for the fight I knew was coming, I closed and locked the bedroom doors. I then stashed the key on the top of a bookshelf out of her reach. At least that was one avenue of escape closed off.

At the sound, Amara came out of the bathroom holding her cloth makeup case and a small glass bottle of perfume. It was obvious she had been crying.

She had changed out of the designer dress I had purchased for her into a simple pale pink skirt which swished around her hips and legs as she walked, and a short black sweater with a pair of matching black ballet slippers. Her hair was now down and fell in soft, combed-out waves over her shoulders and down her back.

She looked so young and vulnerable at that moment.

I just wanted to cradle her in my lap, kiss her forehead, and tell her everything was going to be okay.

But I knew it would not be.

Not unless we could get past what I had done, the choice I had made all those years ago.

My voice was hoarse when I finally spoke. "Amara, look at me, *dolcezza.*"

She flinched at the endearment. Keeping her gaze averted, she shoved her clothing aside and forced her makeup bag inside the suitcase. "I was careful to only pack my own belongings. You can take an inventory of the clothes Gabriella purchased in Rome before I leave if you like."

I flexed my hand at my side, trying to control my anger. She was lashing out. She had every right to be angry. I would not take the bait. "We need to talk."

She reached into her purse and pulled out the mobile phone I had given her. "I also won't have any more need of this." She tossed it onto the top of the bureau.

I inhaled deeply and tried to count to ten. "Amara."

She reached around the suitcase to zip it closed. "I've called Milana. She's leaving with me. I'll stay with her tonight at the cottage and then we'll depart on the first train tomorrow. I'm not telling you where we're going. We'll leave the car at the train station with the keys under the mat."

She tossed her purse over her shoulder and held the suitcase at her side as she faced me. Only then did she finally look me in the eye. She swallowed as her eyes filled with tears. "Goodbye, Barone."

I stayed silent as she stepped around me and crossed the few steps to the closed bedroom doors.

She tried the doorknob.

It was of course locked.

"Unlock the door, Barone."

I stayed facing forward. "No."

"You can't just keep me locked in here."

I turned to face her as I crossed my arms over my chest. "Watch me."

She rattled the doorknob. It didn't budge. She then banged on the door. "Help! Help! Somebody! Open the door!"

She really was adorable. "I think you should know by now, babygirl, that the staff knows better than to pay attention to any screams coming from this bedroom while the two of us are up here."

Her cheeks blushed a beautiful pink, replacing the pale, wan look of her tears.

"Fine!" She marched over to the balcony doors and swung them open. The cool night air rushed in. Stepping out into the darkness, she called out, "I'll just climb down from the terrace."

I flipped open the sterling silver cigarette box on the nearby bureau and selected one. Picking up the heavy matching table lighter, I lit the end and inhaled deeply. I then grabbed her mobile and pocketed it before following her out onto the balcony. I leaned one shoulder against the doorjamb. "Be my guest."

Her eyes widened. "I'll do it," she threatened.

"I know you will."

She jutted out her cute chin with the little divot I liked to

313

lick. "Fine." Picking up her suitcase she hefted it onto the iron railing. After casting a disgruntled look at me over her shoulder, she gave it a hard push. It fell over the side, crashing down the two stories into the bushes below. She then took off her purse and threw it over the railing as well. It landed near the suitcase.

Taking a final leisurely puff of my cigarette, I pinched the end and tossed it aside as I followed her gaze. "That suitcase holds all your worldly possessions," I observed.

She looked at me, then at her suitcase, then back again.

I raised both eyebrows. "And your purse has all your money and identification, I presume."

I could feel the unease settling over her body.

I reached into my trouser pocket, pulled out her mobile, and held it aloft. "And this *was* your only means of communication."

Her eyes widened as realization dawned on her. She lunged for it just as I tossed it over the side. It made a satisfying thump as it fell to the ground.

Amara put her foot on the lower rung of the terrace railing.

"Oh no you don't."

I wrapped an arm around her waist and dragged her back inside our bedroom.

"Let me go!"

"You and I are going to have a talk, *piccola*, whether or not you like it."

She broke free and ran across the bedroom. She turned to face me. Brushing her hair out of her eyes, she was breathing heavily as she placed her hands on her hips. "What did you want to talk about? How you murdered your wife and then made *me* feel guilty for believing the gossip about you?" She pointed at her chest. "Or about how terribly wrong we are for each other.

314

How we come from two completely different worlds, and how all we do is fight, and how eventually you'll probably end up strangling me too!"

My eyes narrowed as I took two menacing steps toward her.

Her mouth opened on a gasp as she stepped back.

Reining in my anger, I asked, "Is that what you truly think, that I'm capable of killing you?"

She threw her hands up in the air. "Yes. No. I don't know. Some days I think I know you and others you are like a stranger to me." She shook her head. "There are times when I delude myself into thinking you might actually lo—"

My brows drew together. "That I might actually what?"

She swiped a tear from her cheek as she looked away. "No, it's stupid."

I crossed my arms over my chest. "I'm not letting you leave here until you tell me."

She crossed her arms over her chest. "Why am I the one having to do all the talking? I'm not the one who *murdered* someone! Probably in some kinky sex game gone wrong, just like the old biddies in the piazza have always claimed."

"You're right. I owe you an explanation."

"I don't want to hear it."

"What?"

She shook her head. "That's what always happened to my mother. The men in her life always had some explanation and she would believe them, and she would take them back, and eventually everything would go to shit again."

"Goddamn it, Amara. I'm not like your piece of shit stepfather."

"No. You're worse. At least with him, you can tell he's a

worthless pig." She waved her hand up and down at me. "You're handsome and intelligent and charming and protective and caring."

I raised my hands, preparing to reach for her as I took a step toward her.

She backed up as she held her arm out defensively. "Oh, no you don't! Those aren't good things! Those are just the bait for the traps you lay. I'm not fooled. Not for one minute. You're also arrogant, overbearing, domineering, stubborn, obstinate, arrogant, and bossy."

My lips quirked. "You said arrogant twice."

"It deserves repeating," she grumbled, then she let out a frustrated sigh. "Just like this argument. Don't you see? We argue so often we are now having the same damn arguments over again! We are no good for one another, Barone. We need to end this now. Before it is too late. *Before we kill one another.*"

I ran a hand over my face. "First off, please stop saying I murdered my wife. And I *really* need you to stop implying I'm going to murder you one day as well. Sit down, we need to talk."

She crossed her arms over her chest. "I prefer to stand."

My patience running thin, I commanded, "Sit. Down."

She scurried around me and sat gingerly on the edge of the bed. "Fine, but only because I changed my mind and am choosing to sit."

Stubborn minx.

I stood before her, choosing my words carefully. "My wife and I married very young. It was not a love match. We both were serving the wishes of our families. Despite that, we cared for one another and tried to make the best of the situation. When the boys were only nine and eleven years old, she became

316

very ill. I flew in the best doctors money could buy, but there was no hope." I grimaced. "We were told it was going to be a very painful and debilitating death with little dignity. She was an extremely devout woman. Suicide was not an option. I never fully understood that. Right until the end she remained obedient to the very God who had been so cruel and heartless to her." I cleared my throat; even all these years later the memories were still painful. "So, one night, when she was ready, she said her final goodbyes to our boys, and I gave her an extra shot of morphine. She died with dignity and in no pain. Shortly afterward, the rumors started. They weren't that far off from the truth, so there was no point in denying them."

Tears were streaming down Amara's cheeks. "Oh, Barone. I'm so very sorry."

I stepped closer and cupped her cheek. I swiped my thumb over her cheekbone, wiping away her tears. "I have felt extreme guilt, but no regrets over my decision. No one should suffer the excruciating pain of a slow death, trapped in their own body. It would have been a living nightmare for her. I know it was the right thing to do. I truly don't believe any god would judge me for that. "

She placed her hand over mine and rested her cheek more firmly against my palm. "Then why burden yourself with the guilt?"

I looked down at Amara's lovely, upturned face. "I didn't love her. I cared for her deeply and hated to see her in so much pain, but I didn't love her. And it tore me apart to think she died being deprived of a husband's love. She deserved that. She should have had it. For years now I guess I was paying a form of penance by denying myself love as well, and then you came along. And I couldn't decide whether you were a beautiful angel sent from heaven or a demon from hell to torture me."

She gasped. "Me? Why? What did I do?"

I stepped close, towering over her small frame and tilted her head back with my finger. Stroking her soft hair back from her face, I said, "You were like the first pink rays of dawn that spread warmth and banish the cold mist that clings to the grapevines after an evening storm. I took one look into those big, beautiful, sad eyes and was lost. For some insane reason, I thought perhaps you would be my salvation. If I could make this sweet, innocent girl smile," I stroked her smooth cheek, "if I could chase the sadness from her eyes, then maybe she would be my redemption."

She closed her eyes as she turned her face into my hand and kissed my palm.

She then rose and walked a few steps away toward the locked doors.

She kept her back to me as she spoke. "Pretty, poetic words are for the rich, who can afford them. I'm sorry, Barone, but I live in the real world, where the lessons I learned from my mother were harsh and cruel. If I stay, I'll fall deeper in love with you. And one day, you'll change your mind about me. You'll decide that I'm too difficult, or too stubborn, or too young, or too much of a pain in the ass. One day we'll have one fight too many and you'll cast me aside, and you'll be able to do that easily, because you're the one with all the power. And I'll be left a hollow shell of myself. That's what happens when only one person is in love and the other is in lust."

She loves me.

After all this bullshit.

318

After all she learned this evening.

This beautiful wild bird I had somehow captured, loves me.

Amara placed her hand on the locked doorknob. Her voice caught as she pleaded, "Please, just open the door and let me leave."

I crossed the distance between us. Turning her around, I backed her body against the door and leaned in. "No fucking way," I growled, before claiming her mouth.

CHAPTER 36

AMARA

I kissed him back.

One final kiss.

My lips were swollen and bruised when he finally released me. I leaned my head back against the door as I stared at his face, trying to memorize every detail. His features blurred as tears filled my eyes. "That was a goodbye kiss, Barone."

Only I didn't want it to be. If I were truly honest with myself, I desperately didn't want to leave this man. I loved him. Even though he drove me crazy, and at times I just wanted to throw something at his head for how overbearing he could be, I couldn't imagine living the rest of my life without him. I didn't want to think about never again feeling his strong arms holding me close as I slept. Or the gentle touch of his lips as he kissed me on the forehead. Or the deep, gravelly sound of his voice when he said *good girl* to me.

I wanted to spend the rest of my life sharing plates of pasta and sipping glasses of wine as we talked about the day's business.

I wanted to fight and then have amazing make-up sex with him.

I wanted to see his face light up with joy as he held our child in his arms.

I wanted a life and a future with him.

The problem was, he wasn't offering me that.

He was only offering me the present. He had made that clear, countless times.

And I needed to decide if that was enough.

If the memories of today would be enough to get me through the coming empty loneliness of tomorrow.

His jaw tightened. "The hell it was."

He swept his arms under my knees and around my back, carrying me over to the bed. He tossed me into the center. I sprang up and crawled over to the edge.

Barone reached for his belt buckle. "Place so much as one toe on the floor, and I will whip your ass with my belt so hard you won't sit for a week."

I sat back on my haunches. "What do you think you're doing?"

Barone kept his hard gaze on me as he shrugged out of his wool blazer then whipped the silk scarf off from around his throat. Holding the scarf between his fists, he raised a single eyebrow and stared down at me.

I shimmied back until my shoulder blades hit the headboard.

He pulled his cashmere sweater over his head, exposing his tanned, muscled chest. "If — how did you put it? My *pretty poetic words* cannot persuade you, then perhaps my *brutal and rough actions* will."

My eyes widened even as my pulse raced. Damn the man. He affected me like no other. I licked my lips as I watched him slowly lower the zipper to his trousers.

This was insanity. Pure insanity. We were like oil and water. Fire and powder. If either of us had any sense, we would run in opposite directions as far as we could from each other.

His trousers fell to the floor. He kicked them and his shoes to the side.

Standing before me naked, he fisted his hard, thick shaft. Jutting his chin in my direction, he ordered, "Take off your sweater."

Arousal pooled between my thighs.

Maybe that is the point of all this craziness.

Life. Love. Lust.

They rarely followed any rational rules.

Maybe the truly foolish part is trying to fight them.

Fuck tomorrow.

If today is all he is offering, then it would have to be enough.

I bit my lower lip. "What happens if I don't?"

He smirked. "Then I'll tear it off you."

I leaned forward on my knees and crawled toward him. I watched as his eyelids lowered. I got so close, I knew he could feel my warm breath on the sensitive tip of his cock as I whispered, "You'll have to catch me first."

I launched myself off the bed and ran full tilt for the terrace. I reached the railing just as his arm wrapped around my waist.

He crushed his warm body against mine as he growled in my ear, "Bad girl."

He lifted my skirt with one hand as he bent me over the railing with the other.

"Are you going to punish me, *daddy?*"

He twisted my panties in his fist and tore them off me. "You're damn right I am."

I gasped at the first spank which sent a hot spike of pain up my spine. His large palm landed on my ass cheeks in quick succession. I could barely catch my breath as I rose on my toes, trying to absorb the hot, prickling pain which radiated over my skin.

Barone shifted to stand behind me. His hips brushed my swollen, punished ass cheeks and upper thighs. He positioned his cock at the wet entrance to my pussy. "This is for thinking, even for one second, that I would let you leave me."

He drove in deep.

I cried out as I gripped the cold metal of the terrace railing. My cheeks burned with the thought that someone from the villa staff could easily hear me, look up, and see what we were doing, but I didn't care. It added to the twisted, taboo thrill of him fucking me outside, in full view of anyone who might wander by.

Barone wound my hair around his fist and pulled, arching my back as he thrust in again and again. He ruthlessly pounded into my body, claiming me. Bruising my delicate inner flesh with the heavy weight of his cock.

He gripped my hip, holding my body in place as he increased the brutal pace of his thrusts. "That's it, babygirl. Take all of daddy's big cock in that sweet, tight pussy of yours."

"Oh God," I moaned. "I'm coming."

Holy shit. Usually, I needed his fingers or his mouth, but he had me so worked up that I was actually coming just from him spanking and then fucking me senseless.

In the same moment my orgasm crashed over me, Barone leaned his body over mine. He wrapped his hand around my throat and tilted my head back. He thrust in one final time as he uttered a guttural growl before harshly whispering in my ear, "From now on, I'm driving my seed in deep until it takes root."

What?

My brain was too fuzzy from the mind-blowing sex and all the twists and turns of this evening to fully process what he just said. I had to have heard him wrong because it almost sounded like he *wanted* me to get pregnant.

I let him scoop me up into his arms and carry me back into our bedroom. He carefully undressed me and laid me under the covers before joining me.

As had become our habit, I laid on my side with him behind me.

He wrapped his arm around my middle and cupped my naked breast in his hand before we both fell into a deep slumber.

* * *

I WOKE to Barone kissing my forehead. "Wake up, *dolcezza*. We have to hurry if we are going to make it to Rome and back today."

I rubbed the sleep from my eyes as I sat up, clutching the sheet to my naked chest. "What? Why are we going to Rome?"

What was going on? I wasn't used to having Barone in the bedroom when I woke up. He usually rose at the crack of dawn to meet his men out in the fields among the vines, especially these last few weeks this close to harvest time.

Harvest time.

It was happening tomorrow.

He called out to me from his dressing room. "We'll take the car, since I don't want to wait on the trains."

"Barone, we can't go to Rome. The harvest starts tomorrow."

The harvest was a huge deal, the most important few days of the entire year for Cavalieri Winery. Everything the winery did all year long led up to this moment. There were still a thousand things to do in preparation. I was actually very excited. Usually, I was stuck in the village working in the tourist shops during the harvest. This would be the first time I would be up at the villa with all the action.

Barone emerged from his dressing room looking devilishly handsome in a dark Dolce & Gabbana suit just as there was a knock on the bedroom door. He unlocked the door and accepted a tray from the servant. He placed the coffee service and platter of pastries on the edge of the bed. This was all very reminiscent of the time Gabriella steamrolled me in Rome to buy that outrageously expensive wardrobe.

He picked his espresso up and drained the contents of the cup. "This is more important. Now get dressed. Sebastian and his sister Arabella are meeting us in three hours."

I wrapped the blanket around me and got out of bed. "Barone, stop! Why are we meeting with the Diamantis? What could possibly be more important than getting ready for the grape harvest?"

He picked me up in his arms and carried me into the bathroom where the shower was already running. He whipped the blanket off me and gave a small nudge to my lower back until I was under the hot stream of water. I turned around to face him, sputtering as the water hit my face.

That is the moment he chose to say, "Your engagement ring of course."

He closed the shower door and walked out of the bathroom.

My engagement what?

Uncaring about my nakedness, I threw open the shower door and raced after him. Standing dripping wet in the middle of our bedroom, I brushed my wet, clinging locks out of my face and said, "What did you just say?"

Barone turned and raised one eyebrow as he surveyed me from head to toe. "I said we're buying your engagement ring today. Actually, the entire wedding set, since I plan on marrying you the moment the harvest is finished. Hopefully, by the end of the week."

I blinked. "Marry me?"

"Yes, *dolcezza*. Marry you."

"You said nothing about marrying you."

He lowered his brow. "What the fuck do you think all that was about last night?"

I threw my hands up in the air. "I don't know. About you, and the scandals in your past, and the crazy bitch Enzo married, and how we would never work out together in the long run because we always fight, and how I love you and you only lust me, and how I don't want to repeat my mother's mistakes, and how—"

He wrapped his arms around my waist and held me close.

"Barone, your suit! I'll get it all wet!"

"Fuck my suit. Say it again."

"What?"

"You know what."

"That we'll never work because we always fight?"

He gave my ass a spank.

"Ow!"

"Try again."

"How you only lust me?"

He spanked me again.

"Ow!"

"One more time."

I pouted as I lowered my eyes. "I don't want to say it because you haven't said it, and I feel silly for saying it, and I never should have said anything because—"

"I love you, *dolcezza*."

I raised my gaze to his. "What?"

"I love you."

"Say it again," I whispered.

He kissed my forehead. "I love you, Amara."

I smiled.

Moments passed.

He raised an eyebrow.

I blinked up at him with feigned innocence.

He narrowed his eyes. "Brat."

I laughed. "Fine. Against *all* my better judgment... I love you too, Barone."

"Now that that is decided... Amara, will you do me the honor of—"

I gave an outraged shriek and pushed him away. "Barone Cavalieri, don't you fucking dare!"

"What?"

I backed away. "Don't you fucking dare propose to me while I'm standing wet and naked in the middle of our bedroom. Besides, it's too soon! We only just said we love one another!" I shouted over my shoulder as I turned and ran back into the bathroom.

He threw his hands up into the air. "You're driving me crazy, Amara, you know that?"

I called out from the shower, *"Ti amo!"*

He called back, *"Anch'io ti amo!"*

CHAPTER 37

AMARA

I stood by Barone's side, clasping his hand, as we watched the stream of villagers coming up the path leading to the winery fields. Some were riding two to a horse, others were walking, still others crammed into the back of a rusted old *Piaggio Ape*. Each carrying handwoven baskets slung over their shoulders or nestled under their arms.

Men, women, and children.

All embracing a centuries-old village tradition.

The grape harvest had arrived.

I looked up at Barone.

He met my gaze, leaned over, and kissed the top of my head.

I closed my eyes and took a deep breath. Tilting my head back, the Italian October sun warmed my face. It was strange to feel as though you were a part of something special.

A legacy.

The Cavalieri legacy.

I looked down at our joined hands. Barone said he would

331

put off talk of marriage until after the harvest, but not for much longer, which meant I had days, not weeks or months, to decide if my future lay with him and his family. Assuming he even gave me a choice. Barone had a way of moving forward, regardless of my feelings on the matter. There was something unsettling about it all.

Like... being trapped in a large glass case that was slowly filling with water. Everyone around could see me through the glass, but instead of realizing the danger I was in, they were admiring how pretty I looked inside the display case.

There are the rich as hell Cavalieris.

There is everyone else below them.

And at the very top is Barone Cavalieri.

Was I stupid to think I could join him at the top? Didn't people like me always eventually get crushed under the weight of all the power, money, and influence of men like Barone Cavalieri?

But he loves me.

I know he loves me.

They always love you... in the beginning, said my mother's voice.

"Amara! Amara! I need you!" called Rosa from where we had set up several long tables for the bonfire and feast that would happen later that evening at sunset. "These two are useless!" she complained as she waved a dismissive hand at Milana and Gabriella who were too busy complimenting each other's outfits to bother with the table settings.

Milana reached over and held up Gabriella's thick hair. "I'm telling you, sweetie. Just a few inches off the bottom. It would really show off your jawline and it would be better suited for chunky statement necklaces which will be all the rage this spring."

Gabriella picked up an empty silver platter and turned it over to admire her reflection as Milana still held up her hair. "I think you may be right. You should come with Amara and me when I take her to Milan next month. You would be much more fun to shop with. I practically had to drag the silly girl into Versace. Can you imagine?"

I shook off my thoughts of doom and gloom and focused on the festive day ahead. "I think I created a double-headed monster introducing those two."

Barone placed a wide-brimmed suede hat on his head. "Have fun with that. See you in a few hours." He gave me a playful swat on the ass before heading into the fields with the rest of his men.

"I'll grab my camera and get some photos for our social media after I help Rosa."

He gave me a wave of his hand over his shoulder without turning around, already focused on the monumental task at hand.

They would all spend the rest of the daylight hours carefully snipping the ripe bunches of grapes from the vines, gathering them in baskets, and then hauling them into the cellars carved deep into the mountains to be processed. There were wineries which used machinery for this process, but the reason Cavalieri wine was so prized was because they still honored the traditional way of making wine, which included carefully harvesting the grapes by hand.

Later, after most of the day's grape bunches had been removed, the older women from the village would be allowed to comb the fields for any forgotten grapes on the vine or ground so they could make chianti at home.

After sending Milana and Gabriella into the garden to pick some late-blooming wildflowers to decorate the tables, I helped Rosa with the table settings and then grabbed my camera and walked out among the vines, taking candid photos of the harvest.

My favorite one captured an unguarded moment between Barone, Enzo, and Cesare. They looked dirty and exhausted. Enzo had grape stains down the front of his shirt. Barone had a smear of dirt across his cheekbone and Cesare's hat was all askew. They were standing in the middle of the ancient Cavalieri grape fields with their heads bent together, laughing.

Life. Laughter. Joy. Love. The future.

It was all there in that one moment.

Barone looked up and saw me. His dark eyes lit up with love.

Cesare beckoned me closer. "Now let's get one with the whole family!"

He took the camera from my hands and set the timer as he stretched his arm up high to capture us all in the frame.

Barone placed me in front of him and wrapped his strong arms securely around my waist.

I closed my eyes and inhaled the perfumed mossy scent of the soil beneath our feet, sweetened with the crushed grapes from the day's harvest, as I leaned back into his comforting strength.

He loves me.

I know he loves me.

Life. Laughter. Joy. Love… and the future.

I wasn't going to run from a man I loved, because I was afraid of the past.

Just before the camera clicked, he leaned down and whispered, "Welcome to the family, *dolcezza*."

My eyes opened as I shivered in the afternoon sun.

No good came from attracting the attention of a man like Barone Cavalieri.

EPILOGUE

CESARE

I helped the men carry the bottles of chianti made just for this purpose out of the cellars, up to the feasting area. It was a Cavalieri tradition to drink the *young wine* of the previous year on the first day of the harvest for the next year. After setting the wooden crates at the end of each table for people to grab, I brushed off my hands and surveyed the scene.

The women had emerged from the lower kitchen with platters of food for everyone who had pitched in to help harvest the grapes. The harvest required a much larger staff than we usually needed so we hired every able-bodied person, including women and children, from the village during the few crucial days they were needed to bring the grapes in.

I heard a rush of air and then a roar of approval from the crowd.

The massive bonfire sprang into life in all its primal glory.

A small band from the village played a rousing rendition of *Tu Vuo' Fa' l'Americano* and everyone joined in the singing.

The feast had begun.

Cork-topped, unlabeled bottles of chianti were passed around as everyone helped themselves to heaping platters of *faraona brasata con cipolline e peperoni, salsiccie con lenticchie e cavolo nero,* and *arosta di masiale al forno.* As our guests ate the savory guinea fowl, sausages with lentils, and roasted pork, they knew there was yet another course of wine-soaked fruits, cheeses, panettone bread pudding, and my personal favorite, baked apples with demerara sugar, mascarpone, and pine nuts. Then later, there would be still more food as many risked singed arm hair and eyebrows to roast *spiedini* and *crostini* near the bonfire.

I tore off a piece of warm focaccia lightly dusted with sea-salt, dipped it in extra-virgin olive oil, and popped it into my mouth as I listened to the men's stories from working in the fields today. And that was when I heard it.

Her laughter.

I narrowed my gaze, searching through the crowd.

I hadn't realized she would be here.

Two women shifted to the right and Milana came into view.

She was standing across the lawn, on the other side of the bonfire.

Her arm was wrapped around her waist, and she was slightly bent over with laughter from something Matteo had just said.

The food in my mouth turned to sawdust.

I marched toward the two of them. Snatching Milana

around the upper arm, I dragged her behind me while I stepped up to Matteo. We were matched in height. I lifted my chin. "Walk away."

Matteo looked over my shoulder, then back at me as he raised his arms. "I didn't know."

My jaw tightened. "Now you do."

I waited until he pivoted on his heel to rejoin the guests before I turned my wrath on Milana. "Stay away from Matteo. Trust me. He's interested in just one thing."

She shook her head as she looked to the side. "You would know."

I looked to the heavens and silently prayed to the Madonna for patience with this woman. "I'm getting tired of this game you're playing, Milana. Either tell me what the fuck I did wrong so I can apologize or get over it."

Her head turned slowly back to focus on me. She lifted her wineglass to her lips and took a long sip as she glared daggers at me over the rim. She then lifted the glass high in the air before she smashed it to the ground at my feet. "It will be a cold day in hell before I ever... ever... forgive you, Cesare Cavalieri."

Her curvy hips swayed as she stormed off.

I sighed as I glanced at my watch.

It was only fair to give her a head start.

I had warned her.

My patience was now officially at an end.

We settled this tonight.

With a final glance over my shoulder at the bonfire and guests, I headed in the same direction as Milana. Time to finally claim what was mine.

· · ·

To be continued...
Sins of the Son
Cavalieri Billionaire Legacy, Book Two

ABOUT ZOE BLAKE

Zoe Blake is the USA Today Bestselling Author of the romantic suspense sagas *The Diamanti Billionaire Dynasty* & *The Cavalieri Billionaire Legacy* inspired by her own heritage as well as her obsession with jewelry, travel, and the salacious gossip of history's most infamous families.

She delights in writing Dark Romance books filled with overly possessive billionaires, taboo scenes, and unexpected twists. She usually spends her ill-gotten gains on martinis, travels, and red lipstick. Since she can barely boil water, she's lucky enough to be married to a sexy Chef.

ALSO BY ZOE BLAKE

CAVALIERI BILLIONAIRE LEGACY

A Dark Enemies to Lovers Romance

Scandals of the Father

Cavalieri Billionaire Legacy, Book One

Being attracted to her wasn't wrong… but acting on it would be.

As the patriarch of the powerful and wealthy Cavalieri family, my choices came with consequences for everyone around me.

The roots of my ancestral, billionaire-dollar winery stretch deep into the rich, Italian soil, as does our legacy for ruthlessness and scandal.

It wasn't the fact she was half my age that made her off limits.

Nothing was off limits for me.

A wounded bird, caught in a trap not of her own making, she posed no risk to me.

My obsessive desire to possess her was the real problem.

For both of us.

But now that I've seen her, tasted her lips, I can't let her go.

Whether she likes it or not, she needs my protection.

I'm doing this for her own good, yet, she fights me at every turn.

Refusing the luxury I offer, desperately trying to escape my grasp.

I need to teach her to obey before the dark rumors of my past reach her.

Ruin her.

She cannot find out what I've done, not before I make her mine.

Sins of the Son

Cavalieri Billionaire Legacy, Book Two

She's hated me for years... now it's past time to give her a reason to.

When you are a son, and one of the heirs, to the legacy of the Cavalieri name, you need to be more vicious than your enemies.

And sometimes, the lines get blurred.

Years ago, they tried to use her as a pawn in a revenge scheme against me.

Even though I cared about her, I let them treat her as if she were nothing.

I was too arrogant and self-involved to protect her then.

But I'm here now. Ready to risk my life tracking down every single one of them.

They'll pay for what they've done as surely as I'll pay for my sins against her.

Too bad it won't be enough for her to let go of her hatred of me,

To get her to stop fighting me.

Because whether she likes it or not, I have the power, wealth, and connections to keep her by my side

And every intention of ruthlessly using all three to make her mine.

Secrets of the Brother

Cavalieri Billionaire Legacy, Book Three

We were not meant to be together... then a dark twist of fate stepped in, and we're the ones who will pay for it.

As the eldest son and heir of the Cavalieri name, I inherit a great deal more than a billion dollar empire.

I receive a legacy of secrets, lies, and scandal.

After enduring a childhood filled with malicious rumors about my father, I have fallen prey to his very same sin.

I married a woman I didn't love out of a false sense of family honor.

Now she has died under mysterious circumstances.

And I am left to play the widowed groom.

For no one can know the truth about my wife...

Especially her sister.

The only way to protect her from danger is to keep her close, and yet, her very nearness tortures me.

She is my sister in name only, but I have no right to desire her.

Not after what I have done.

It's too much to hope she would understand that it was all for her.

It's always been about her.

Only her.

I am, after all, my father's son.

And there is nothing on this earth more ruthless than a Cavalieri man in love.

IVANOV CRIME FAMILY TRILOGY

A Dark Mafia Romance

Savage Vow

Gregor & Samara's story

I took her innocence as payment.

She was far too young and naïve to be betrothed to a monster like me.

I would bring only pain and darkness into her sheltered world.

That's why she ran.

I should've just let her go...

She never asked to marry into a powerful Russian mafia family.

None of this was her choice.

Unfortunately for her, I don't care.

I own her... and after three years of searching... I've found her.

My runaway bride was about to learn disobedience has consequences... punishing ones.

Having her in my arms and under my control had become an obsession.

Nothing was going to keep me from claiming her before the eyes of God and man.

She's finally mine... and I'm never letting her go.

Vicious Oath

Damien & Yelena's story

When I give an order, I expect it to be obeyed.

She's too smart for her own good, and it's going to get her killed.

Against my better judgement, I put her under the protection of my powerful Russian mafia family.

So imagine my anger when the little minx ran.

For three long years I've been on her trail, always one step behind.

Finding and claiming her had become an obsession.

It was getting harder to rein in my driving need to possess her... to own her.

But now the chase is over.

I've found her.

Soon she will be mine.

And I plan to make it official, even if I have to drag her kicking and screaming to the altar.

This time... there will be no escape from me.

Betrayed Honor

Mikhail & Nadia's story

Her innocence was going to get her killed.

That was if I didn't get to her first.

She's the protected little sister of the powerful Ivanov Russian mafia family - the very definition of forbidden.

It's always been my job, as their Head of Security, to watch over her but never to touch.

That ends today.

She disobeyed me and put herself in danger.

It was time to take her in hand.

I'm the only one who can save her and I will fight anyone who tries to stop me, including her brothers.

Honor and loyalty be damned.

She's mine now.

RUTHLESS OBSESSION SERIES

A Dark Mafia Romance

Sweet Cruelty

Dimitri & Emma's story

It was an innocent mistake.

She knocked on the wrong door.

Mine.

If I were a better man, I would've just let her go.

But I'm not.

I'm a cruel bastard.

I ruthlessly claimed her virtue for my own.

It should have been enough.

But it wasn't.

I needed more.

Craved it.

She became my obsession.

Her sweetness and purity taunted my dark soul.

The need to possess her nearly drove me mad.

A Russian arms dealer had no business pursuing a naive librarian student.

She didn't belong in my world.

I would bring her only pain.

But it was too late…

She was mine and I was keeping her.

Sweet Depravity

Vaska & Mary's story

The moment she opened those gorgeous red lips to tell me no, she was mine.

I was a powerful Russian arms dealer and she was an innocent schoolteacher.

If she had a choice, she'd run as far away from me as possible.

Unfortunately for her, I wasn't giving her one.

I wasn't just going to take her; I was going to take over her entire world.

Where she lived.

What she ate.

Where she worked.

All would be under my control.

Call it obsession.

Call it depravity.

I don't give a damn… as long as you call her mine.

Sweet Savagery

Ivan & Dylan's Story

I was a savage bent on claiming her as punishment for her family's mistakes.

As a powerful Russian Arms dealer, no one steals from me and gets away with it.

She was an innocent pawn in a dangerous game.

She had no idea the package her uncle sent her from Russia contained my stolen money.

If I were a good man, I would let her return the money and leave.

If I were a gentleman, I might even let her keep some of it just for frightening her.

As I stared down at the beautiful living doll stretched out before me like a virgin sacrifice,

I thanked God for every sin and misdeed that had blackened my cold heart.

I was not a good man.

I sure as hell wasn't a gentleman… and I had no intention of letting her go.

She was mine now.

And no one takes what's mine.

Sweet Brutality

Maxim & Carinna's story

The more she fights me, the more I want her.

It's that beautiful, sassy mouth of hers.

It makes me want to push her to her knees and dominate her, like the brutal savage I am.

As a Russian Arms dealer, I should not be ruthlessly pursuing an innocent college student like her, but that would not stop me.

A twist of fate may have brought us together, but it is my twisted obsession that will hold her captive as my own treasured possession.

She is mine now.

I dare you to try and take her from me.

Sweet Ferocity

Luka & Katie's Story

I was a mafia mercenary only hired to find her, but now I'm going to keep her.

She is a Russian mafia princess, kidnapped to be used as a pawn in a dangerous territory war.

Saving her was my job. Keeping her safe had become my obsession.

Every move she makes, I am in the shadows, watching.

I was like a feral animal: cruel, violent, and selfishly out for my own needs. Until her.

Now, I will make her mine by any means necessary.

I am her protector, but no one is going to protect her from me.

Made in the USA
Monee, IL
13 August 2024

63797673R00197